NEW YORK NIGHT

By Stephen Leather

D1584119

Teenagers are being possessed and turning into sadistic murderers. Priests can't help, nor can psychiatrists. So who is behind the demonic possessions? Jack Nightingale is called in to investigate, and finds his own soul is on the line.

Jack Nightingale appears in the full-length novels *Nightfall, Midnight, Nightmare, Nightshade, Lastnight* and *San Francisco Night*. He also appears in several short stories including *Blood Bath, Cursed, Still Bleeding, I Know Who Did It, Tracks* and *My Name Is Lydia*.

CHAPTER 1

It had been so easy to get the boy to come with her that she almost felt guilty. Almost, but not quite. She had undone the top two buttons of her shirt and he could barely take his eyes off her cleavage. Normally she'd have poured scorn on him but that wasn't the plan so she'd sat down next to him and asked him his name. Like she cared. His name was Matt and he was seventeen which made him a year older than she was. He was good looking in a surfer dude sort of way, curly blonde hair and blue eyes and a sprinkling of freckles across a snub nose. They talked about school –he went to an upmarket private school and his parents wanted him to go to an Ivy League college. He was interested in bands she'd never heard of and liked graphic novels. She feigned interest and made the right noises but nothing he said was of any interest to her. Everything she told him was a lie. Everything. She didn't want him to know a single thing about her. Not that he cared, he could barely take his eyes away from her cleavage.

She wanted his body, nothing more.

She offered to buy him a burger and they walked to McDonalds. He had a cheeseburger and fries and a Coke while she nibbled on chicken nuggets.

'I'm going to be a lapdancer,' she said, and he lifted his eyes and looked into hers.

'Seriously?'

'Sure,' she said. 'I've got the equipment. Might as well make money from them.'

His eyes went back to her breasts. 'How old are you?' he asked.

'Eighteen,' she lied.

'You can work as a lapdancer when you're eighteen?'

'Sure, why not? The clubs don't care.'

'And you take off your clothes and everything?'

'I'm not ashamed of my body.' She dipped a nugget into a tub of barbecue sauce and bit into it. 'The problem is, I need to practise.'

'Practise?'

'Sure. You have to audition. You have to show you have the moves. So I need to practise.'

He grinned. 'You could practise on me.'

'Are you serious?'

His grin widened. 'Sure. Why not? You could come to my apartment.'

She frowned. 'What about your parents? What if they walked in on us?'

'Where then? In the park?'

'You think I can give you a lapdance in the park? How would that work exactly?'

His cheeks reddened and he covered his embarrassment by taking a bite out of his burger.

'I know a place,' she said. 'An empty loft in a building not far from here. My dad's a real estate agent and I've got the keys.' She reached into the pocket of her jeans and pulled out a key ring with two keys on it. She jingled them in front of him.

'Are you serious?' he asked.

'As cancer,' she said.

He swallowed. 'A lapdance?'

'As many lapdances as you want,' she said. 'I need the practice.'

He nodded enthusiastically. 'Sure, Yes. Absolutely. Wow. Yes.'

She had to fight to stop herself sneering at him. Instead she smiled and winked. 'Finish your burger, then,' she said.

He bolted down the rest of his burger and fries, took a gulp of Coke, and stood up. 'Let's go.'

CHAPTER 2

The loft was a ten-minute walk from McDonalds. The building was six storeys high with a delicatessen and a discount shoe shop on the ground floor, and between them a metal door that was unlocked by tapping in a four-digit code into a steel intercom unit. The door clicked and she pushed it open. Matt followed her into the hallway, panting with anticipation. In front of them was an old-fashioned delivery elevator. It opened by pulling on a length of rope that lifted a wooden panel. A pulley system meant it moved smoothly up with a slight whisper. They stepped inside. She pulled the rope and the panel whispered down, then she pressed a brass button with the number 3 on it. The elevator jerked and then rattled upwards.

'This is so cool,' he said.

'It used to be a factory,' she said. 'Full of sewing machines.'

The elevator shuddered to a halt. She pulled on the rope and the panel slid up. There was a metal grille that had to be pushed to the side before she stepped out into a brick-lined hallway. He followed her. There was a single wooden door with a peephole in the centre. She took out the keys and unlocked it, then stepped to the side to let him go in first.

The apartment was long and narrow. To the left were three floor to ceiling windows overlooking the street. Blinds had been drawn and she flicked the light switch. A dozen ceiling lights came on. To the right was an open-plan kitchen with stainless steel appliances and beyond it was a metal staircase leading up to the bedrooms. There was only one item of furniture, a single wooden chair in the centre of the living area.

The girl walked over to it, her sneakers squeaking on the bare oak floorboards. 'You can sit here,' she said.

He looked up. Black-painted pipes and wiring conduits criss-crossed the double-height ceiling. The floor vibrated under his feet as a truck drove by outside.

He hesitated, suddenly unsure. 'Do you want to do this or not?' she asked, taking off her jacket and tossing it onto the kitchen counter.

'Sure, yeah,' he mumbled. He took off his jacket and tossed it onto the floor, then sat down and rubbed his hands together.

She opened one of the kitchen drawers and took out a pale green scarf. He didn't see it until she walked in front of him. 'What's that?'

'I need to tie you up,' she said.

He put up his hands. 'You never said anything about tying me up,' he said.

'I have to,' she said. 'Those are the rules.'

'Why do you have to tie me up?'

'Because if I don't, you'll touch me. And I don't want you to touch me.'

'Why not?'

'Because those are the rules of a lapdance. The girl can touch the guy but the guy can't touch the girl.'

'That's stupid.'

'It's not stupid. It's the rule. If the guy tries to touch the girl they beat him up and throw him out of the club.'

'Who does?'

'Security. That's their job. To make sure that the girls aren't touched.'

The boy licked his lips. 'So if you tie me up then I get the lapdance?'

She smiled. 'That's why we're here, isn't it?'

'And you'll give me French?'

'French?'

'You know. Kiss me.'

'That's not what French means.'

'Yes it does. It's when you kiss on the lips.'

She shook her head. 'That's a French kiss. French is oral sex. Greek is anal sex.'

The boy frowned. 'Anal sex? What's that?'

'It doesn't matter. Do you want a lap dance or not?' She undid another two buttons of her shirt and his eyes widened as he stared at her cleavage. 'If you don't, I can find someone else to practise on.'

He nodded, his eyes glued to her breasts as he held up his left wrist. She tied the scarf around it, then moved his arm behind his back before threading the scarf under the chair and tying it to his other wrist. 'How does that feel?' she asked. 'Can you get out?'

He pulled his arms but the scarf held tight. He shook his head. 'No.'

She stepped back. 'I'd better make sure,' she said. She went over to the kitchen and pulled open one of the drawers. Inside there was a length of plastic-covered rope. She took it and tied his left leg to the chair, then looped it around his right leg.

'Why are you doing that?' he asked.

'I'm going to make you really horny and I don't want you to get free,' she said. 'Because if you touch me I'll have to stop.' She wound the rope around his stomach and chest.

'I don't like this,' he said.

'You will do soon,' she said. She finished tying the rope and stepped back. 'Perfect,' she said. She undid the rest of the buttons on her shirt and took it off. She wasn't wearing a bra and her breasts swung free and she smiled at the look of anticipation in his eyes. 'You like them, huh?'

He licked his lips. 'You're beautiful.'

'No need for sweet talk,' she said. She put the shirt on the kitchen counter, undid her jeans and pulled them off.

'Oh my god, this is really happening,' he said, his voice catching in his throat.

'Yes,' she said, dropping her jeans on top of her shirt.

'You are so sexy, baby.'

Her eyes hardened. 'I told you, there's no need for any sweet talk. Just shut up and let me do what I have to do.'

He nodded. 'Okay, okay. Just get on with it.'

She slid off her panties and tossed them on the floor. She put her hands on her hips and stood watching him, a slight smile on her face.

'What?' he said. 'What are you waiting for?'

She could see the bump in the crotch of his jeans and her smile widened. 'Nothing,' she said. She went over to the kitchen drawer again and took out a pack of chalk. She selected a piece and began to draw a circle with him in the centre.

'What are you doing?'

She stopped drawing and sat back on her heels. 'You need to shut up,' she said. 'I have to concentrate on what I'm doing.'

'You said I could have a lapdance.' He strained at his bonds. 'Look, I've changed my mind. Untie me.'

She sighed and stood up. She picked up her panties off the floor and walked over to him.

'I want out!' he shouted.

She held his nose with her left hand and when he opened his mouth to breathe she pushed the panties between his lips. She pushed until they filled his mouth then pointed a warning finger at his face. 'One more sound out of you and I'll tape your mouth shut,' she said. 'Just shut up and let me do what I have to do.' She turned around and she went back to drawing the circle. He stared at the ridges on her spine as she bent forward. Her skin

glistened under the overhead lights and he could feel his erection grow
harder even though he was more frightened than he'd ever been. She was
muttering to herself, he realised, but he couldn't make out what she was
saying. It didn't sound like English. She shuffled forward and he caught a
glimpse of the pale blonde hair between her legs. He moaned but the
panties in his mouth muffled any sound.

CHAPTER 3

Jack Nightingale had never been a fan of aeroplanes, but if he did have to fly he preferred to be up at the front end in a big seat rather at the back near the toilets with barely enough space to stretch out his legs. Joshua Wainwright's assistant Valerie had made the booking and he figured it was no coincidence that he was crammed into a middle seat close to the toilets. Valerie had never really warmed to him, even though they only met a couple of times a year at most.

He boarded the flight in Chicago so he was only in the air for just under two hours, twenty minutes of which they were in a holding pattern above JFK airport. He flew with no luggage so within ten minutes of the wheels touching the ground he was outside, looking for his ride.

There was a black stretch Humvee parked by the kerb and as Nightingale walked up to it the back door opened and a cloud of bluish cigar smoke billowed out. Joshua Wainwright was sprawled across the buttery leather seat with his hand-tooled cowboy boots propped up on the seat opposite and a large cigar in his right hand. 'Climb on in, Jack,' he said. 'Time's a wasting.'

Wainwright's Texas drawl and cowboy boots were at odds with the New York Yankees baseball cap on his head. In his left hand was a crystal tumbler of malt whisky. There was a gold Patek Philippe watch on his left wrist and a thick gold chain on the right.

Nightingale climbed in next to Wainwright and the door closed on its own. Wainwright waved his glass at a polished oak cabinet. 'Help yourself to a beer if you want one.'

'I'd rather smoke, if that's okay.'

Wainwright grinned and gestured with his cigar. 'Go ahead.'

As the driver edged into the traffic leaving the terminal, Nightingale took out his pack of Marlboro and lit one.

'First time in New York?' asked Wainwright.

Nightingale nodded.

'Hell of a city,' said Wainwright. 'Never sleeps. There's something going on around the clock.'

Nightingale blew smoke. 'And why am I here?'

Wainwright put his whisky down on a polished wood side table and pulled a sheet of paper from the inside pocket of his jacket. 'A young girl was murdered a couple of days ago. Kate Walker. They found her body in an empty apartment. Butchered. And there was a sigil carved into her back. A sigil I'd never seen before.' He gave the paper to Nightingale. 'The one on the left.'

There were two line drawings on the piece of paper. Nightingale frowned as he stared at the hand-written symbols. A sigil was a magic sign, effectively a devil's signature, peculiar to that devil and often necessary for summoning it from the bowels of Hell. This one was angular, like a reversed letter G with added cross-strokes and a jagged tail that pointed up. 'It's a new one to me, too,' said Nightingale.

'That's not surprising, considering how many devils there are,' said Wainwright.

'And it was carved on a body?'

'On her back. There were lots of other cuts, too. But I think they were there to disguise the sigil.'

'What do the cops think?'

'They're looking for a killer but they don't know that's a sigil.'

'How come you know and they don't?'

'I got it from a guy who works in the city morgue. He keeps a watching brief for things like this and tips me off.'

Nightingale nodded at the second sigil. 'And this one?'

'Two weeks ago. In Philadelphia. Once the New York case was brought to my attention I had my people do some digging. That's all they've come up with so far.'

Nightingale nodded as he looked at the sigil. It was like a hashtag with a triangle in the centre. 'Have the cops made a connection?'

'No, and it doesn't look as if they will. The Philadelphia murder was a boy, in his twenties. And there were lots of other cuts and slashes. The fact that the two deaths were in different states means the cops are unlikely to make a connection.'

'Is there any way of identifying the sigils?' Sigils were as individual as fingerprints. There was one for every devil and the last time Nightingale checked there were close to three billion devils in Hell. There were 66 princes under Satan, each commanding 6,666 legions, and each legion consists of 6,666 devils.

'Only one way I can think of,' said Wainwright.

Nightingale frowned. 'What do you mean?'

'You know someone who can identify them, remember?'

Nightingale looked up. 'Are you serious?'

'We need to know what's going on here, Jack. And Proserpine can tell you.'

'She doesn't take kindly to being summoned just to be questioned.'

'She doesn't have a choice.'

Nightingale grimaced. 'I really don't like messing with her.'

'Can you think of another way of finding out who's behind this?'

'Maybe. I'll have to give it some thought.'

'Jack, I need you to put a stop to these killings. If they continue they're going to be linked eventually. Some cop is going to spot the connection and then the occult link will come out and that makes it difficult for all of us.'

'This is about keeping Satanism below the radar?'

'It belongs in the shadows and that's where it needs to stay,' said Wainwright. 'You need to find out what's going on – and stop it.'

Nightingale folded up the sheet of paper and slid it into the inside pocket of his raincoat. 'What about case notes, or a briefing on how far the cops have got?'

'I don't have contacts close to the case,' said Wainwright. 'I've got a decent private eye on the payroll here but she's not aware of the background, shall we say.'

'She doesn't know you're a devil worshiper, you mean?'

'She knows I'm a wealthy guy who likes to know what's going on in the city,' said Wainwright. 'But she's a former cop so she'll be able to hook you up.'

'And what do I tell her my role is?'

'You can tell her you're a researcher working on a documentary about murders. I own a studio out in LA, I can get you fixed up with credentials.'

'I'm working on a movie? That's my story?'

'Not a movie. A documentary. Or a book. I own a publishing company too. Whatever you feel most comfortable with. She's not going to overthink it. I pay her a good retainer.'

'What's her name?'

Wainwright fished a card from his jacket and handed it to him. 'Her name's Cheryl Perez. She worked homicide for almost ten years before going private. Don't ask her why.'

'Because?'

'Because it was a bit messy and you don't want to get on the wrong side of her.'

Nightingale studied the card. Cheryl Perez, Private Investigator. An office address on Broadway, a cell phone number and an email address. Wainwright was sipping his whisky again. 'What do you think's happening, Joshua? Why would someone carve sigils into corpses.'

'I'm not sure they were,' said Wainwright.

Nightingale frowned. 'Now you're confusing me.'

'Corpses,' said Wainwright. 'Certainly the case in Manhattan, the cuts were made while the girl was still alive. Then she was killed. Then more cuts were made to cover up the sigil.'

'So the sigil is important, obviously. But sigils are the way of contacting devils, aren't they? They're the direct line.'

'That's right,' said Wainwright. 'For most devils, their sigil is the only way to summon them.'

'So the deaths are part of the summoning? A sacrifice?'

'Perhaps. But it's way above my pay grade. I've never heard of it being done. Human sacrifice is rare, Jack. As rare as hen's teeth.'

Nightingale looked out of the window. The sky was threatening rain. 'Where are we going?'

'I've fixed you up with a place to stay.'

'Nothing high. You know how I hate elevators.'

'Sixth floor. But there are stairs.'

Nightingale settled back in his seat. He could manage six floors.

CHAPTER 4

The Humvee dropped Nightingale outside a tall steel and glass building two blocks from Central Park. Wainwright gave him a key card. 'There's security downstairs, 24-7. Your name is on the list so you're good to go. The card will get you in.'

'It's an office block, Joshua. I thought you were taking me to a hotel.'

'You've got the whole floor. There's an executive bathroom with a shower and a couple of sofas, and a kitchen area. You'll be fine. You're always talking about maintaining a low profile, and this is low profile.'

'Where will you be?'

'I'm flying out tonight but you can always reach me by phone.'

Nightingale climbed out of the Humvee and ground what was left of his cigarette into the pavement as it drove away. He went inside. There was a security guard in a dark blue uniform and peaked cap. He tilted his head on one side and narrowed his eyes but before he could say anything Nightingale flashed the key card. 'Jack Nightingale, I'm on the sixth floor.'

The guard looked at a clipboard and nodded. 'The card will operate the elevator, just tap it on the keypad to open the door and again on the keypad inside to get to your floor.'

'Where are the stairs?' asked Nightingale.

The security guard gestured over to the elevator lobby. 'Elevators are over there.'

'Yeah, I can see. I prefer the stairs.'

'Why?'

'Claustrophobic.'

'The emergency stairs are there,' said the security guard, pointing at a door at the end of the lobby. 'Watch out for rats, we've had the pest control people in but they're still around.'

Nightingale thanked him and walked up the stairs. There were trays of rat poison dotted around along with warning notices not to touch them. He reached the sixth floor and pushed open a door that opened onto the elevator lobby. There was a glass door leading to the office and he slid the keycard through the reader and pushed it open.

In the reception area was a white counter with holes cut in the top for computer wiring and a grey wall behind it on which were stainless steel letters spelling out CFG WORLDWIDE. There were hallways to either side of the counter which led to an open plan office that took up most of the floor. The carpeting was grey and was smooth and unmarked as if it had just been laid. Every few yards there were stainless steel flaps covering the power and communications sockets but there was nothing in the way of furniture. To his left was a line of glass-sided offices and to his right a kitchen area with a microwave, a large fridge and a sink. Next to it were three toilets – male, female and handicapped. Nightingale went into all three but didn't see a shower. He went over to the offices. Two were meeting rooms. One was empty but the other had a large oval table with a dozen steel and leather chairs around it and a whiteboard on one wall. Next to it was an office with two desks and a row of filing cabinets, beyond it was another office with one large desk and there was a linking door to the final office. That obviously belonged to the boss, it was in the corner and there were two leather sofas angled around a coffee table, a massive modern desk with a high-backed chair. There was a door that led to a wood-panelled bathroom with a small shower. 'Home sweet home,' muttered Nightingale.

The floor-to-ceiling windows were all covered with white horizontal blinds but they had been angled so that the light streamed in. Nightingale walked around and closed them all before going back to the executive office and doing the same there. He sat down in the high-backed chair and swung his feet up onto the desk, then pulled his cell phone from the pocket of his raincoat. Cheryl Perez answered on the third ring.

'Mr Wainwright said you'd call,' she said. 'I'm around whenever. He said you're my main priority so long as you're in town.'

Nightingale looked at his watch. It was just before five. 'Drink?'

'Thought you'd never ask. Where are you?'

'96th Street.'

'West or East?'

'I didn't realise there was a difference.'

'Which side of the park are you?'

'It's to my left. I think.'

She laughed. 'First time in New York?'

'Yeah. Is it that obvious?'

'There's an Irish bar on 87th and Columbus,' she said. 'O'Malley's. That's 87th West. I'll see you there at six.'

'AM or PM?' said Nightingale.

'This is English humour, I suppose?'

'What passes for it.'

'Very impressive,' said Perez. 'Oh, wear a red rose so I'll recognise you.'

'Are you serious?' The line went dead. Nightingale stared at the phone wondering if she meant it or not.

He went downstairs and found a CVS pharmacy where he bought toiletries, a shaving kit and towels. He went back to the office and showered and shaved and at just before six he was sitting at the bar in O'Malley's nursing a pint of Guinness.

'You passed on the rose?' asked Perez as she appeared at his side. She was quite short, five feet four at the most, with shoulder-length black wavy hair and skin the colour of the peanuts in the bowl by his Guinness. She had high cheekbones and full lips and perfect teeth and Nightingale realised he was staring so he slid off his stool and held out his hand.

'I thought it was American humour,' he said.

'It's okay, the raincoat was the giveaway. It's very English.' She shook his hand. She was wearing a black overcoat with the collar turned up and as she took back her hand and undid the buttons he caught a glimpse of a white shirt and a small gold crucifix. She looked around the bar. There were half a dozen circular tables at the far end of the room, mainly unoccupied, and beyond it a pool table. 'Have you eaten?'

'Aeroplane food at thirty-five thousand feet,' he said.

'Fish or chicken?'

'Could have been either. No way of telling.'

'They do a great Irish stew here.'

'Sounds like a plan.' Perez ordered a glass of red wine and two Irish stews they went over to sit at a table by the wall. There were framed photographs of Irish movie stars, artists and writers dotted between Irish pub memorabilia It looked as if it had been put together by a Hollywood set designer. 'You're a fan of Ireland, then?'

'Something wrong with that? Should I have asked to meet in a tapas bar?'

'What? No. I just meant…'

She laughed. 'I'm just busting your balls, Jack.' She raised her glass. 'Sláinte.'

He clinked his glass against hers. 'Sláinte.'

She leant forward and lowered her voice. 'So Mr Wainwright says you want some info on a case. That murdered girl.'

'Yeah. Kate Walker. And a look at the crime scene if that's possible. Or at least copies of the crime scene photos. Can you do that?'

'I can try,' she said. 'I asked around and I know a cop who knows a cop.' She sipped her wine. 'Mr Wainwright didn't say why you were interested.'

She looked at him steadily. She had a cop's eyes, Nightingale realised. And she was weighing him up. He took a deep breath and sighed. 'How much do you know about him?'

'He's as rich as God. Runs a slew of companies but keeps a low profile. You Google him and nothing comes up.'

'And what do you do for him?'

'Don't think I haven't noticed you changing the subject,' she said. 'Like most wealthy men, he has enemies. He needs to know what's going on around him. I'm sure he has dozens like me on the payroll. He pays us a retainer and from time to time he asks us to do things for him. I've a number of clients like that.' She sat back in her chair. 'You don't get away that easily. Why the interest?'

'I'm supposed to give you some bullshit story about me researching a book or a movie, but I can see you're nobody's fool so I won't insult you by lying to you. I'm a private eye, same as you. I was a cop before that. And a police negotiator. I'm on Joshua's payroll too.'

'You see right there there's a difference. You call him Joshua. I call him Mr Wainwright. So I'm not convinced we are the same, you and I.'

'I've known him for a while,' said Nightingale. 'He uses me to check up on things that spark his interest.'

'And he's interested in a dead girl?'

'Your case and another that's similar. In Philadelphia. A young guy was cut to pieces there.'

'And he thinks there's a connection?'

'He's not sure. Which is why he wants me to take a look.'

'And why's he interested?'

Nightingale ran a hand through his hair. 'I hate being questioned by cops,' he said.

'And there you go changing the subject again.'

Nightingale laughed. 'Okay, how about this? He just is. I can't tell you why. He's paying me to look at the cases and report back to him. He wants to know what happened. You get paid and I get paid. Nobody gets hurt.'

She sipped her wine and smiled. 'Maybe you should have just lied, because now I'm more confused than ever. But like you said, I get paid and we're not doing anything illegal.' She took another sip of wine. 'Are we?'

'Cross my heart and hope to die.'

'That's all right, then.'

A waiter came over and placed two plates of Irish stew on the table. Nightingale picked up his knife and fork.

'Do you mind if I say grace?' she asked Nightingale.

Nightingale started to smile, thinking that she was joking, but then realised she was serious. He put down his knife and fork. 'Sure.'

She nodded her thanks and then lowered her head. 'Bless us, O Lord, and these, Thy gifts, which we are about to receive from Thy bounty. Through Christ, our Lord. Amen.' She crossed herself.

'Amen,' said Nightingale, and did the same.

CHAPTER 5

Sara could see that he was afraid so she smiled what she hoped was a comforting smile. 'It's a game,' she said. 'It's just a game.'

'If you want to play a game, let's play Grand Theft Auto,' said her brother. Luke was ten, six years younger than she was. They rarely played together but she needed another pair of hands for the Ouija board and Luke could be relied on to do as he was told.

'Because I want to play this,' she said.

'It's stupid,' he said. 'I've never heard of a game like this before.' He sat back on his heels. They were in her bedroom. He was rarely allowed into her room and had looked at her suspiciously when she had first suggested they play a game together.

'You liked Charlie Charlie didn't you? Well this is the same. You can ask it a question and it'll answer.'

'Charlie Charlie is for fun,' said the boy.

'So is this. But with Charlie Charlie you can only pick one of four answers, right? This way the spirits can talk to us.'

'Spirits? You mean ghosts?'

'It's all the same. Look, it's a game. Just a game. Do you want to play or shall I tell mom you haven't done your homework?'

Okay, okay,' mumbled Luke. 'Don't give me a hard time.'

'Put your fingers on the planchette. Just the tips.'

He frowned. 'Planchette?'

She nodded at the heart shaped piece of wood on the board. It was dark brown, oak maybe, that had once been varnished but most of the varnish had been worn off over the years. 'It means little plank. It's French. You put your fingers on it and it spells out words.'

'How?'

'Does it matter? Just do it.'

Luke put out his hands and touched the planchette, then jerked his fingers back as if he had been stung.

'What's wrong?'

'Nothing.'

'It won't bite.'

He reached out again and this time his fingers stayed on the piece of wood.

'Good boy,' she said. She reached across the board and her fingers joined his.

'Now what?' he said.

'Just keep quiet. Let me do the talking. But no matter what happens, keep your fingers on the planchette.'

He nodded and stared down at the board. The letters of the alphabet ran across the board in two rows, A to M on the top and N to Z below it. Below the letters were the numbers from 0 to 9 and below that was GOOD BYE in capital letters. In the top left hand corner was the word YES and NO was in the top right corner.

'Nothing's happening,' he said.

'Hush. Let me do the talking.' She looked up at the ceiling. 'Are you there?' she said.

'Who?' asked Luke. 'Who are you talking to?'

'Hush,' she said, her eyes fixed to the ceiling. 'Keep quiet.' She took a deep breath. 'Are you there?' Almost immediately she felt the planchette twitch under her fingers. 'It's Sara. I'm here,' she said, louder this time. The planchette twitched again.

'Are you doing that?' asked the boy.

'Hush,' said Sara. She closed her eyes and took a deep breath, then slowly exhaled. 'Daniel, are you here?'

The planchette twitched and then scraped across the board.

'You're talking to Daniel?' asked Luke. 'That's what this is about?' The planchette stopped moving.

'Luke, shut up, okay?'

'Daniel's dead, Sara. We went to his funeral.'

'Luke, seriously, shut the fuck up,' she snapped. She looked up at the ceiling again. 'Daniel, are you here?'

The planchette began to move again, scraping slowly across the board until the tip touched the E in YES.

'Really? It's you?'

The planchette jerked away from the YES and then slowly crept back until it was nudging the E again.

Sara beamed. 'I knew it would work, I knew it.'

'You're pushing it,' said Luke. 'I can feel you pushing it.'

'Shut up!' snapped Sara. 'I'm not.'

The planchette began to move again. First it went back to the bottom of the board, then it shook from side to side, then it moved up and to the left. It stopped just under the letter B. Then it went back down, hesitated for a few seconds and scraped up to point at L. It began to move faster as if it was gaining confidence.

I-N-D-F-O-L-D T-H-E B-O-Y.

Luke's eyes widened.

'What does it mean? Why does it want to blindfold me?'

Sara stood up. 'Don't worry,' she said. 'It just means it has a message it only wants me to see.' She went over to her wardrobe and pulled out a silk scarf. It had been a birthday present from one of her aunts. It was expensive – Chanel - and it was pure silk but she had never worn it. Sara stood behind Luke and tied the scarf around his eyes.

'I don't like this,' he said, his voice quivering.

'Don't be a cry baby,' she said. She sat down and put her fingertips back on the planchette. She tilted her head back and stared up at the ceiling. 'I'm ready, Daniel,' she whispered. The planchette began to slowly scrape itself across the board as if it had a life of its own.

CHAPTER 6

Perez arranged a meeting with the detective for a briefing on the Kate Walker case. His name was Andy Horowitz and he was a big guy who looked like he could handle himself and almost certainly had a military background. He had a crew cut and broad shoulders that strained at the shoulders of his overcoat. His eyes were a pale blue and he didn't seem to blink much. There was a small scar on his left cheek and when he offered his hand to shake, Nightingale could see the flesh was puckered around the thumb. An old burn scar. 'You were a cop, in London?' Horowitz asked. They were standing inside a diner close to the station where the detective was based, waiting to be seated.

'For a while.'

'Cops don't carry guns in England? How does that work? What do you do if someone pulls a gun on you?'

'I did carry a gun. I was an armed cop. But only specially trained police are armed, and they get called out when there's a problem.'

Horowitz frowned. 'I don't get that,' he said. 'A cop stumbles across a robbery. What does he do? Ask the perp to wait until reinforcements arrive.'

Nightingale grinned. 'Pretty much, yeah. It sounds crazy but it works. Plus, most of our criminals don't carry guns.'

A waitress showed them to a booth by the window, handed them menus and asked them what they wanted to drink. They all asked for coffee and she headed for the counter. Horowitz and Perez sat opposite him.

'And now you're a PI?'

'Yeah, but I don't have a licence in the States.'

'That's not the issue, licence or not we're not supposed to talk to private investigators.' He looked over at Perez and for the first time he smiled. 'Unless they're family.'

'Family?'

'He's my honorary big brother,' said Perez. 'We worked Robbery Homicide together a few years ago.'

'My first time out of uniform,' said Horowitz. 'She kept me on the straight and narrow.' He looked back at Nightingale. 'So, I'm happy enough to help family, but I'm not sure how helpful I can be because the Kate Walker case is still wide open.'

'Is it your case?'

Horowitz shook his head. 'No, but I reached out to the guys who caught it. Between you and me I think they'd be grateful for any help.'

'So what happened?'

'It was a third floor loft in 95th Street. Girl called Kate Walker. Sixteen years old. High school cheerleader, dad's in real estate, in fact he was trying to sell the loft. We think that's how she got access. The body was found within twenty-four hours of her death by one of his partners. She opened the door and Kate was lying in the middle of the main room in a pool of blood.'

'Cause of death?'

'Blood loss. Multiple wounds and by multiple I mean a lot. More than fifty cuts and stab wounds, at least half a dozen of which would have been fatal.'

The waitress came over and they ordered. Horowitz wanted pancakes, Perez ordered an omelette and Nightingale asked for toast.

'No eggs, hun?' asked the waitress. Nightingale shook his head and she went off to the counter where a short-order cook was scraping scrambled eggs across a hotplate.

'Any motive? Sexual?'

'No signs of sexual contact, no violence in that area.'

'But she was naked?'

Horowitz nodded. 'Her clothes were in a pile in the kitchen.'

'So she'd taken them off?'

'Almost certainly.'

'Under duress?'

'There were some defence wounds on her hands but no blood on the clothes, so we're assuming the attack came after she undressed.'

'Forensics?'

Horowitz shook his head. 'Nothing.'

'Do you have a theory?'

'Murdered by person or persons unknown.'

'But she knew her killer, right?'

Horowitz's eyes narrowed. 'What makes you say that?'

'Her dad was selling the flat so she must have taken the killer there.'

'Or she went around and disturbed him.'

'Evidence for that?'

Horowitz flashed him a tight smile. 'Supposition,' he said. 'Same as your supposition that she knew her killer.'

'Fair point,' said Nightingale. 'But do you think a random killer is more likely?'

Horowitz shrugged. 'If I was a betting man I'd say it wasn't random but we haven't come up with a motive yet.'

'Can you show me the crime scene?'

The detective nodded. 'I've brought the keys with me.'

CHAPTER 7

Horowitz drove them to the crime scene in a grey saloon. Perez sat up front and they chatted about old times for the fifteen minutes it took to get to the apartment building. They parked on the street and Horowitz let them in through a door sandwiched between a delicatessen and a discount shoe shop.

The detective walked towards an old-fashioned delivery elevator. He pulled on a length of rope that lifted a wooden panel. Perez stepped in.

'I'd prefer the stairs,' said Nightingale.

'Say what?' said Horowitz.

'I'm not a big fan of lifts. Or elevators as you call them.'

'It's only the third floor,' said Horowitz.

'Can I walk up?'

'There aren't any internal stairs,' he said. 'There's a fire escape running down the back of the building but you've got to go down an alley to reach it and even then I'm not sure you'll be able to pull it down.'

'What's wrong, Jack?'

'I just don't like elevators. Never have done.'

'Don't see you've got a choice,' said Perez.

Nightingale sighed and stepped in. He took out his cigarettes but Perez shook her head. 'Not indoors, Jack,' she said. 'Not in New York.'

Horowitz pulled the door closed and pressed the button for the third floor. The elevator jerked and Nightingale yelped. Perez grinned as the elevator rattled upwards for almost thirty seconds before it shuddered to a stop. Horowitz opened the door and Nightingale hurried out.

Perez followed him and Horowitz closed the door and took out a set of keys to open the door to the apartment.

It was long and narrow with floor to ceiling windows to the left and an open-plan kitchen to the right. There was no furniture, just bare wooden floorboards. The sound of the traffic was like a dull throb in the background. Above their heads were black-painted pipes and wiring conduits.

'Where was the body?' asked Nightingale.

Horowitz took a couple of crime scene photographs from his overcoat pocket, studied them and gestured towards the middle of the room.

'Can I have a look?' asked Nightingale, holding out his hand.

'You can keep them,' said Horowitz. 'Cheryl said you'd want them.'

Nightingale flicked through the photographs. They were all shots of the body, lying face down on the floor. He compared the pictures to the scene one by one, rotating them to match what he was seeing. The girl was face down, her back and legs a mass of cuts. He stared closely at the photographs but there was no way of making out the sigil among all the flayed flesh and blood.

'He really went to work on her,' said Horowitz. 'It's either a sadistic serial killer who gets off on torture, or it's personal.'

Nightingale's Hush Puppies squeaked on the bare boards as he walked across the floor. He stopped when he saw the dried blood stain in the centre of the room. He stopped and stared down at the rust-red marks.

'Did the guys who caught the case tell you much?'

'Just that it was an unholy mess. The woman who found the body was in a right state. They found her outside, pale as a sheet and shaking.'

Nightingale flicked through the photographs again. Perez walked over to stand next to him and she grimaced as she looked at the pictures. 'What sort of sick fuck does that?' she asked.

Nightingale figured the question was rhetorical so he didn't answer. 'Was the knife left behind?' he asked Horowitz.

The detective nodded and then gestured at the kitchen area. 'It was one of a set. They got decent prints off it and DNA but no match to anyone in the system.'

'There was no furniture, you said?'

'The guys who caught the case said there was just a wooden chair. That was taken for examination. Same prints and DNA.'

'Her clothes?'

'On the kitchen counter.'

'And did anyone clean up after the body was taken away?'

'I don't see how they could have, any professional cleaners would have gotten rid of the stain.'

Nightingale crouched down and tilted his head from side to side.

'Looking for something in particular?' asked Perez.

Nightingale ignored the question. 'Had she been tied?' he asked Horowitz.

'Not that they could see. She'd been here a day before she was found so there was a fair bit of swelling, but there didn't seem to be any evidence that she'd been bound.'

'Defense wounds?'

Horowitz nodded. 'A few.'

Nightingale stood up, moved a couple of feet to his right and squatted down again.

'Looks to me like she knew her killer,' said Nightingale.

'Like I said, that's supposition,' said Horowitz. 'He could have got in somehow and she disturbed him. He grabs a knife. She fights back and goes into overkill mode.'

'And tells her to remove her clothes?'

'She was a pretty girl. Maybe he decides to rape her?'

'At the diner you said there was no evidence of sexual assault.'

'None. But he could have changed his mind. He's here, hiding maybe. She lets herself in. He grabs a knife. Makes her undress. When she's naked she panics and fights back. He kills her and rape is no longer an option.'

'There's no blood spatter. Just a pool.'

'So?'

'So if there was a struggle they'd be blood spatter across the floor and the walls. There isn't.'

'So he hit her and she went down and he killed her.' The detective frowned. 'Do you have a different theory?'

Nightingale stood up and shook his head. 'I wish I did. What about a suspect?'

'They've checked all the local CCTV but they don't even have her arriving. There aren't many cameras in this part of town and as you saw there's nothing in the lobby. They're canvasing the area with her photograph but no one remembers seeing her arrive. It's frustrating having the killer's fingerprints and DNA but not everyone is in the system.'

'So the case has gone cold?'

'I wouldn't say that. But it's not hot, that's for sure.'

'And what about looking at her family and friends, just in case it was someone she knew.'

'She was a good, stay-at-home girl. No issues at school, no problems with drink or drugs. She had a boyfriend but he died three months ago.'

'Died how?'

'Boating accident. On the river in a canoe or a kayak or whatever they call them. He wasn't wearing his life vest, overturned and the current dragged him away. It was in the papers. A tragic accident.'

'And you checked the family?'

'You're thinking the father?' Horowitz shook his head. 'I asked the guys and it's a definite no. He was devastated when they broke the news to him. He's still in shock. Took it harder than the mother. And before you start jumping to any conclusions, he was with people the whole day, either in his office or with clients. He wasn't alone for a single second. The mother was at home. She had a brother. A younger brother, Eddie. He was with friends all day. But that's just ticking the boxes because it wasn't a family member who did this.'

'Why do you say that?'

'The degree of violence. And the fact the body was naked. When family members kill each other it tends to be short and sweet. The mutilation here was so extreme that we're looking for a psychopath. Someone who takes pleasure from causing pain.'

'But most of the cuts were post mortem, right?'

'According to the ME it was hard to tell. Some before, definitely. But the blood loss was so catastrophic she would have died quickly anyway. For sure he carried on cutting after she'd died.'

'He? Definitely a man?'

'Not many women kill like this, Jack. But I take your point. Could be either.'

Nightingale nodded at the bedroom door. 'Okay if I look there?'

'The bedroom's empty. But sure.'

Nightingale opened the door. Unlike the rest of the apartment the floor was carpeted. There was no furniture but there were built-in closets, all empty. Another door led to a bathroom, so pristine it looked as if it had never been used.

'If she was here for sex, why not use the bedroom?' said Nightingale.

'There's no bed,' said Perez. 'And you're making assumptions again. If he forced her to remove her clothes, would he care which room he was in?'

'The carpet has got to be a better choice than a wooden floor.'

'Is that the voice of experience, Jack?'

He flashed her a tight smile. 'I'm just trying to get into the mind of whoever did this,' he said.

'It's a fair point,' said Horowitz at the doorway. 'It's all very organised. It didn't look as if there was any sort of struggle prior to the attack. But if it was sex they came for Jack's right, you'd go for the carpet. Less wear and tear on the knees.' Perez turned to look at him and he shrugged. 'It happens.'

Perez shook her head sadly. 'That's far more information than I needed, Andy.'

'Plus, if this was a social meeting, there'd be booze or drugs or something,' said Nightingale.

'The killer could have taken everything with them,' said Perez.

'Sure. But it was Kate's father who was showing the place,' said Horowitz. 'We have to assume that if it was a social thing then she would have brought him here and not the other way around. That being the case, why would the killer take anything away?'

'She could have bought a bottle of wine and a couple of glasses,' said Perez. 'Killer realised there'd be prints and took them with him.'

'They checked nearby dumpsters,' said Horowitz. 'They didn't find anything that had been dumped. And why take a bottle and glasses and leave the knife? We have his DNA and prints from that. So I'd say no, he didn't take anything with him. Again, assuming it's a he.'

'So nothing strange in the dumpsters?' said Nightingale.

'I wouldn't say that,' said the detective. 'This is New York. But nothing that suggests it came from this crime scene.'

Nightingale went back to the main room and over to the bloodstain. He bent down and moved his head from side to side. Perez grinned. 'You know, give you a magnifying glass and a funny hat and you'd be the spitting image of Sherlock Holmes.'

Nightingale didn't say anything but walked around to the other side of the stain, squatted down, and peered at the floor again. Eventually he straightened up. 'Okay,' he said.

'Okay what?' said Perez.

'Okay we're done here.'

CHAPTER 8

Horowitz dropped them off outside Perez's office. Perez leant over and gave him a peck on the cheek. 'Thanks, I owe you one,' she said.

Horowitz laughed. 'You owe me more than one,' he replied.

'If ever you need the services of a Private Eye, you know who to call,' she said, opening the door.

'Yeah, the Pinkertons. You be careful.'

'Always,' she said, climbing out.

Nightingale thanked him and joined Perez on the sidewalk. Horowitz drove off, heading north. 'Andy seems like a good guy,' said Nightingale. 'Very on the ball.'

'He's a good cop. A straight arrow.' She looked at her watch. 'You want a coffee?'

'Sounds good.'

'There's an Italian place around the corner.'

As Nightingale walked with her, he lit a cigarette, taking care not to blow smoke in her direction. 'I wish the cops in the UK were as helpful when it came to off-the-books help?'

'We go back a long way,' said Perez.

'Former boyfriend?'

She laughed. 'Why would you say that?'

'I just thought there was – you know – heat.'

'Heat?'

'Between you.'

She laughed louder and shook her head. 'If only you knew,' she said.

'Knew what?'

They reached the coffee shop and he held the door open for her. She laughed. 'British manners? I love it.'

'Don't New York men open doors?'

'Not so much, and certainly not when they're after coffee. A girl's more likely to get trampled in the rush.'

Nightingale followed her inside. 'I'll get them,' he said.

'Latte,' she said.

Nightingale went over to the counter as Perez threw her coat onto the back of a chair and sat down. He carried the coffees over on a tray. She smiled as she saw that he'd bought chocolate muffins. 'To keep you sweet,' he said.

He sat down opposite her, broke a piece off his muffin and popped it into his mouth. 'So, you were telling me about Andy…'

'That's not strictly speaking true.'

'You said "if only I knew" as if there was something there.'

She laughed and took a sip of her latte. 'It's none of your business, so I don't know why I'm even telling you this, but he was best man at my wedding. My husband's best friend. I mean best friends forever, they were next door neighbours, born in the same hospital ward on the same day. They joined the army together, served in Iraq together, became cops together, worked out of the same precinct. They were practically joined at the hip.' She smiled ruefully. 'What's funny is that if things had gone differently, Andy and I could well have got married.'

'Husband?' said Nightingale, frowning. She wasn't wearing a ring and hadn't mentioned being married, but then they hadn't had much in the way of chit-chat.

'Ex-husband.' She smiled thinly. 'Dead husband, to be one hundred per cent accurate.'

'Oh, sorry.'

She looked at him, her head tilted to one side. 'Why are you sorry? You didn't know him. You barely know me.'

'I just meant.. you know. Sorry for your loss.' He popped another piece of muffin into his mouth to cover his confusion.

She nodded and took another sip of coffee. 'I'm still a bit raw. But you can see that.'

'What happened? Line of duty?'

She shook her head. 'Eric killed himself. Took his gun and put it in his mouth and pulled the trigger.'

'Hell, I'm sorry.'

She shrugged. 'Yeah. Me too.' She shrugged again. 'I met Eric through Andy. Andy was partnered with me when he first moved to homicide. He introduced me to Eric one night in a bar after work.' She smiled ruefully. 'Andy always said it was the biggest mistake he ever made.'

'In what way?'

'You're going to make me spell it out? Andy always wished he'd asked me out first. But Eric beat him to the punch and Andy was too good a guy to do anything after that.'

'You okay to talk about it?'

'Why?'

'Just wondered why he'd kill himself, that's all. I dealt with a few suicides during my time with the Met.'

'You said you were a negotiator.'

'In the UK negotiators deal with any person whose in a crisis. Hostage negotiation is a very small part of it, generally it's domestic disputes or people who want to hurt themselves.'

'Eric didn't want to hurt himself. He wanted to die, period.'

'Did he leave a note?'

She shook her head. 'He just sat down, drank half a bottle of bourbon, stuck his gun in his mouth and pulled the trigger. I found the body. No note, no nothing.'

'And he never said anything?'

'What, like "honey I'm going to blow my head off, catch you later?" No, he never said anything. Not a word.'

'Genuine suicides often don't,' said Nightingale. 'The ones that talk about it are generally the ones that don't do it. Did he have money problems?'

'No more than any other cops. He played poker for a while, mainly on-line, and he ran up a few grand on his credit card, but he came to his senses and stopped.' She sipped her drink. 'He had flashbacks, to what he saw in Iraq. Night sweats sometimes. I'd wake up and the sheets would be soaked, and he'd be mumbling to himself. But I never imagined he was so troubled that he'd...' She shuddered.

'I'm sorry,' he said.

'Don't keep saying that,' she said.

Nightingale nodded. 'Okay.'

She picked up her muffin, held it to her mouth, then seemed to change her mind and put it back on the plate. 'You dealt with many suicides?'

'Not many. If by suicide you mean someone who actually went through with it. As a general rule, if they hang around long enough for the negotiators to arrive, then they're not really committed.'

'But some died in front of you?'

'A few'

'Why would they do it?"

'Kill themselves, or kill themselves while someone is watching?'

'Both.'

Nightingale shrugged. 'People kill themselves because they're in pain and they think that ending their lives will end their pain. As a negotiator, your job is to point out the alternatives. To show them that life is worth living. That their life is worth living. Sometimes you can't convince them. Sometimes there are no arguments. Then they do it. And they do it with someone watching because they're scared of dying alone, I guess.'

Perez sipped her coffee. 'Eric made sure I was at work when he did it.'

'He'd decided to go through with it and didn't want you to try to stop him.'

'I just wish I knew why. We were planning to have a baby. We'd talked about it. And then he just…' She gritted her teeth. 'It makes me so fucking angry sometimes. How the fuck could he do that to me? If he'd just left a note, if he'd just told me why he did it. It's the not knowing that hurts, you know?'

Nightingale nodded. 'I know.'

'Bastard.'

'Yeah.' He raised his mug. 'Cheers.'

She forced a smile. 'Cheers,' she said, and clinked her mug against his.

'Are you up for taking me to see the girl's parents?' he asked.

'What on earth for? Can you imagine what they're going through?'

'I don't buy that this was a stranger killing. I'm pretty sure that Kate knew her killer. She probably even took him to the apartment.'

'Like Andy said, there's nothing to suggest that.'

'No evidence, no. But she had the key, so she must have taken that from her dad. That must have been planned. She removed her clothes. If she was expecting violence she'd probably have resisted at that point and the killer would have cut her then. There was no blood on the clothes so she removed them before the attack.'

'The killer could have forced her to do that.'

'Could have, would have, should have,' said Nightingale. 'What's more likely, then? She decided to visit one of her father's properties on her own? For what? There was no furniture there, no TV to watch, why would she bother?'

'Right back at you if she knew her attacker,' she said. 'Suppose it was a new boyfriend. Why choose an apartment with no furniture? Wouldn't she have taken any boyfriend to a place with a bed at least?'

Nightingale shrugged. 'Maybe. Maybe she didn't know there wasn't any furniture. Or maybe she didn't care.'

'You're suggesting she took someone there, someone who then killed her. How could she make an error like that? If what you're suggesting is right, it had to be someone she knew well, someone she trusted. How could she make a call so wrong that she ended up dead?'

'I don't know, Cheryl. I was hoping that her parents might have the answers.'

Her eyes narrowed. 'Are you telling me everything, Jack?'

He flashed her his most innocent smile. 'I don't know much, to be honest.'

She nodded thoughtfully. 'What were you looking for? On the floor? You bent down a couple of times to check out the floorboards.'

'Anything. Something the cops might have missed.'

'And did you see anything?'

'Nothing useful,' he said. He figured better not to tell her that he'd seen black candle wax on the floorboards, and traces of chalk. Someone had done a pretty good job of cleaning up after themselves, but he was fairly sure someone had constructed a magic circle in the apartment, and that the girl had been in the centre of it when she had died. Nightingale guessed that the magic circle was the reason Kate had been in the unfurnished flat. But what he didn't know was whether it had been Kate, or her killer, who had drawn the pentagram and lit the candles.

Perez continued to stare at him for several seconds, then she nodded. 'I'll see if I can arrange something.'

CHAPTER 9

Dee-anne looked at the photograph and wrinkled her nose. Too young. She was looking for someone in their forties, at least. Someone with their own place. She flicked the picture to the left and another face appeared. She chuckled to herself. Too damn ugly. She flicked left. A pale-faced guy with long blonde hair. Too girlish. She flicked left. The next picture on her phone was in his fifties, wearing a suit and tie. His name was Nate. She flicked the picture to the right and smiled when she saw that he was a match. He already liked her. Cool. The next picture was a man also in his fifties but repulsively fat and Dee-anne shuddered. Even for what she was after she had standards. Reject. The next five Tinder profiles were all of teenagers, on skateboards, throwing gangster signs and generally being idiots. Reject, reject, reject, reject, reject. And still they kept coming, profile after profile. Dee-anne was sitting in a Starbucks on Broadway, south of Central Park, with a double espresso in front of her. It was her third. She had been in the coffee shop for the best part of an hour and had scanned hundreds of photographs on Tinder. Most of them had been rejections. More than a dozen of the one's she'd accepted had been in touch already. Usually it started with a short message. 'Hey.' Or 'How are you doing?'

Dee-anne's reply was always the same. 'I'm horny now. Where are you?' She had posted six photographs. None of them were actually her –

she had used photographs she'd taken off the internet of a girl who was a close match to her own looks – olive skin, dark brown eyes, full lips, shoulder-length curly chestnut hair. The girl in the photographs had longer legs and fuller breasts and was happy to show them off. Three of the pictures she'd downloaded had been bikini shots.

Most of the contacts wanted to arrange a meeting much later that evening. Dee-anne would send them a single text – WHAT PART OF NOW DON'T YOU UNDERSTAND? – and then delete them. One guy was available now but was in New Jersey and she didn't want to leave Manhattan. Another suggested meeting in a motel but she wanted it to happen in their home so he was rejected, too.

She left-flicked another six photos in quick succession. Too old. Too cheap. Too fat. Too ugly. Too young. Too short. Number seven was perfect. Forty-eight he said but looked ten years older. Tall, greying hair, wearing a blazer and a red and white striped tie. She accepted him and rejected three more.

Her phone beeped as she received a message. CUTE PICTURES. It was Nate. She sent him a text back. I'M HORNY NOW. WHERE ARE YOU?

WEST 52ND STREET.

YOU STAY ALONE?

SURE. YOU WANT TO COME ROUND?

SEND ME YOUR ADDRESS.

Less than a minute later his address arrived. Then another message. I WILL FUCK YOU SO HARD YOU WILL SCREAM.

Dee-anne smiled and sipped her coffee before texting him back. LET'S SEE WHO SCREAMS LOUDEST. She added a smiley face. She put her phone away, finished her coffee, and went off in search of a taxi.

CHAPTER 10

The yellow cab driver was from Sierra Leone originally and during the drive he told Dee-anne how his family had been hacked to death by teenagers with machetes and that he had been lucky to escape with his life. Dee-anne had listened to the man's story and had nodded and made encouraging noises at the right places but there was something definitely off about what the man was saying. It sounded too rehearsed as if he'd gone over it time and time again to make sure it had the ring of authenticity. Her fingers touched his as she handed over the fare and she instantly knew the truth. The man had been one of the attackers, he had killed and mutilated hundreds of men, women and children and had used the money he had stolen from his victims to pay for his passage to the United States.

'I know what you did, Emmanuel,' she said as she took her change. 'You should keep up the good work here in America, Get yourself a big knife and have some fun.'

His mouth opened and he nodded slowly. 'I will, mistress' he said.

'Enjoy yourself,' said Dee-anne. She climbed out of the taxi and slammed the door. Dee-anne had told the taxi to stop a block away from where Nate lived and she walked the rest of the way. It was a modern block of condominiums with a glass-fronted reception area. There was a door entry system that meant she had to tap in the number of the condo and the hash key. There was no CCTV covering the door but there was a small black lens staring down at her above the keypad.

'Hello,' said a voice.

'Nate?'

'Dee-anne?'

'Sure.'

'Come on up. Fourth floor.'

The door buzzed and she pushed it open. There was a CCTV camera covering the elevator lobby but it was a simple matter to keep her face turned away as she stepped into the nearest one. She looked down at the floor as she pressed the button. There were another two cameras covering the hallway on the fourth floor, one left and one right. She kept her head down as she walked towards Nate's apartment. She pressed the doorbell with the knuckle of her index finger. The door opened and Nate smiled at her. His face was a bit more wrinkled than his Tinder picture and she figured he had probably Photoshopped it. Or more likely paid someone to Photoshop it for him. He didn't look computer savvy. 'Welcome,' he said, and held the door open. She stepped inside. Music was playing. Something classical. 'Can I take your coat?'

'Thank you.' She took off her coat and he took it from her. She walked down a narrow hallway which opened out into a large sitting room. The blinds were drawn and the lights had been turned down and there was an ice bucket with a bottle of wine in it and two glasses on the coffee table. There were also two bowls, one with olives, the other containing nachos.

'Please, sit down, make yourself comfortable,' said Nate.

There was a low grey sofa and two matching armchairs with black cushions. She sat on the sofa and he joined her. He was wearing grey trousers that looked as if they belonged to a suit and a white shirt with large gold cufflinks in the shape of mini golfballs. There was a smear of shaving foam under his left ear.

'Tinder's fun, isn't it?' he asked, pouring her glass of wine.

'It certainly speeds things up,' said Dee-anne. 'But you have to go through an awful lot of chaff.'

'Chaff?'

'Chaff. As in separating wheat from.' She took the glass from him and raised it in salute. 'Or in other words, you have to work your way through a hell of a lot of frogs to find a prince.'

'Is that what I am?' he asked. 'A prince?'

'We'll see,' she said, and they clinked glasses.

'Your profile says you're twenty-one,' he said.

'Yes.'

'You look younger.'

'That's good to know.' She giggled and sipped her wine. 'I love your condo.'

'Thank you.'

'And you live alone?'

'I'm divorced. The children flew the nest years ago, so, yes...' He sipped his wine. 'You really don't look twenty-one,' he said. 'My youngest boy is twenty-two and you look much younger than him.'

'I've always looked young for my age,' she said. 'Does that worry you?'

'Of course not.'

'Do you want me to call you daddy while you're fucking me?'

He looked startled, then slowly smiled. 'Maybe.'

She sipped her wine. 'I do worry about the screaming,' she said.

'The what?'

'The screaming. Your text. You said you'd make me scream.'

'It was a joke.'

'But what about the neighbours? What if there's a lot of noise.'

Nate chuckled. 'Mrs Gonzales below me is as deaf as a post. The guy above me is a divorced dentist and he's out at work all day. I never hear the guy who lives next door, I don't think he's home much. Plus the soundproofing is as good as it gets.'

'So you can play your music as loud as you want?'

'Sure,' he said. He stood up and went over to a Bang and Olufsen sound system. 'What do you like?'

'You choose,' she said.

'I'm a jazz fan.'

'Jazz is cool.'

'You like jazz?'

'I didn't say I like it. I said it's cool. Rock would also be cool.'

There were several shelves of LPs on the wall above the sound system. He went over and ran fingers along the covers. 'I've got Springsteen. The Stones. U2.'

'I hate U2,' she said. 'That Bono, how pretentious is he? An audience with the Pope, what was that about?'

Nate laughed. 'No U2, then.' He pulled out an album. 'Linkin Park?'

'Sure.'

He opened the Perspex cover of his record player and took the vinyl disc from its sleeve. Dee-anne smiled to herself as she saw how his hands were shaking. She figured that Nate didn't get too many pretty young girls in his condo. From the look of it he'd Photoshopped out his gut, too. Not that it mattered. Looks weren't that important. Soundproofing, and no witnesses, that was what mattered. He put the record on the turntable and a few seconds later music filled the condo. He came back and sat on the sofa again, closer to her this time. He smiled and she smelled toothpaste on his breath. He ran his fingers through her hair. 'How old are you?' he asked. 'Tell me the truth. I'm going to fuck you anyway.'

'Even if I'm under age?' His jaw dropped and she laughed at his reaction. She ran her hand down his chest and played with the buckle of his belt. 'Don't worry, I'm not.'

He kissed her on her the lips and she tasted something sour, underneath the mint of the toothpaste. 'So tell me,' he said, pulling away. 'How old are you?'

Her hand slipped between his legs and she smiled at how easily he got hard. She figured he'd probably taken a Viagra tablet or two in anticipation of her arrival. 'I'm a lot older than you think, Nate,' she said. 'A lot older.' She gave him a soft squeeze and he gasped.

'How old?' he asked.

She grinned at him. 'I've been around since the beginning of time, pretty much,' she said.

He frowned, confused. 'I don't understand.'

She squeezed his testicles hard and he yelped. His erection vanished. She grinned at his discomfort and squeezed again.

'What the fuck!' he shouted and pushed himself away. 'What the fuck are you doing?'

'I wanted to hear you scream,' she said quietly. She sipped her wine.

He stood up and pointed at the door. 'Get the fuck out!' he shouted.

'Make me,' she said.

He frowned. 'What?'

'Make me,' she repeated. 'You're a big strong man and I'm a poor weak defenceless girl. Make me.'

'What the fuck is wrong with you?'

Dee-anne shrugged and took another sip of wine.

Nate jabbed his finger at the door. 'Get the fuck out or I'll call the police!'

She smiled sweetly at him. 'And tell them what exactly, Nate? That you've got an underage girl in your apartment and you're plying her with wine.' She raised her glass.

'You said you were twenty-one.'

'I lied.'

His eyes widened and he looked flustered, then he pulled out his wallet. 'Look, if it's money you want, I'll pay you to go...' He took out a handful of banknotes and offered them to her. She ignored the money and her smile widened. Eventually he dropped the bills on the coffee table next to the ice bucket. 'Just take it and go,' he said.

'So you don't want to fuck me any more?'

He put a hand up to his forehead. 'What the fuck are you playing at?'

'Girls just wanna have fun, right?' She sipped her wine and then placed her glass on the table.

He clasped his hands together as if he was praying. 'Please, just go.'

She stood up slowly. 'But I haven't had my fun, yet.'

'I just want you to go. Take the money, and go.'

'I don't want your money, Nate. Take off your clothes.'

His jaw dropped. 'What?'

'Take off your clothes.'

'Why?'

'You'll find out why. You asked me around because I turned you on, right? That's why I'm here. Now take off your clothes.'

He stood looking at her, transfixed to the spot.

'Or you can call the cops and we'll do that whole underage girl drinking wine in your apartment thing.'

'If I undress, you'll go?'

'Of course. After I've kissed you.'

'Kissed me?'

'Sure. That's why I'm here, isn't it?' She bent down and picked up her glass. She sipped her wine as Nate took off his clothes, carefully placing them on one of the grey armchairs. Eventually he was down to his socks and underwear. They matched, a pale green with darker green stripes. 'You buy your socks to match your underwear?' she said.

'They came as a set.'

'Seriously?'

He nodded.

'Take the socks off, Nate. Let's do this properly.' He did as he was told, then stood facing her with his hands cupped over his groin. She put the glass down and walked slowly towards him. He swallowed nervously. She reached up to stroke his face and he flinched. 'How do you feel, Nate?'

He tried to speak but his voice caught in his throat. He coughed. 'Scared.'

'Scared? Or excited?'

His Adam's apple bobbed as he swallowed again. 'Both.'

'But it feels good, doesn't it?' She put her right hand flat against his chest. She could feel his heart pounding and she bit down on her lower lip. She ran her fingers down towards his groin and he let his hands swing by his side. She could feel him getting hard despite his obvious discomfort and she licked her lips. 'Are you ready?' she asked.

'Please don't hurt me again,' he whispered.

She knelt down slowly, blowing along his flesh as she moved. Then she pulled his underwear down until it was around his ankles.

She pursed her lips and blew his pubic hair and her eyes sparkled as she saw the way he hardened. He began to tremble. She looked up at him and opened her mouth. Her teeth were sharp, he realised. Yellowed and pointed. As he stared at her in horror her brown eyes turned a bright red. He moved his hands to push her away but he was too slow and she lunged forward, her mouth opening wider. As she bit he felt the flesh sever and the blood flow and he tilted back his head and screamed at the ceiling. She shook her head from side to side as she bit down, then pulled back and spat out the chunk of bloody flesh. He fell backwards and hit the floor hard, his groin a red mess. She stood up and wiped her lips with the back of her arm, then walked over to the sound system and turned up the volume.

He tried to shuffle away from her, leaving a trail of glistening blood on the carpet, like a slug moving across a sidewalk. She grinned down at him, blood dripping from her yellow fangs, and began unbuttoning her shirt. 'Let me get undressed first, because I don't want to get blood on my clothes,' she explained as he stared up at her in horror. 'There's going to be a lot of blood, Nate. A lot.'

CHAPTER 11

Perez phoned Nightingale first thing in the morning. He had showered and changed into some new clothes that he'd bought at a local Macys and was making himself a coffee. 'Still want to see Kate Walker's parents?' she asked.

'Sure.'

'I'll pick you up in fifteen minutes.'

Nightingale finished making his coffee, grabbed his coat and was outside a couple of minutes before Perez turned up in a white Toyota Prius. He climbed in. She was wearing a dark blue suit over a grey shirt and had her hair clipped back.

'Mrs Walker will see us, but her husband's out,' she said as she edged into the traffic, heading east.

'What did you tell her?'

'Just that we wanted to ask her a few more questions. I skated over the fact I wasn't a cop and she didn't ask.'

'What about my British accent?'

'I was hoping you could sound American.'

'Like this you mean?' said Nightingale, putting on his best American accent.

Perez grimaced. 'That sounded like an Englishman pretending to be a Canadian.'

'How about this?'

She shook her head. 'Worse.'

'So we'll just say I'm a profiler on secondment from Scotland Yard. Like a modern-day Sherlock Holmes.'

'Yeah, that'll work,' said Perez sarcastically.

'I was joking about the Sherlock Holmes, but it's not so far-fetched that the NYPD would bring in a British profiler.' He took out his cigarettes but saw from the look that flashed across her face that the car was a no-smoking area and put them away. 'So where are we going?' he asked.

'Queens.'

'So Kate didn't live in New York?'

'Queens is one of the five boroughs. The island is Manhattan but it's all New York.' She laughed. 'But a lot of people would agree with you that New York is Manhattan and everywhere else isn't.'

'So what was she doing in Manhattan?'

'Her home is in Forest Hills, it's less than thirty minutes on the Subway from there to Central Park. Thirty bucks or so in a cab. It wouldn't be unusual for a teenager to pop into Manhattan for shopping or to see friends.'

They drove across the Queensboro Bridge, passing over Roosevelt Island. 'We are now officially in Queens,' said Perez.

'No need to show my passport, then?' said Nightingale.

'I'm warming to your English humour,' she said.

'Are you?'

'No,' she said. 'That was New York sarcasm.'

Ten minutes later they pulled up in front of a mock Tudor house, the sort that looked as if it belonged in the English countryside, with decorative half-timbering, a steeply-pitched red-tiled roof, tall, narrow windows and decorative chimney pots.

There was a black BMW parked outside a three-car garage.

Perez and Nightingale climbed out. The house was in the middle of a quarter-acre site with a neatly manicured lawn and half a dozen mature trees. There was a child's swing hanging from one of the branches. 'Nice house,' said Nightingale.

'Oh yes.'

'Expensive?'

'Hell, yeah. Way out of my price range. Mr Wainwright could afford it, if he wanted.'

'So the Walkers were doing well.'

'He's good at his job but the wife comes from money. Banking.'

'How many kids?'

'Two. Kate and a son. He's fifteen.'

They walked up to the house. There was an old-fashioned bell-pull in the shape of a stirrup. Perez pulled it and a bell rang somewhere inside the house. The door opened a few seconds later. A young dark-skinned housekeeper in a black and white uniform opened the door. Perez immediately switched to Spanish. Nightingale didn't speak the language but it was clear that Perez was telling her who they were and that Mrs Walker was expecting them. The housekeeper closed the door. Perez looked at Nightingale. 'What?' she said. 'You don't have maids in England?'

'In stately homes, maybe. I didn't say anything.'

'I could see the look on your face. People out here, they have help.'

'And where's she from?'

'South America or Central America maybe.'

The door opened and the woman showed Perez and Nightingale into a large marble-lined hallway, a minimalist interior that was at odds with the fake Tudor exterior.

Mrs Walker was sitting in a minimalist living room on one of two white sofas either side of a large white fireplace containing a TV screen that showed a video of a flickering fire. She was in her late thirties, blonde and slim and with a face that would have been model-pretty if it hadn't been for the hollow cheeks and deep set eyes that suggested she wasn't eating or sleeping much. She stood up and shook hands with them both. Her hand was more like a bony claw with bright pink nails and Nightingale could see the veins through near-translucent skin. She was older than he'd first thought, Nightingale realised,

Perez did the talking, introducing herself and Nightingale. She kept her reason for being there vague and skated over the fact that they weren't there officially. 'We just need a little more information about Kate,' said Perez as she perched on the sofa opposite Mrs Walker. Nightingale had remained standing and was holding a pen and notepad to at least give the appearance of officialdom. 'In the days leading up to what happened, was Kate upset about something?' Perez asked.

'Why do you ask that?' said Mrs Walker, squinting as if she had a headache.

'We're trying to work out what reason she might have had to have gone to the apartment in Manhattan.'

'I've been asked that so many times,' said Mrs Walker. 'We don't know why. The keys were here in my husband's study. He'd shown some clients around that morning and hadn't gone back to the office.'

'He does that a lot?' asked Perez.

'Leave keys here? Of course. There are probably half a dozen in there right now.'

'All in Manhattan?'

'Some in Manhattan. Mostly here in Queens.'

'We were wondering if she had gone to Manhattan to meet someone,' said Nightingale. 'Someone she wanted to talk to.'

Mrs Walker shook her head. 'If she wanted to talk to someone, she'd have talked to me.'

'But teenagers…' He grimaced. 'Sometimes there are things they don't want to share with their parents, right?'

Her eyes narrowed. 'Do you have children, Mr Nightingale? You don't strike me as a father.'

'I'm not. But I know how they are.'

'Based on what? That you were one yourself once? You're a man without children so I don't see that you could have any idea of the relationship between a mother and daughter.'

'I'm sorry, Mrs Walker, I didn't mean to minimise the bond you have with Kate.' He was going to correct himself and say 'had' but he self-censored himself immediately. 'So she was perfectly happy? No problems that you knew of?'

'I'm not saying that. I'm just saying that when something was worrying her, she'd talk to me.'

Nightingale nodded. 'Anything in particular?'

Mrs Walker forced a smile but her forehead remained perfectly smooth. 'There was Ryan's accident, of course. She still hasn't gotten over that.' She closed her eyes and Nightingale knew that she was also struggling with tenses. Mrs Walker opened her eyes. 'Ryan died twelve weeks ago. She broke down at his funeral and she's been on edge ever since.'

'It was a boating accident?'

'They call it an accident but to be honest it was down to his own stupidity. He was a lovely boy but he had a crazy streak. Cycling without a helmet, never wearing his seatbelt in the car. He was with a group of friends kayaking and he wasn't wearing a life vest. And he'd been drinking, it turned out later. They all had. I'm just glad that Kate wasn't with him at the time.' Tears were welling up in her eyes and she grabbed a tissue from a box on the table by her side and dabbed her eyes.

'So it hit Kate hard?'

Mrs Walker nodded. 'She was off school for two weeks. We couldn't get her out of her room. Then she went a bit...'

Nightingale waited for her to finish, but when she didn't he prompted her. 'A bit..?'

'She said she was trying to talk to him. Have you heard of this game, Charlie Charlie?'

Nightingale nodded. 'She was using Charlie Charlie?'

'It was going around the school apparently. All the kids were doing it, usually for fun. But she seemed to think Ryan was talking to her.'

'I'm sorry, I'm not following,' said Perez. 'Charlie Charlie?'

'It's a kid's game,' said Nightingale. 'Well, it's more than that but it tends to be kids who do it. You put two pencils in the shape of a cross on a piece of paper. In the four sections you write yes and no. Then you ask Charlie Charlie to answer questions. The top pencil is supposed to point to the answer.'

'But who is Charlie Charlie?'

'He's supposed to be a Mexican demon or something.'

'That makes no sense,' said Perez. 'Charlie isn't a Mexican name. It'd be Carlitos Carlitos if it was anything.'

'None of it makes sense,' said Nightingale. 'It's just kids scaring each other. Once you get a yes or no answer you can ask other questions and write different answers on the paper. Supposedly Charlie Charlie will answer anything. It's only recently taken hold in the US and UK, but it's been around for years in Latin America. Before that it was in Spain where they called it the Juego de la Lapicera. Pen Game. The thing is, the slightest vibration or draught makes the pen move, and often a form of mass hysteria kicks in, children start screaming and fainting. Schools then ban it and the media picks it up and then of course every kid wants to do it.'

'You seem to know a lot about it,' said Mrs Walker.

'I've come across it a few times, but as I said it's usually a result of mass hysteria. Where did Kate learn about it?'

'School. They banned it a few months ago. Before Ryan passed away. Then after the funeral I found her playing Charlie Charlie with her brother. I took it as a sign of how much she missed Ryan. I told her it was nonsense but she insisted that sometimes Ryan communicated with her. I took her to see a therapist and after a few sessions she seemed to come to her senses.' She dabbed at her eyes again.

'Mrs Walker, could Ms Perez and I take a look at Kate's bedroom?' asked Nightingale.

Mrs Walker flinched as if she'd been stung. 'Why?'

'It would give us a better idea of who she was, which might point us in the direction of her killer.'

Mrs Walker tilted her head to one side. 'I don't understand. The police were here the day she was found and they spent hours asking me and my husband about her.'

'I understand. But there might be something that wasn't noticed before.'

'Such as?'

'It might be anything. Say she has a poster of a band on her wall. Maybe that band was doing a personal appearance on the day she went into Manhattan. That would give us somewhere to look.'

'She doesn't have posters on her wall,' said Mrs Walker.

'That's just an example.'

Mrs Walker was clearly uncomfortable at the thought of them going into her dead daughter's bedroom so Nightingale looked over at Perez for support.

'We'd only need a few minutes,' she said. 'We wouldn't need to touch anything. We just need a look.'

Mrs Walker nodded. 'Okay. Fine.' She dabbed her eyes. 'I haven't tidied it up, it's just the way she left it when…' She moaned and closed her eyes. 'Maria can take you up.' She opened her eyes again. 'Maria!'

The housekeeper appeared from the hallway. 'Yes, Mrs Walker.'

'Please show them upstairs to Kate's room.' She blew her nose as the housekeeper led Nightingale and Perez through the hallway and up a marble staircase at the top of which was a hallway running left and right. She took them to the left, walked by three white-painted doors and opened the fourth. She stood to the side to let them go in.

It was a large room with two windows overlooking the rear garden. There was a white four-poster bed with a crumpled duvet and the pillows carelessly tossed against the headboard. There was a mirrored built-in closet to the left and to the right was a door that led to a bathroom. Nightingale looked over his shoulder. The housekeeper was standing in the hallway. She had taken out a smartphone and was looking at it. He went over to the bathroom. It was large and airy with a window with frosted glass, a walk-in shower with glass sides that matched the window, and a roll-top bath. There was a line of yellow ducks on the window sill. There was a mirrored cabinet above the sink and Nightingale opened it. Inside was a pack of sanitary towels on the top shelf and some Pepto-Bismol on the shelf below it.

'What are you looking for, Jack?' asked Perez.

'I'm not sure,' he said, closing the cabinet. He walked past her, back into the bedroom. Mrs Walker was right, there were no pop posters on the wall. There was a map of the world and photographs stuck to it. He looked at the pictures. They were all of Kate, smiling and happy, in places she'd visited, presumably with her parents. There was a picture of her in front of the pyramids in Egypt, on safari in Africa, in front of a Thai temple, skiing in Austria, on a yacht in the Mediterranean.'

'She had a good life,' said Perez, coming up behind him. 'I don't even have a passport.'

'I'm not a fan of planes,' said Nightingale.

'What is it with you? You don't like planes, you don't like elevators. But you're okay with cars?'

'It's not about transport. It's about being in confined spaces where I have no control over what's happening.'

'You're a passenger in my car.'

'Yeah, but I can always grab the wheel.'

'Good to know.'

Nightingale turned around. 'I don't see any pictures of the boyfriend, do you?'

There was a framed photograph of Kate and her brother with their parents on a bedside table. It was a formal picture, taken in a studio by a professional. On the wall above it was a framed photograph of her class at school, another formal pose with a teacher standing at the side. Stripped across the bottom was FOREST HILLS HIGH SCHOOL, CLASS 11K.

'Maybe she didn't want a reminder?'

'She was trying to contact him. That doesn't sound like she was trying to forget him.' He went over to the closet and slid back the right hand mirrored door. It was full of dresses and shirts hanging from a rail and at the bottom were six drawers. He pulled the top one open. It was full of underwear. 'Ah,' he said, stepping back. 'Maybe you should check here.'

There was desk by the window with a top-of-the-range Apple computer and a pair of expensive headphones. He switched it on but it was password protected. Nightingale switched off the computer. There was a white chest of drawers against one wall with a collection of soft toys on it. One was a white bear holding a heart on which were the words LOVE YOU. Nightingale picked it up and showed it to Perez. 'Sweet,' she said.

Nightingale worked his way down the drawers. There were t-shirts in the top one, sweaters in the second, shorts in the third, and in the bottom one, a Ouija board, white candles and a box of matches. 'There you go,' he said.

Perez came over and looked down at it. 'What is it?'

'It's an Ouija board. They sell it as a kid's game but it's basically a way of communicating with spirits. I'm guessing Mrs Walker didn't know about this.' He bent down and picked it up. He took it over to the bed and took off the lid to show her the board and the white plastic planchette that came with it.

'It's a game?' asked Perez. 'How does it work?'

'You put your fingers on the plastic thing, the planchette, and ask a spirit to spell out messages.'

'So this isn't Charlie Charlie?'

'It's like a step up from that.'

'You think she used this to try to talk to her dead boyfriend?'

'Maybe. Or it could have been in the drawer for years and forgotten about. But the candles in there suggest that she's been using it recently.' He put the lid back on the box and took it back to the drawer.

'So she was still grieving for the boyfriend. She was trying to talk to him beyond the grave. What's that got to do with her going to Manhattan and getting into an empty apartment?'

'Maybe someone was offering to help her. She arranges to meet him in the apartment for a séance or something.'

'A séance? Are you serious?'

'She tried Charlie Charlie. Her mum told us that. She's been using a Ouija board. Maybe neither worked and she wanted to move up to the next level.'

'A séance?'

'Or a medium. Someone who channels spirits.'

'You believe in that nonsense?'

'You're a Catholic, Cheryl. You believe in an immortal soul, in Heaven and Hell?'

'Me believing in God and believing in holding hands around the table to talk to the dead are two different things.'

'In my experience there are mediums who can make contact with spirits,' said Nightingale. 'There are a lot of charlatans, sure, but there are a few who are genuine. But that isn't the point, the point is whether or not Kate believed it. If she did, she might have contacted someone who offered to help.' He turned to look at the computer. 'We could do with looking at her files.'

'We'd need a warrant and that's not going to happen because I'm not a cop any more.'

'Even if Mrs Walker agreed to letting us have a look?'

'It's password protected.'

'I'm sure you've got computer experts, haven't you?'

She thought about it for a couple of seconds, then nodded. 'Okay, it's worth a try,' she said.

They went back downstairs. Mrs Walker was still sitting on the sofa, dabbing her eyes. 'Thank you for that, Mrs Walker,' said Perez. 'We won't take up any more of your time?'

'Did you find anything useful?'

Perez shook her head. 'Unfortunately not. Mrs Walker, did the investigating officers examine your daughter's computer?'

'Her computer?'

'In the bedroom. The Apple.'

'The detectives who came here didn't go upstairs. They spoke to me and my husband and we gave them...' She blew her nose before continuing. 'We gave them a DNA sample. Her toothbrush. But I went upstairs to get it. They stayed here.'

'Can we borrow the computer, just for a few days?' asked Perez.

'Why?'

'We'd like to check her emails, that's all. It'd be easier for the technician to do it in our office rather than send them here.'

'You think she might have emailed the person who killed her??'

'That's a big leap, Mrs Walker,' said Perez. 'But it might help us to know if she was talking to anyone before she went to Manhattan.'

'What about her cellphone, Mrs Walker?' asked Nightingale.

'That was with her, in the loft,' said Mrs Walker. 'The police took it with them and they still have it.'

'But you're okay for us to take the computer?' asked Perez. 'I'll get it back to you in a few days.'

Mrs Walker nodded but didn't say anything. She was dabbing at her eyes as Perez and Nightingale left.

CHAPTER 12

The technician was a Korean girl in her twenties with a fringe that overlapped the top of her black-rimmed spectacles. Her name was Yung-yi and it took her less than ten minutes to crack the password of Kate Walker's desktop computer. Nightingale and Perez had given her the computer and gone off to get coffees and by the time they returned she was printing out a dozen or so sheets of Kate's emails.

'There's everything she sent over the week before she died,' said Yung-yi. 'Most of it is school-related.'

'What about social media?'

'Not a problem, she stored all her passwords so I can log onto anything,' said the technician.

'Facebook, Instagram, Twitter, give me everything you can find,' said Perez. 'Also I need a list of everything she searched for and any websites she visited.'

'I'm on it,' said Yung-yi. She had a bowl of popcorn next to the computer and she tossed a couple of pieces into the air and caught them in her mouth.'

'Show off,' laughed Perez.

There was a large white-topped table at the far end of Yung-yi's office and Perez sat down with Nightingale and gave him half the printed sheets. The technician was right, they were mostly involved school assignments.

There were a few personal emails to friends making arrangements to meet but they were always local meetings. 'I'm guessing she was more chatty on her phone,' said Nightingale.

Perez nodded. 'The cops will have been straight onto that so we can assume they didn't find anything,' she said.

'Can you ask Andy? Just to be sure.'

'Andy's not an idiot,' said Perez. 'But yes, okay, I'll ask.'

'Nothing in those?' asked Nightingale, nodding at the papers she was holding.

She shook her head.

'I'd really like to talk to Kate's brother,' said Nightingale.

'Why?'

'The Ouija board was in her room. Maybe she had her brother help her with it. It needs at least two people, ideally three.'

'You seriously think the Ouija board has something to do with her death?'

'It's possible. The brother would be able to tell us if she was using it. For all we know it could have been in that drawer for years. An unwanted Christmas present maybe.'

'So why didn't you ask Mrs Walker about it?'

Nightingale shrugged. 'I didn't want to worry her.'

'Ouija boards are nonsense, right? A toy.'

'They were sold as a toy, back in the sixties,' said Nightingale. 'But they're a serious occult tool.'

'To talk to the dead?'

'Sometimes. But it's an open channel. Anyone can use it. Devils. Demons. If you use one, you're leaving yourself open to be contacted by anyone or anything. It's a lot like an internet chat room. You're never sure who you're really talking to. They became popular at the same time as automatic writing, where you hold a pen and close your eyes and let a spirit write through you. That's one on one and takes a lot of practice. A talking board is easier. Pretty much anyone can do it.'

'Talking board?'

'That's the generic name. The word Ouija was patented but there had already been talking boards around for years. Ouija was a made-up word, combing the French and German words for Yes.'

'Someone always pushes, I thought that's how they work.'

'When it's a game, yes. Either consciously or subconsciously, someone moves the planchette. But when a spirit is present….' He left the sentence unfinished.

'So what do you think happened? You think she used the board and tried to contact her boyfriend?'

'Perhaps.'

'But how do we get from there to her being sliced to death in a Manhattan loft?'

'I don't know. I'm taking this one step at a time.'

'From the look on your face I'd say you weren't telling me everything, Jack.'

'All I have is theories. Nothing concrete. But as soon as I know for sure, I'll tell you.'

'Okay, I have her Google history now,' said Yung-yi. She pressed a button and her printer kicked into life. 'And just so you know, she has Tor software on here.'

'Which means what?' asked Perez.

'The Tor browser lets you access the dark web,' said Nightingale. 'It's a shadow internet that runs through a network of relays around the world. No one can see what sites you visit and the sites can't learn anything about you. There's a lot of illegal stuff on the dark web. Drugs, killers for hire, money laundering.'

'What would a Forest Hills teenager be doing on the dark web?' asked Perez.

Nightingale left the question unanswered and went over to the printer. It had already churned out half a dozen sheets and he picked them up. Most of her search engine queries were homework-related and he smiled at the fact that several times she had Googled 'pre-written essays' for several subjects. She had Googled reviews of restaurants in Forest Hills and had spent some time looking at the drug ecstasy and its chemical name, methylenedioxy-metamphetamine. Which suggested either she was using it or someone she knew was.

'When did the boyfriend die?' he asked Perez.

'Three months ago, Mrs Walker said. I don't have the actual date. Why?'

'Because two months ago she was Googling "séances" and "Ouija board" "contacting the dead" and a lot of spiritualist stuff.' He handed her the sheets and picked up more from the printer's tray. He flicked through them. 'Then suddenly she stopped.'

'That was when she downloaded Tor,' said Yung-yi.

'Which means what?' asked Perez.

'It means she stopped using the internet and went into the dark web.'

'What did she look at there?'

Nightingale smiled. 'That's the point. There's no way of telling. And because it's all anonymous and untraceable, there's some seriously disturbed stuff there.

Perez looked over at the technician. 'He's right,' said Yung-yi. 'She's cleared her cache so there's no way of knowing what sites she went to and what she downloaded.'

'But we do know her interest in the Ouija board was recent and so almost certainly tied in with her dead boyfriend,' said Nightingale.

Perez sighed in exasperation. 'But I don't see how that gets us any closer to finding her killer.'

'That's why we need to talk to her brother,' said Nightingale. 'I'm hoping he'll be able to tell us what she did with the Ouija board.'

CHAPTER 13

Nightingale wasn't sure what he expected Forest Hills High School to look like, but the main building took him by surprise. It was in a Georgian style with a red brick exterior trimmed with limestone and pitched grey-black slate roofs. There were towering white columns supporting a triangular pediment with a clock in the centre and at the top of the building was a circular tower made of columns. It looked for all the world as if it had been lifted straight out of London and dropped into the Queen's landscape.

'How old is the school?' Nightingale asked Perez as they climbed out of her car.

'1940s,' she said. 'It's got a good reputation.'

Perez had phoned ahead and Eddie Walker was waiting for them in the principal's office. The principal's secretary was a pretty young girl in her twenties wearing a black blazer over a yellow dress. She seemed to think that Perez and Nightingale were with the NYPD but Perez was immediately upfront that they were private detectives but they were looking at the Kate Walker case.

'Does Mrs Walker know that you're talking to Eddie?' she asked.

'We were just at her house,' said Nightingale, which didn't answer her question but seemed to satisfy the secretary.

'Am I in trouble?' asked Eddie. He was a good-looking boy with a strong jaw and a mop of dark brown hair that he kept flicking away from his eyes. He was wearing a red and black plaid shirt over a white t-shirt, and black jeans, He had a rash of white spots across his forehead and a larger spot on his chin that he kept scratching as he looked at them. He was sitting on a sofa at the far end of the room by the window.

'Not at all,' said Perez. 'We just need to ask you about your sister.'

'Do you need me to be here or can I get on with my work?' asked the secretary.

'Whatever you're happy with,' said Perez.

The secretary nodded at her work station, close to the door that led to the Principal's office. 'I've some emails that have to go out this afternoon,' she said. 'Just let me know if you need anything.'

She went over to her computer and sat down. Perez joined Eddie on the sofa while Nightingale pulled up a chair.

'Eddie, we need to know what Kate was doing with the Ouija board,' said Nightingale.

'Are you Australian?' asked the boy.

Nightingale smiled. 'English.'

'You sound Australian.'

'I get that a lot.' The boy's attempt to change the subject was transparent and he was rubbing his hands together nervously. Nightingale leaned closer to him and lowered his voice. 'This is just between you and us, Eddie. We won't be telling your mom or your dad or anyone. That's why we've come here to talk to you and not your home. Do you understand?'

The boy nodded. 'Sure. But I don't know anything about a Ouija board.' He looked over at Perez, smiling and nodding as if he could make her believe him by sheer force of will.

'We found the board, in your sister's bedroom,' said Perez.

'There has to be at least two people using it,' said Nightingale. 'She had the board in her room and she wouldn't use it with your mom and dad, would she?'

'They'd go crazy,' said Eddie.

'Of course they would. That's why she asked you. Just tell us what happened, Eddie. No one else needs to know.'

The boy folded his arms and stared at Nightingale's Hush Puppies. 'I told her I didn't want to do it. It was stupid. But she kept on and on. She wouldn't stop.'

'What did she want you to do?' asked Perez.

'She wanted to talk to Ryan. We'd been playing that stupid Charlie Charlie game and she seemed to think he was trying to get a message to her.'

'Did you play Charlie Charlie with Kate?' asked Nightingale.

Eddie shook his head, still staring at Nightingale's shoes. 'It's stupid. The wind blows the pencil. That's all.'

'But Kate thought there was more to it?' asked Nightingale.

Eddie nodded. 'She showed me the Ouija board. Said it would let Ryan talk to her. I told her, Ryan's dead, the dead don't say anything to anyone because that's what dead means. She kept on at me and on at me. Then she said she'd tell my mom that I'd been smoking pot.' He looked up guiltily. 'Forget I said that, please.'

'Eddie, we don't care about pot,' said Nightingale. 'We don't care about anything other than what happened to your sister. Anything you tell us stays here, it goes no further. I promise.'

Eddie nodded. 'She found a joint and said she'd show it to mom. Mom would have freaked, and I mean freaked. So I did what she wanted.' He looked over at Perez. 'You mustn't tell my mom.'

'We won't,' said Perez.

'Swear?'

'I swear,' she said, and touched the small gold cross at her throat.

Eddie looked back at Nightingale. 'She said it had to be done at midnight. She did it on a night when mom and dad were asleep. She came to get me and took me to her bedroom. She had the board set out on the floor and these candles around it. She lit the candles and had me touch the pointer thing.'

'The planchette?'

'I don't know what it was called. It was a bit like a heart with a hole in it.'

'Did she say a prayer before you started? Or sprinkle anything on the board?'

Eddie shook his head. 'Just made me put my hands on it and then she asked to talk to Ryan. She asked if Ryan was there and the pointer thing began to move. To YES. I was sure she was pushing it and I told her and she got really angry with me. She said I'd spoil it if I kept talking. She asked if Ryan was really there and it went to YES again. Then it started to spell out words.' He sat back on the sofa and ran his hands over his face. 'Can I have a drink of water?' he asked Perez. 'Or a soda would be better. A Pepsi. Or a Mountain Dew.'

'Sure,' said Perez. 'Is there a machine or something?'

Eddie nodded at the door. 'Outside. In the corridor.'

Perez went out to fetch a soda. 'Are you okay?' asked Nightingale.

'Not really,' he said. He shuddered. 'I still can't believe that Kate's dead. And the way she died.'

'So what did it spell out, Eddie? What did the board say?'

Eddie took a deep breath. 'Blindfold the boy.'

'She wanted to blindfold you?'

'It wasn't her. It was him. Ryan.'

'Or it was her pushing the planchette.'

Eddie shook his head. 'She wasn't pushing. She was talking to Ryan. He was making us move the thing. Even when she put the blindfold on me it kept moving.' Eddie stared at Nightingale, his face fearful. 'It works, doesn't it? The Ouija board. You can use it to talk to the dead?'

'Don't even think about it, Eddie.' He pointed a warning finger at the boy's face. 'Kate's dead. She's gone. Don't even think about using the board to contact her.'

'I wasn't,' he said.

'Well don't.'

Perez returned with a can of Mountain Dew. Eddie mumbled his thanks as he took it from her. He popped the tab and drank as she sat down next to him. 'So where are we?' she asked Nightingale.

'Whoever they contacted, they asked Kate to blindfold Eddie,' said Nightingale. 'Once Kate had done that, Eddie wasn't able to see the messages.'

'How long did this go on for?' Perez asked the boy.

'A while,' he said. 'I lost track of time.'

'And you had your fingers on the planchette all the time?'

'Kate said I had to. She said it wouldn't work if only one person was touching it.'

'She didn't spell the words out loud?'

Eddie shook his head. 'All I heard was when she asked him questions.'

'What sort of questions was she asking?' said Perez.

'I heard her say when. And what she'd need. She stopped at one point to get a pen, I think.'

'A pen?'

'She told him to wait and then she got up and went away. She came back after a bit and she started taking notes. A lot of notes.'

'What did it sound to you like they were talking about?' asked Nightingale.

Eddie sipped his soda then rubbed his mouth with his sleeve. 'I don't know. She didn't say much. And she put whatever she was writing on away before she took the blindfold off.'

'What happened then?' asked Nightingale.

'She put the board away and made me promise never to tell anyone what had happened. She said if I did she'd tell my parents about the weed.'

'And you never said anything to your parents?' asked Nightingale. 'Not even after Kate was found?'

Eddie shook his head. He sipped his soda.

'And she never mentioned it again? She never told you what she'd written?'

The boy shook his head again.

Perez patted him on the shoulder. 'Are you okay?'

He nodded. 'You won't tell my parents?'

'Of course not,' she said. 'We won't even tell them we've spoken to you, if you'd prefer it that way. Like we were never here.'

'That would be good,' he said. 'Thank you.'

Perez stood up and nodded at Nightingale. 'I think we're done, aren't we?'

'Sure.'

'The Ouija board, you think it has something to do with what happened to Kate?' asked Eddie.

'It shows that she wanted to contact Ryan,' said Nightingale. 'She might have tried other ways. We'll ask around.'

'You have to catch him,' said Eddie. 'You have to get whoever it is.'

'We will,' said Nightingale.

CHAPTER 14

Nightingale and Perez walked out of the school and over to Perez's car. Nightingale lit a cigarette as they walked. 'See now I'm confused,' said Perez.

'About what?'

'Does this Ouija board work or not? Because you're sending me mixed signals.'

'It depends.'

'On what?'

'On who's using it. It's sold as a toy and it works just fine that way. You get a group of kids playing it and someone will push. Maybe more than one. And once someone starts pushing everyone joins in. Not always deliberately, sometimes it happens subconsciously, but it's a game.'

'You're very good at evading questions, Jack.' They reached the car and she took out her keys. 'But what Kate did, it wasn't a game. And she blindfolded her brother so he couldn't be pushing it. The way I see it that leaves two choices. She was talking to herself or she was talking to the spirit.'

'A spirit,' said Nightingale. 'Maybe not the spirit she thought she was talking to. There's no way of knowing who had contacted her.'

She stared at him over the top of the car. 'So now you're saying it's real. That she was talking to the dead?'

'I don't know who or what she was talking to.'

'But it's more than a game, that's what you're saying.'

Nightingale sighed. He took a long drag on his cigarette and blew smoke before replying. 'It's a game. But it can be more than that. It's like a pen. You can write a poem with it, or a blackmail letter. It's the same pen, what matters is the use you put it to.'

'But you're telling me that a Ouija board can be used to talk to the dead.'

'To the spirits of the dead, yes. But you have to know what you're doing. I'd say ninety-nine per cent of the time people are either playing around or subconsciously pushing.'

'And Kate Walker?'

Nightingale blew smoke again. 'That blindfold thing worries me. I've never heard of that before. It doesn't mean that she wasn't pushing, consciously or subconsciously, but...' He shrugged.

'But what?'

'If she was communicating with someone or something, what would they have to say that they didn't want the brother knowing about?' He shrugged. 'I don't know, Cheryl. This is a new one on me.'

Perez climbed into the car. Nightingale threw away what was left of his cigarette and joined her.

She sat with her hands on the wheel but made no attempt to start the car. 'I don't understand what's going on here,' she said.

Nightingale said nothing and she turned to look at him, eyes narrowed. 'Did Wainwright know about this occult stuff when he brought you in? Because it's starting to look to me as if you're some sort of expert on all this.'

'He didn't know. He wanted me to check it out. That's what I'm doing.'

'Let me ask you a direct question, Jack. You believe you can talk to the dead?'

He returned her stare for several seconds. 'Yes.'

'And that's personal experience talking?'

Nightingale nodded. 'Yes.'

She closed her eyes, sighed, and then cursed under her breath. 'What the hell have you got me into?'

Nightingale wasn't sure if the question was rhetorical or not so he didn't answer. Eventually she started the car but she drove him back to where he was staying without saying a word and didn't say goodbye when she left him on the sidewalk.

CHAPTER 15

Dee-anne was wearing a black leather jacket and tight-fitting jeans and a white t-shirt that said in very small letters – IF YOU CAN READ THIS 1) YOU ARE STARING AT MY BREASTS AND 2) YOU ARE WAY TOO CLOSE. Her hair was tied back in a ponytail and several heads turned as she walked the length of the bar, her heels clicking on the wooden floor, and slid onto a stool at the far end. She was carrying a small black Michael Kors bag and she put it on the bar next to her.

There was a single barman working, a guy in his thirties with bulging arms that strained at a black t-shirt. He had slicked-back hair and a goatee beard and was chewing on a toothpick as he walked up to her.

'Jack, rocks,' she said.

'Jack as in orange juice?'

She frowned. 'Jack as in JD. Jack Daniels. Rocks as in ice.'

Four bikers wearing denim vests with SATAN'S SOLDIERS on the back were playing pool and one of them, bald with a bushy ginger beard, turned to see what was going on.

'I'll need to see some ID,' said the barman.

She held out her hand and he reached out but then he frowned when he realised she wasn't holding anything. She grabbed his wrist and smiled. 'You don't need to see any ID, Billy. Just get me the fucking drink.'

He sneered at her and tried to pull his hand away, but realised he couldn't move his arm. He pulled harder but her nails dug into his flesh making him wince. He stared at her hand. It was small, not much bigger than a child's. He frowned, trying to work out how she could hold him so tightly.

'See, Billy, you don't want your wife knowing that you like to suck bikers' dicks in your spare time. Or that now and again you pay them to fuck you up the arse. You're not gay, obviously, you being married and all, it's just you like the feel of flesh against flesh. I mean who doesn't, right? Live and let live, that's what I always say. So you run off and get me a drink or I'll phone your wife and let her know what you do in your spare time.'

The barman tried to pull his arm away but she refused to release him. A vein began to throb in his temple as he strained against her grip, but she held him fast.

'Or maybe I'll call the cops and tell them about the meth you sell. The little bags you've got behind the bar there and the half kilo upstairs behind the TV. That's prison time, Billy. Mind you, plenty of dicks to suck behind bars, right? An ill wind and all that.' She let go of his arm and he struggled to maintain his balance. 'Get me my Jack rocks, Billy. And be quick about it.'

Dee-anne stared at him until he nodded and went over to a line of spirit bottles. He returned with a Jack Daniels and ice, put it down in front of her and retreated to the other end of the bar. The biker with the ginger beard said something to his pool companions and they all looked over at the girl but she didn't seem to notice.

She took out her phone and spent a few minutes flicking through Tinder, selecting likely candidates and rejecting the chaff. She felt him outside several seconds before the door opened. She didn't recognise the body he was in, of course, but she knew it was Xaphan.

He recognised her for who she was, grinned and waved and headed towards her. 'Isn't this fucking amazing?' he said.

She grinned back. 'I'm loving it.'

'You feel so much more alive, don't you? Even though every cell is dying. You know you're dying but that just makes everything so intense.' He slid onto the stool next to her and nodded at her drink. 'What is that?'

'Jack Daniels.'

'I tried that. What else is good?'

'Scotch.'

'I'll have a Scotch, then.'

Dee-anne waved over at the barman. 'Hey, Billy, a Scotch rocks for my friend here. A malt. A good one.'

The barman poured the drink and brought it over.

'This is my friend, Matt,' she said. 'Matt this is Billy.'

Matt held out his hand. The barman stared at it.

'Don't be a prick, Billy,' said the girl. 'Shake hands with your customer.'

The barman shook hands and Matt grinned. 'Nice to meet you Billy.' He let go of the barman's hand and Billy hurried away. Matt looked over at the girl. 'He likes to suck dick, huh?'

She laughed. 'Who knew?' She picked up her glass and clinked it against Matt's. Or Xaphan's. It was confusing. The face she was looking at belonged to a good-looking teenage boy. But behind the eyes was Xaphan, a second-order demon who was supposed to spend all eternity stoking the fires of Hell.

And she knew that Xaphan saw her as a pretty teenage girl, even though she was Lilith, a princess of Hell who could take many forms, most of which would send the occupants of the bar out into the streets screaming with terror. 'What do you want to do?' asked Dee-anne.

Matt grinned. 'Let's have some fun,' he said. 'Nasty fun.'

'Anything in particular?'

'Let's play it by ear.'

The girl nodded. 'We can trawl a few clubs, see what's out there.'

Matt downed his glass in one, and shuddered with pleasure. 'It's like drinking fire,' he said. 'You can feel it spreading through your body.'

'Have you tried vodka?'

He shook his head.

'Vodka does the same but quicker. You don't get the same flavour in your mouth but you get more of a burn.' She waved at the barman. 'Billy, give my friend a vodka. Snow Queen.'

'Snow Queen?' repeated Matt.

'From Kazakhstan. They use artesian spring water from the Himalayas and then distil it five times. It's as pure as the driven snow.'

The barman poured a measure of vodka and put the glass down in front of him.

'Leave the bottle. Billy, there's a good man,' said Dee-anne. The barman did as he was told then beat a hasty retreat to the far end of the bar.

Matt drank it in one and then gasped and patted his chest with the flat of his hand. 'Oh yes, now that I like,' he said. He refilled his glass. 'So you've been here a few days now. How much fun have you been having?'

She grinned. 'A lot,' she said. She held up her smartphone. 'There's this app they use to arrange sex. You put up your picture and your details and then if someone likes your profile you can talk to them. Mainly it's just sad men looking for sex.'

He took the phone from her and looked at the screen. 'So I could use it?'

'You might have to use a different picture, you look too young.'

'What about you?'

She grinned. 'Old men like young girls. It works like a charm.' She took the phone back from him. 'It's perfect, you can check hundreds of possibilities in an hour or so and you know where they live and you can find out if they're alone or whatever.'

'I love it,' said Matt, and drained his glass. 'Fuck me that's good.'

One of the bikers walked over from the pool table, swinging his cue. He was tall, well over six feet four, his head shaved and with four steel studs in his right ear. He had a small tuft of black hair sprouting from under his lower lip. The sleeves had been hacked off his jacket to show off the intricate tattoos of skulls, naked women and snakes that covered both arms. He leered at Dee-anne. 'Hey sexy, if ever you fancy a real man, give me a call.'

Dee-anne smiled, showing perfect teeth, and swivelled around on her stool to face him. 'You're a real man?'

'Damn right.' He dropped his hands between his legs and squeezed his own groin. 'This'll satisfy you more than his tiny pecker will.'

Matt slid off his stool. He was a head shorter than the biker and had to lift his chin to look him in the eye. 'Are you saying I've got a small penis?' He looked over at the girl. 'Is he saying I've got a small penis?'

The biker laughed, though it was more like the growl of an attack dog. 'If you've got one at all, which I doubt. You look like a virgin to me. Have you ever even kissed a girl?'

'Are you really a soldier of Satan?' said Dee-anne. 'That's what it says on your back, right?'

'You can read, that's good.'

'Nah, the reason I ask is that I know most of Satan's troops and you I don't recognise.'

'What the fuck are you talking about, bitch?'

'I'm just saying, I don't see that a pussy like you would ever be one of the master's soldiers.'

'You're calling me a pussy? Me? A pussy?'

'I think she is,' said Matt. 'And I think she's right.'

'Fuck you,' said the biker, raising the pool cue. He brought it down hard towards Matt's face and it was just inches away from landing when Matt's hand flew up. There was a loud 'thwack' and the pool cue was locked in Matt's hand. The biker's jaw dropped in astonishment. Matt grinned at his surprise. Then his left arm flew up and his forearm pushed under the biker's chin and forced him back against the wall. The biker struggled but couldn't move. The pool cue fell from his hand and clattered on the floor.

Two of the bikers stepped away from the pool table, their cues raised high. The girl turned and pointed at them. 'Stay where you are, boys, or I'll rip your fucking heads off.' They froze and looked at her, clearly confused. She slid off her stool and took a step towards them. 'I mean it. Get back to your fucking game or I will rip you apart.' Her voice had become suddenly deeper and rougher and her eyes had turned a vivid scarlet. She bent down, picked up the dropped cue, and broke it in half as if it was nothing more than a twig. The two men backed away. As they reached the pool table her eyes returned to their usual blue colour and she smiled sweetly. 'Thank you so much,' she said, and tossed the broken cue away.

'So I've got a tiny dick, have I?' Matt asked the biker that he had pinned up against the wall.

The biker glared down at him. Even if he'd wanted to speak the arm across his throat prevented him from saying anything. Matt thrust his left hand between the biker's legs. Matt looked over his shoulder at Dee-anne. 'He does have a very large penis,' he said. 'It's big. So are his balls. They're huge.'

'Good to know,' said Dee-anne.

'Hey Billy, have you sucked this guy's dick?' shouted Matt. 'Tell me, have you had Reggie's dick in your mouth?' The biker's eyes widened at the mention of his name. 'Yeah, I know you Reggie. I know everything about you. I know what you did to that young girl in Phoenix and I know what your dad did to you when you were nine. I know about that hooker you kicked to death when you were high on crack and how you burnt down your father's house with him in it when you were sixteen.'

The biker gritted his teeth together and grunted. He struggled but Matt's left arm under his chin kept him locked against the wall.

The boy grinned up at the biker. 'Yeah, they're one set of balls you've got there.' He squeezed harder and the biker's face went crimson. Spittle was spurting from between his closed lips. 'I wonder what sound they'll make when they burst?' Matt squeezed harder and the biker screamed. 'They're going,' said the boy, increasing the pressure. 'I can feel it.' The biker was roaring in pain now and banging the back of his head against the wall. The boy started to roar along with him as he clenched his fist tighter, then he laughed as he felt the balls collapse. The biker slumped and the boy stepped back and let him fall to the floor. The boy stood looking down at the unconscious man, grinning in triumph. 'Not so big now, are they?' he said. He put his hand to his nose and sniffed, then pulled a face. He smiled at the girl. 'That was fun,' he said.

'Nasty fun?' she said.

He laughed out loud. 'Oh yeah, real nasty fun.' He put his arm around her shoulder. 'Let's go.'

The girl winked at the barman, then gestured at the unconscious biker. 'My friend with the busted balls there's paying, Billy' she said. 'Take a nice tip for yourself while you're at it.'

They headed out together. 'Did you hear them pop?' Matt asked as they stepped into the street. 'They popped like grapes.'

She laughed. 'Yeah, I heard.' The door slammed shut behind them.

CHAPTER 16

There were six of them on the path, standing in a circle and laughing and swearing. They looked up as Dee-anne and Matt approached. One of them said something and they all laughed, though there was now a harder edge to the laughter.

'What do you think?' asked Dee-anne. They were walking across Central Park. The sun had gone down and the moon was hanging overhead, a perfect white circle, the sky so clear they could make out the craters.

'I think they think we're prey,' said Matt.

'Big mistake.'

'Huge.'

'We could turn around and walk away.'

'We could,' she agreed.

'But we're not going to, are we?'

She grinned and slipped her arm through his. 'Hell, no.'

The gang split into two as they approached, standing either side of the path. They were all dressed in baggy jeans, gleaming new Nike high-tops and hoodies. They had their hoods up and their hands deep in their pockets. All six were now staring at the two of them. The tallest had the New York Yankees logo stripped across his hoodie and was chewing on a toothpick. He gestured with his chin at Matt. 'She your bitch?' He was in his late teens but had the eyes of a man much older. Bored and lifeless.

'I'm nobody's bitch,' said Dee-anne.

'I wasn't talking to you, bitch.'

'Are you hard of hearing?' said Dee-anne.

The teenager stepped forward and lifted his hand to strike her. She stared at him with unblinking eyes. 'I dare you,' she said.

'Bitch!' shouted the man and went to slap her. She didn't start moving until the hand was inches from her face but when she did it was a blur. One moment she was standing staring at him, the next his arm was at his side, a jagged piece of his ulna sticking out through the sleeve of his hoodie. His mouth opened and closed and his eyes widened as he stared in horror at the shard of bone.

'Bitch broke his arm!' shouted the teenager next to him. 'Did you see that? Snapped it like it was nothing!'

The teenager with the broken arm slowly knelt down, the colour draining from his face.

Matt moved towards the boy nearest him and grabbed him by the throat. The boy tried to scream but Matt's grip was so strong no sound escaped. The boy tried to claw at Matt's face but Matt lifted him off the ground so that his feet dangled in the air. Matt grinned up at him. 'Cat got your tongue?' he said.

The boy's eyes were bulging and spittle was dribbling from between his lips. One of his companions grabbed at Matt's arm but Matt kicked him between the legs. The attacker flew backwards, across the path and smacked into a large rock at the side of the path. His head hit the rock with a loud thwack and blood sprayed across the grass. Matt laughed out loud, turned and in one smooth movement threw the boy he was holding at the rock. His aim was slightly off and the boy fell to the side of the rock, scrambled to his feet and began running away as fast as he could.

The three remaining teenagers had huddled together like sheep. Their hands were out of their pockets. One had his hands up to his face, his mouth open in shock, the other reached behind his back and pulled out a hunting knife. The third turned to run but Dee-anne kicked his legs out from underneath him and he fell on the path. She stamped down on his right knee and grinned savagely at it cracked. The teenager screamed and curled into a foetal ball. Dee-anne drew back her leg and kicked him hard in the kidneys.

The teenager with the knife was slashing it back and forth as he moved towards Matt. 'Oh no, please don't hurt me with your big bad knife,' said Matt.

'Fuck you, man,' said the teenager. He stepped forward and lunged with the blade but Matt had already moved to the side and the knife went wide. Matt's eyes turned a bright red and when he grinned his teeth had turned into sharp points that gave him the look of a shark about to strike. The teenager pulled back the knife but Matt reached out and grabbed the boy's wrist and broke it with a single twist. He carried on twisting and flipped the boy into the air and then brought him crashing down onto the path.

The final teenager was backing away, his hands up defensively. 'I don't want no trouble, man,' he stammered.

'It's no trouble,' said Matt. He sprang forward as the boy turned to run. He grabbed his head with both hands and twisted savagely. The spine cracked and he felt the body go limp. He tossed him to the side and as he turned to smile at Dee-anne his eyes returned to their usual blue colour and his teeth went back to their normal all-American smile. 'That was fun.'

Dee-anne grabbed his arm. 'We need to go.'

'Why the rush? No one can hurt us.'

'We don't want to cause a fuss. Low profile, remember? Until it's time.'

She hurried him down the path.

'But it was fun, right?' he asked.

'Hell, yeah,' she said.

'The sound when their bones break, isn't it the best sound ever? And the way they react to pain. The terror in their eyes.' He shuddered. 'You can feel the fear, can't you? It's better than anything.'

'Where are you staying?' asked Dee-anne.

'I'm still at home.'

'You should move out.'

Matt shrugged. 'They might call the cops. And it's easier just to be there.'

'Suit yourself.'

'What about Baalberith?'

'He's here already. He'll be coming to Manhattan soon.'

'And the Master?'

'That's more complicated. He needs to get all his ducks in a row. But when he does arrive, we can take it up to the next level.'

Matt laughed and wiped his mouth with the back of his hand. 'I can't wait,' he said.

A woman with two small poodles was walking their way. She was small and almost circular, wrapped up in a fur coat. Dee-anne smiled at her. 'Lovely dogs,' she said, with a smile.

'Thank you,' said the woman. Her face was unnaturally smooth but her hands were liver-spotted and wrinkled.

'I wonder if they taste like chicken,' said Matt. The woman's jaw dropped but her forehead stayed perfectly smooth as Dee-anne hurried Matt down the path.

'You need to stop drawing attention to yourself,' she said. 'We have to stay below the radar. How are you getting home?'

Matt shrugged. 'I was going to walk.'

'We'll get a taxi. I'll drop you.'

'What about you? Where do you stay?'

She held up her phone. 'I'll find somewhere,' she said. 'I usually do.'

CHAPTER 17

Matt unlocked the front door and stepped into the hallway. He didn't bother switching on the light and headed for the stairs. He was half way up the staircase when the lights came on. 'Not so fast, young man,' said a voice. 'Down you come.'

It was his mother, and it was clear from the look on her face that she wasn't happy.

'It's late,' he said.

'Exactly.' She snapped her fingers and pointed at the sitting room door. 'We need to talk.'

Matt sighed and walked slowly down the stairs. His mother stood in the Japanese kimono she wore as a dressing gown, her arms folded.

'I'm tired,' he said.

'And I'm tired of you treating this house like a hotel.'

Matt walked into the sitting room and stood by the fireplace. His mother went over to the sofa and sat down. There was a glass of red wine on the coffee table in front of her. 'Now, young man, what time do you call this?'

Matt made a show of looking at his watch. 'One o'clock,' he said.

'One forty-five,' she said. 'Almost two o'clock.'

Matt shrugged but didn't say anything.

'And Mrs Cohen phoned this afternoon. She wanted to know when you'd be back in school. Apparently you told her you were sick.'

'I am.'

'You don't look sick to me.' She frowned as she saw the grazes on the knuckles of his right hand. 'What have you done to your hand?'

'Nothing.'

'Show me.'

'There's nothing to show.'

'Have you been fighting?'

Matt glared at her. 'I'm sick of your fucking nagging.'

Her jaw dropped. 'What did you say?'

'I'm going to bed,' said Matt. He started walking to the door but his mother jumped to her feet and blocked his way.

'How dare you talk to me like that!' she said.

He tried to get past her but she grabbed him by the shoulders. 'Matt, will you sit down and talk to me.'

'Fuck off!' he shouted, spittle peppering her face.

She let go of his shoulder with her right hand, drew it back and slapped him across the cheek, hard.

He grinned, then head-butted her. She fell backwards, crashed onto the coffee table and rolled onto the floor. The glass of wine fell over and wine spilled over her legs.

Matt moved to stand over her. 'Are you happy now, bitch?' He kicked her in the ribs.

Matt's father burst into the room, his eyes blazing. He was a small man, just over five foot six, but he had a weightlifter's build with wide shoulders and muscled forearms. He was wearing silk pyjamas, his feet bare. 'What the hell's going on?' he shouted. He saw his wife sprawled on the floor and hurried over to help her up.

He saw the red mark on her forehead. 'Honey, what happened? Did you fall?'

She sniffed and wiped away tears. 'He hit me,' she said, her voice a hoarse whisper. 'Matt hit me.'

'He what?'

'He hit me.'

She began to sob and he eased her over to the sofa. 'Did you lay hands on your mother?' he asked, turning to face Matt.

'She asked for it,' snarled the boy

'Asked for it? You never hit a woman and you never, ever, touch your mother, do you hear me?'

'Fuck off,' growled Matt.

His father rushed over and hit Matt full in the face, knocking him flat on his back. 'You bastard!' screamed his father. 'Get up so I can knock you back down again.'

Matt chuckled and wiped his mouth. His hand came away wet with blood.

'Allan, no!' shouted Matt's mother.

He ignored her. 'Get the fuck up!' he shouted.

Matt rolled over and got to his feet, his back to Allan. He turned slowly, his head down so that his fringe hung over his face.

'You apologise to your mother right now!' shouted Allan.

Matt said nothing. He slowly raised his head. His eyes, usually a pale blue, had turned crimson red. He bared his teeth. Matt's teeth had always been perfect with a smile that would have done credit to a toothpaste commercial but now they were yellow, like fangs. Matt took a step towards him. His nails seemed longer and sharper, like the claws of a predator.

'Please, just stop it, both of you!' screamed the woman.

'You need to calm down,' said Allan, but he could hear the uncertainty in his voice. The thing that was moving towards him looked like his son, but he'd changed.

Matt's lip curled back in a wolf-like snarl. He took another step towards his father. Allan turned to run but Matt was too fast for him, he sprang forward and grabbed the neck of his pyjamas, pulling him back. Then he stamped down on the back of Allan's right knee. The joint snapped like a chicken bone and Allan screamed and went down.

'Stop!' shouted Matt's mother. 'Just stop!'

Matt lifted his right foot and stamped on his father's head. 'How do you like that?' he shouted. 'How does that feel?' He stamped down again. And again.

'Matt, stop, you're killing him!' shouted his mother.

Matt grinned over at her. 'Well that is sort of the point,' he said.

His mother stood up and backed towards the door. 'Stay where you are, mom,' said Matt.

Her whole body was shaking and she continued to move to the door, tears streaming down her face. Matt jumped over his father's body and grabbed a large marble sculpture, a symbolic depiction of a woman holding a baby. He swung it over his head and smashed it down on his mother's head. The skull exploded like a watermelon and blood sprayed across the carpet behind her. She slumped without a sound. Matt stood over her and hit her again, and again, until her head was bloody mass of broken skull, blood and splattered brain matter.

He heard his father moan behind him and he tossed the sculpture to the floor. He went over to where his father was curling up into a ball, his head covered with blood. Allan shuddered and coughed and two teeth fell from between his lips on to the carpet. 'Please... stop...' he said, and coughed again. Bloody phlegm trickled from his mouth.

'Stop?' said Matt. 'Why would I stop? I've only just started.'

CHAPTER 18

Nightingale's cellphone rang and he rolled over and grabbed at it. It was just after eight o'clock in the morning and it was Perez calling. 'Are you up?' she asked.

'I am now,' said Nightingale, sitting up and rubbing his face.

'Andy wants to see us, now.'

'What's happened?'

'A double murder.'

'Yeah, well I didn't kill anybody.'

'Can the English humour, Jack. He'll meet us in a coffee shop down the road from where you are. Italian place called Rossi's. Eight thirty.'

'I'll be there,' said Nightingale. He ended the call, lit and smoked a cigarette while he looked out through the window at the street below, then headed into the bathroom to shave and shower.

Perez was sitting outside at a table with a latte in front of her and a croissant in her hand. 'Andy's inside,' she said.

'I'll buy his coffee, see if that helps.' Nightingale went inside where a bald, portly man with a sweeping moustache and an apron in the colours of the Italian flag was giving Horowitz an Americano. 'I'll have the same,' said Nightingale. 'And I'll get his.'

'Thanks,' said the detective and he headed outside to join Perez. Nightingale ordered a ham and cheese Panini and took it and his coffee outside where Horowitz was already deep in conversation with Perez.

Nightingale pulled over a chair from the neighbouring table and joined them. 'So what's the story?' he asked, before taking a large bite out of his Panini.

'There's been a double murder on the Upper West Side,' said Horowitz. 'A Mister Allan Donaldson and his wife Emma. Beaten to death. Kicked, punched, stamped on. Both bodies are in a real mess. Their son Matthew is missing and as of an hour ago we're treating him as the suspect.'

Nightingale swallowed. 'Because?'

'Because the bloody footprints all around the bodies are a match to his shoe size. And his fingerprints are on a sculpture that was used to kill Mrs Donaldson.'

'If he lived there, his fingerprints would be on everything anyway,' said Nightingale. 'How do you know he didn't disturb the attackers and ran away?'

'You think we're amateurs, Nightingale?' asked Horowitz. 'For one, if he did escape he'd have gone to the cops. Two his were the only bloody footprints we found. Three there's CCTV footage of Matt returning just after one forty-five in the morning and then leaving in a hurry ten minutes later.' He counted the points off on his fingers and then looked at Nightingale expectantly. 'Now does that satisfy your English criteria for putting someone on the list of suspects?'

Nightingale held up his hand. 'Sorry, I'm not a morning person. I need caffeine to kick-start my day.' He sipped his coffee. 'And this involves me because..?'

Horowitz sat back in his chair and folded his arms. 'Because Matthew Donaldson's fingerprints and DNA are a match to what we found on the knife that killed Kate Walker.'

Nightingale's jaw dropped. 'What?'

'Matthew Donaldson killed Kate Walker. And at around two o'clock this morning he killed his parents.'

'Motive?'

'We're looking for one, obviously. But at the moment it's looking as if he's a serial killer. And he shouldn't be too difficult to find. Case closed.'

Perez looked over at Nightingale. 'That's good news, right?'

'I guess so,' said Nightingale.

'You don't seem thrilled,' said Horowitz.

Nightingale wrinkled his nose. 'It throws up more questions than it answers,' he said. 'I mean, it's great that you have a suspect, and that we've identified him as Kate's killer. But how did he know her? What was he doing with her in the apartment? Have you found anything to link him to Kate? Other than the prints and his DNA of course.'

'It's early days. We'll check phone records, emails, the works.'

'Yeah about that,' said Nightingale. 'Why didn't you check Kate's desktop for emails?'

Horowitz's eyes narrowed. 'How do you know we didn't?'

Nightingale forced a smile, realising he'd made a mistake. 'I just assumed, you didn't mention it.'

Horowitz continued to stare at Nightingale. 'Did you go around to the house?' Nightingale sipped his coffee and Horowitz turned to glare at Perez. 'Please don't tell me you went around to the Walker's house.'

'We just wanted a chat, for background,' said Perez.

Horowitz shook his head in exasperation. 'Cheryl, come on. I said I'd help, but your messing with an ongoing investigation.'

'We weren't messing. We had a brief conversation with Mrs Walker.'

'You're not authorised to do that.' Horowitz cursed. 'I was doing you a favour and you go an piss all over me.'

'We weren't there long. And we said we were looking for background on Kate, that's all. We didn't claim to be anything we're not.'

Horowitz jerked a thumb at Nightingale. 'How does he know about the computer?'

'We asked Mrs Walker if we could take a look at the hard-drive.'

Horowitz's eyes widened. 'Please tell me she said no.'

'She was okay with it, Andy.'

'You removed evidence?'

'The house isn't a crime scene and you guys had already been. And it's a fair point, why didn't you check the computer?'

'Because Kate was the victim and we'd already checked her phone.' He gritted his teeth and shook his head. 'I can't believe you did that.'

'It was no biggie, Andy. And Mrs Walker was happy enough.'

Horowitz shook his head again. 'Well at least tell me if you found anything?'

'No emails out of the ordinary. School stuff mainly.'

'No contact with a Matthew Donaldson?'

'Not that I remember.' She looked over at Nightingale.

'I'm pretty sure not,' said Nightingale.

'Where's the computer now?' asked Horowitz.

'My office,' said Perez.

'Well get it back to the Walker house today,' said Horowitz. 'Look, this seems to be open and shut. We have all the forensics we need to convict Matthew Donaldson of all three murders. We're looking for him now and I doubt a seventeen-year old High School student is going to be evading New York's finest for long.'

'Don't suppose he went to Kate's school, did he?'

Horowitz's jaw tightened for a second, then he forced himself to relax. 'You really need to stop second-guessing me, Nightingale. It's as annoying as hell.'

This time Nightingale raised both hands in apology. 'Andy, again, I'm sorry. No offence intended.' He lowered his hands. 'It's just that the whole thing is weird and I'm sure you know that. There are serial killers, we know that. Plenty of predators around who get a kick out of killing. And there are plenty of family members who kill family members. Happens all the time. But what we have here is a killer who does both. He killed Kate at random and then he kills his parents. That's unusual. Very unusual.'

'Agreed,' said the detective. 'But maybe one led to the other. The boy snaps and kills Kate, for whatever reason. That's the trigger that starts him killing and a few days later he snaps again, this time with his parents.' He shrugged. 'Let's be honest, most killers have mental health issues to start with. And to be equally honest I don't care, all I want to do is arrest him, the shrinks can work out what makes him tick once we've got him behind bars.' He finished his coffee and stood up. 'Anyway, looks to me as if your case is solved so hopefully your client will be satisfied. With any luck we'll have Donaldson in custody today so I'll have three solved murders and a cast-iron case, so all's well that ends well.'

Perez stood up and hugged him. 'Thanks, Andy. I owe you.'

'Yes you do,' said Horowitz. 'Big time.' He nodded at Nightingale and walked away, his long coat flapping around his ankles.

Perez sat down and took the half of the Panini that Nightingale hadn't touched. 'You didn't tell him about the Dark Web or the Ouija board,' said Nightingale.

'He was upset enough without me going into that,' said Perez. She bit into the sandwich and spoke with her mouth full. 'Besides, if Matthew Donaldson is the killer it makes the occult stuff irrelevant, doesn't it?'

'You think?'

'Donaldson's on a spree. He killed Kate and then he killed his parents. Who knows who else he's killed.'

'So you think, what? He chose her at random? How likely is that, Cheryl? She met him in the apartment her father was showing. She had to have known him.'

'We still don't know that. Maybe he broke in and she disturbed him. He kills her and later he kills her parents. Like Andy said.'

'We know he didn't break in.'

'Then maybe he just picked her at random and knocked on her door.'

'The one time she just happened to be in the apartment? She had to make an effort to be there, she had to take her father's key, travel all the way from Queens. And all that happens at the exact time that a random serial killer is looking for a victim? Unlikely.'

'Coincidences happen all the time, Jack. Wrong time, wrong place.' She took another bite of the Panini and washed it down with coffee.'

'There's something else going on. I'm sure of it.'

'You're like a dog with a bone. Let it go.'

'I can't.' He sipped his coffee. 'We need to go to Philadelphia.'

'Okay.'

'But first we need to find out what set Matthew Donaldson off.'

'And how do we do that?'

Nightingale grinned. 'Good old fashioned detective work.'

CHAPTER 19

The Donaldsons lived in an apartment block in a quiet street about three blocks from Central Park. Perez managed to park her car close to the entrance to the building which had a white and brown striped awning that reached across the sidewalk to the road so that residents didn't have to get wet when it was raining. There were no police cars or emergency vehicles in the road so clearly all the excitement was over. 'How do you want to play this?' asked Nightingale as they climbed out of the car.

'If there's a doorman we do it the traditional way and pay him,' said Perez. 'The doormen know everything there is to know about the residents.'

The doorman was a portly man in his fifties who had a ramrod straight back that suggested he'd spent time in the military. He was wearing a black coat with chrome buttons and black leather gloves. Perez introduced herself as a private eye but didn't mention Nightingale.

'You were in the Job?' asked the doorman.

Perez nodded. 'Almost ten years.'

'Ever come across a Sergeant Lombardi?'

'I know a Rocco Lombardi. Rocky, worked out of the 33rd Precinct.'

'Still does. My cousin. Black sheep of the family but ended up a cop, life's funny like that.'

Perez held out a hand and the doorman pocketed a couple of bills without even looking at them, 'You working the Donaldson case?' he asked.

'Just trying to get some background,' she said.

'Can we do it outside?' asked the doorman. 'I could do with a smoke.'

They went and stood under the awning by the street. Nightingale took out his Marlboro, gave one to the doorman and lit it and one for himself. 'It all happened last night,' said the doorman. 'We work two shifts, six till two, two till ten. There's no doorman at night. Seems that the son came home in the early hours and there was a ruckus in the apartment. Shouts and screams and a lot of banging. That's unusual for the Donaldsons, they're a quiet family.' He grimaced and corrected himself. 'Were a quiet family, I should say. Mrs Peters who lives on the same floor called the cops and when they came everything had quietened down but no one would answer the door. They broke in and found Mr and Mrs Donaldson dead.'

'Have you been inside?'

The doorman shook his head. 'They had that tape up and said no one was to go inside. They had the full crime scene team in and later they took away two bodybags.'

'You've got CCTV?' asked Perez.

The doorman nodded. 'The detectives took the disc with them. It shows Matt coming back at just before two o'clock and leaving fifteen minutes later. No one else came or went at the same time so there doesn't seem to be any doubt.'

'What sort of boy was he?' asked Perez.

'If you'd asked me last month I would have said he was a great kid. Quiet, unassuming, wouldn't say boo to a goose.' He scratched his nose. 'That's always what they say about the kids who shoot their classmates, isn't it? Quiet kids who keep to themselves. But that's exactly what he was.

Until about two weeks ago. Then he started coming in late, missing school, behaving like an arsehole.'

'In what way?'

'He always used to have a smile for me. I keep a pack of gum behind the desk and I'd always give him a piece. But then he started cutting me dead, didn't even look at me. He used to be a real polite kid and would hold the door open for anybody but I saw him practically push Mrs Gonzales out of the way when she was laden down with parcels. Just pushed right by her without a word. I heard him cursing, too, and he never used to do that.'

'How old is he?'

'Seventeen, going on eighteen. But it wasn't a teenage thing. It was something else. He'd changed. He looked scruffier, he'd stopped combing his hair and to be honest he smelt bad, as if he wasn't showering. I think he was cutting school. He'd leave with his school bag but he started coming back at different times.'

'Must have been upsetting for his parents?' said Perez.

The doorman blew smoke and nodded. 'Saw Mrs Donaldson leaving in tears a few times. And Mr Donaldson would come back from work looking pretty angry. He'd say hello to me but I could see he had something on his mind. I know they took him to a therapist at least once. They both went with him and he was shouting at them as they went to the car.'

'Why do you think they were taking him to a therapist?'

'Because he screamed at them that he didn't need to see a stinking therapist,' said the doorman. He took a long pull on his cigarette and then blew smoke at the road. 'Father Mulligan was here once. He went upstairs and was there for an hour or so.'

'Father Mulligan?'

'The priest at Holy Trinity on West 82nd , near Amsterdam.'

'Any idea why he was here?' asked Nightingale.

The doorman frowned. 'You Irish?'

'English. I'm guessing it wasn't a social call?'

'He didn't say why he was here, just that he needed to go up to their condo.'

'They were Catholics?' asked Perez.

'They went to church, but I wouldn't say they were regular churchgoers.' He took a final drag on his cigarette and flicked the butt away. 'Not sure there's much more I can tell you.'

Perez handed him a business card. 'Just on the off chance Matthew comes back, let me know yeah.'

'The cops asked me to do the same.'

'Yeah, well the cops won't give you a hundred bucks. I will.'

CHAPTER 20

There were grey stone steps leading up to the entrance of the Holy Trinity Church. The church had been built in Byzantium style, the exterior constructed from layers of cream and brown brick giving it the look of a layer cake, with two tiled domes either side of a massive stone cross at the top. There were three large squarish wooden doors set in archways, flanked by narrower doors. In between the doors were large lamps that looked as if they would be more at home outside a mosque. The middle door was open and Perez and Nightingale went inside. Nightingale was immediately hit by the size of the place, as the front of the building was deceptively small. There was a row of massive stained glass windows around the altar at the far end of the church down a long aisle flanked by heavy wooden pews.

There was a stone font to the right of the door containing Holy Water. Perez dipped her fingers in it, knelt and crossed herself. She looked over at Nightingale as she stood up.

He shrugged. 'I'm not a Catholic.'

'What are you?'

He shrugged again. 'A pragmatist.'

There was a priest busying himself at the altar at the far end of the church. He was wearing a simple black cassock. He turned to look at them as he heard them approach. He was in his thirties with receding hair and circular spectacles perched on the end of a hooked nose that reminded

Nightingale of a hawk on the look out for prey. 'Are you Father Mulligan?' asked Perez.

'I am indeed,' said the priest. 'How can I be of help, officers?'

'We're not police, father,' said Perez. 'We're private investigators.'

'You look like detectives.'

'Well, we are, it's just that the city doesn't pay our wages,' said Perez. 'We'd like to talk to you about the Donaldsons.'

The priest nodded and crossed himself. 'A terrible business,' he said. 'Terrible.'

'So you've heard what happened?' asked Perez.

'The whole neighbourhood is in shock,' said the priest.

'They were parishioners?'

'I would say they were occasional worshippers,' said the priest. 'I wouldn't see them every week. Or indeed every month.'

'You went to their home recently?' said Perez.

The priest frowned at the question. 'Yes,,,' he said, hesitantly.

'About Matthew, correct?'

The priest scrunched up his face as if he was in pain. 'Anything we discussed would be covered by priest-penitent privilege, of course.'

'Only if you heard their confessions, and for that they would have come to the church.'

'My view would be that any conversation where I am carrying out the function of a priest would be confidential.'

'Well, if you visited their home as a friend or an adviser and not as a spiritual adviser, priest-penitent privilege wouldn't apply,' said Nightingale.

'Are you a lawyer as well as a private investigator?" asked the priest.

Nightingale smiled. 'I've come across issues with the confessional before,' he said. 'But this is a bit different as Mr and Mrs Donaldson are now dead so privilege isn't an issue.'

'Perhaps,' said the priest.

'And you know that the police think that it was Matthew who killed them?' asked Nightingale.

The priest nodded. 'He was a troubled boy when I saw him.'

'Mr and Mrs Donaldson wanted to talk to you about Matthew, is that right?' asked Perez. 'You can tell us that much, surely.'

'Last week, yes.'

'Do you think you could tell us why? As Jack says, the parents are now dead so telling us doesn't cause them any problems.'

The priest sighed and nodded. 'You're right, of course,' he said. 'The fact that the Donaldsons are dead changes everything.' He shrugged. 'But I'm not sure that what I have to say will be of any help to you, or to anybody. Mrs Donaldson thought that her son might have been possessed. A ridiculous notion, of course. And I told her so, in as many words. Too many movies about possession, Hollywood has a lot to answer for.'

'Possession?' repeated Perez. 'By what?'

'Exactly,' said the priest. 'That's the question I asked her. In the Middle Ages, mental illness was blamed on possession by demons because they didn't understand clinical depression and bipolar disorders. Everything got blamed on the devil and they looked to the local parish priest for a cure. I told her, I said, she needed to see a therapist or a doctor.'

'Did you talk to Matthew?' asked Perez.

The priest nodded. 'Yes, and he seemed fine to me. A bit rebellious but then what seventeen year old boy isn't?'

'What did Mrs Donaldson want from you, Father?'

The priest sighed. 'She wanted me to make her son better,' he said. 'But what she asked me for was an exorcism. She thought that he had become possessed and that I would cast the demon out for her. Those were her exact words. Cast the demon out.' He shook his head. 'She was at the end of her tether. Obviously.'

'And did you do it?' asked Nightingale.

'Of course I didn't do it. The boy almost certainly had psychological issues, an exorcism wouldn't help that. It might even make things worse. We're not talking baptism here. She wanted a full exorcism.'

'But you could do that, surely?' said Nightingale.

'Most definitely not,' said the priest. 'Not all priests are allowed to carry out exorcisms. First of all the church has to be sure that it's a genuine case of possession and trust me, they are few and far between. Plus there's a child involved. The church has to be very careful with children. As you can imagine. I couldn't make a decision to carry out an exorcism, that authority would have to come from the bishop. And I wasn't going to approach the bishop without being absolutely sure that Matthew was genuinely possessed.'

'What are the signs of possession?' asked Perez.

'Many and varied,' said the priest. 'Lack of appetite, scratches on the skin, unnatural body postures, a change in a person's voice. But all those things could be medical conditions. Supernatural strength, speaking in another language, being able to foretell the future, being able to move things by force of will, yes they could well be symptoms of possession but outside horror films who sees that?'

'Did Matthew show any of those symptoms?'

The priest shook his head. 'He just seemed like an unhappy kid. He spoke to me quite civilly though he clearly wasn't happy that I was there.'

'Did you try him with Holy Water?' asked Nightingale.

'Did I what?'

'Did you see how he reacted to Holy Water?'

The priest shook his head in amazement. 'He's a troubled boy. Not a vampire.'

'We're not talking about vampires, Father Mulligan. We're talking about a boy who might be possessed and Holy Water might have confirmed that.'

'I didn't for one moment think that Matthew Donaldson was possessed,' said the priest.

'So how do you explain the fact that he killed his parents?'

'You think the devil made him do it?'

'You believe in the devil, don't you, Father?'

'I believe the devil is always with us and that we must always be on our guard. But that doesn't mean I can go around performing exorcisms on a whim. Matthew Donaldson is clearly a very disturbed individual and once he's caught he can hopefully be treated. But that treatment almost certainly needs to be in a hospital in the care of professionals.' He looked at his watch. 'I have to prepare for Mass,' he said.

'Thank you for your time, Father,' said Perez.

'Bless you,' said the priest, and he hurried back to the altar.

'What is wrong with you?' hissed Perez as she and Nightingale walked outside.

'What do you mean?'

'That crack about Holy Water?'

'It was a serious question. If Matthew had been possessed, he might well have reacted to the Holy Water. Now we'll never know.'

'You're serious about this? The whole possession thing?'

'Something set him off,' said Nightingale. 'You heard what the doorman said. He was the all-American kid one moment, a homicidal killer the next.'

'And you believe that some sort of possession did that?'

Nightingale shrugged. 'I'm not ruling anything out,' he said.

CHAPTER 21

Perez picked Nightingale up outside the office block at just after nine o'clock in the morning. Philadelphia was just over a hundred miles away and it took two and a half hours to get there. Leon Budd's address was a public housing block in a run down part of the city. Opposite the block was a play area with two basketball courts surrounded by high wire fences and a grassy area peppered with signs that suggested that any activity that was remotely fun shouldn't take place there. A group of black kids in basketball shirts and baggy pants watched as Perez and Nightingale climbed out of their car and looked up at the block. 'Seventh floor,' said Perez.

'My lucky number,' said Nightingale.

'Seriously?'

'No. It was a joke.'

'How is that a joke?'

Nightingale shrugged and lit a cigarette. As he blew smoke up at the clouds one of the boys walked over, his hands thrust deep into his pockets. 'Check your car,' he mumbled. He was a teenager, short and stocky with his hair braided and platted into geometric patterns across his scalp.

'What, valet service?' asked Perez.

The boy shrugged. 'Kind of.'

Nightingale looked around. There was plenty of curb-side parking spaces. 'Doesn't seem like parking's a problem around here,' he said.

'It's a rough neighbourhood,' said the boy. 'Cars get stolen. Paintwork gets scratched. Tyres get slashed.' He shrugged. 'Lots of undesirables around.'

Perez nodded. 'I can see that.'

The boy looked over at his companions. They were all looking in his direction. One of them was bouncing a basketball on the ground. The boy looked back at Perez. 'So what do you say?'

'How much would keep my car in tip-top condition?' she asked.

'Twenty would do it.'

'How about ten?' asked Perez.

The boy looked pained. 'I've got overheads.'

Perez went to take out her wallet but Nightingale beat her to it and held out a twenty-dollar bill to the teenager. His hand emerged from his pocket, grabbed it and disappeared again in one smooth motion. He shrugged and walked back across the road.

'That's how extortion works in the City of Brotherly Love,' said Perez.

'He was nice about it,' agreed Nightingale.

They went inside and Nightingale wrinkled his nose at the stench of stale urine. Perez stabbed at the button to call the elevator. 'I'll catch you up there,' said Nightingale, heading for the stairs. He finished his cigarette on the sixth floor, stamped out the butt on the concrete, then hurried up the last few stairs. He still got there before Perez. She scowled as she stepped out of the elevator. 'It stopped at every floor,' she growled. 'Some kid pressed all the buttons.'

'The scenic route,' said Nightingale.

'English humour, Jack?' She shook her head. 'It's wearing thin.'

The smell of stale urine was just as strong in the hallway as it had been downstairs. There was litter strewn across the tiled floor and plaster was peeling off the walls. As they walked down the hallway most of the doors they passed had been damaged and repaired, and most had a minimum of three locks.

'This is it,' said Perez, stopping at a pale green door that had the number 664 on it, though the six was missing one of its screws and had swung upside down. Perez knocked on the door and when there was no answer she knocked again. She put her head against the door and frowned. 'I can hear voices,' she said. 'The TV maybe.' She banged the flat of her hand against the door several times. Eventually a middle-aged black man with tribal scars on his cheeks opened it. He was shirtless and shoeless and stared at Perez through thick-lensed spectacles. There was a screwed up scar on his left shoulder that looked like an old bullet wound, and a thick rope-like scar on his right side.

'Who are you?' he said.

'Mr Budd?'

'I know who I am, who are you?'

'My name's Cheryl Perez. I want to talk to you about Leon.'

'You the police?' He pronounced it po-lees.

'No, Mr Budd. We're not with the police.'

'You with the city?'

'No, we're private investigators, we want to....' The door closed in her face and she heard a bolt being drawn. She knocked on the door half a dozen times but Mr Budd was clearly ignoring her. They heard him boost the volume of the TV.

'I get the feeling he doesn't want to talk,' said Nightingale.

'Do you think?'

'I guess the people here only ever get knocks on the door when it's bad news,' said Nightingale.

Perez nodded. 'Yeah. Shit. That was a wasted journey.' She walked back to the elevator and pressed the button. 'What about going down? You okay with that?''

'Up, down, it makes no difference. It's not the direction, it's the being in a small box suspended by a wire.'

'You know that elevators are the safest form of transport, period.'

'Let's agree to differ on that.'

She frowned. 'What do you mean?'

'I mean you and I have different opinions on the subject and it's not worth arguing about.'

'I meant what are you implying – I said that elevators are as safe as houses and you give me that "agree to differ" bullshit.'

'I'm just saying, I don't feel comfortable using them, but if you do, go ahead. It's like cigarettes. Some people smoke and others don't.'

'Smoking cigarettes is nothing like using an elevator,' she said. She pressed the button again. 'What the hell is taking so long?'

'Probably broken down,' said Nightingale with a grin. He headed for the stairs. He lit a cigarette when he was half way down the stairwell and was still smoking it when he emerged outside the building. He was taking his final drag when Perez finally joined him.

'Stopped on every floor again, but this time no one pressed the buttons.'

Nightingale shrugged. 'It happens.'

Perez looked over at her car. 'At least the valet service seems to have worked.'

Nightingale looked over at the group of teenagers standing on the other side of the road. The one with the basketball was still bouncing it hand to hand. Nightingale dropped his cigarette butt on the ground and strode over to them.

'Jack, no...' said Perez but he ignored her.

The teenagers formed a line as Nightingale approached them, the tallest one in the middle was the guy with the basketball. 'How's it going guys?' he asked brightly. He took out his pack of Marlboro and lit one. He could see that two of the boys had the hungry look of smokers and he offered them the pack and lit cigarettes for them with his Zippo.

'You look like 5-0,' said the guy with the basketball.

'I'm not.'

'What about her?' asked the teenager, nodding at Perez who was walking across the road towards them.

'She used to be, but she's a private eye now. Did you know Leon Budd?'

The teenager's eyes narrowed. 'You Australian?'

'British.'

'Yeah? From where?'

'London. Mainly.'

The teenager nodded. 'They call it the Big Smoke, don't they?'

Nightingale nodded. 'Some do, yeah.'

'You know what they call Philly?'

'The City Of Brotherly Love,' said Nightingale, and smiled at the look of disappointment on the teenager's face.

Perez joined him. 'How are you doing?' she asked the guy with the ball.

'All good,' he said. 'You're private eyes? So you pay money for information, don't you?'

'It's been known,' said Perez. 'But it'd have to be good information.'

'So what do you want to know about Leon?'

'You knew him?'

'Sure. We know everyone. These are our streets. No one walks down here we don't know.' The teenagers either side of him nodded in agreement.

'Tell you what, how about a game of one on one?' asked Perez. 'Every time I score you answer a question, every time you score I give you ten bucks?'

'Ten bucks?'

'Absolutely.'

'What are you? Five six?'

'Five six and a half,' said Perez.

'I'm six one, and I'm black. You're five six and a half and you're…'

'Careful,' said Perez, pointing a finger at him.

'And a girl is what I was going to say,' said the teenager, with a sly grin.

'What's your name?' asked Perez.

'They call me Flames.'

'Because you're shit hot?'

The teenagers all laughed. 'Nah, because he used to set fire to things when he was a kid,' said one.

'So what's it going to be, Flames? You ready for a game of one on one?'

'Hell yeah,' said Flames, bouncing the ball.

'Cheryl, maybe I should…' started Nightingale.

'Should what, Jack? You play hoops?'

'Well, no, but…'

'But what?'

'Well, I'm taller for a start.'

She laughed, took off her jacket and tossed it at him before jogging onto the court.

'This is gonna be easy money,' said Flames. He bounced the ball as he turned in a tight circle, then joined her on the court. He bounced the ball at her and she fumbled the catch. It slipped from her fingers and she chased after it. Flames turned to his friends and pumped the air. 'Easy money!' He was so busy celebrating that he didn't even see Perez scoop up the ball, run with it bouncing it as she went, and then jumping and smoothly dropping it through the hoop.

Flames turned just as Perez scooped up the ball. 'What the fuck?' he said.

'First question. Do you know who killed Leon?'

'No I do not,' said Flames. 'And I wasn't ready.'

'What, you want someone to blow the whistle?' She threw the ball at him and it hit him, mid chest. He grabbed it, nodded, and bounced it half a dozen times before moving towards the hoop. He feinted left and she went with him but when he moved right she was already there and before he could take a step she had taken the ball from him, bounced it as she went by and then bounced it twice again until she was under the hoop. She jumped and dropped it through.

'No fucking way!' shouted Flames. His companions were shrieking with laughter.

'Did Leon use drugs?' asked Perez.

Flames shook his head. 'Never did. He was working two jobs to pay his way through college. His brother and sister used. Sister died of an overdose a while back. But Leon?' He shook his head. 'Nah.' Perez threw the ball to him and he began to bounce it at his side.

Perez moved to stand between him and the hoop. He started to move, switching hands, bouncing the ball hard and fast. He ran towards her, twisted so that his left shoulder barged into her chest, then ran through her. She fell backwards, hitting the ground hard, and he jumped over her and threw the ball at the hoop. It hit the backboard, bounced against the rim and dropped through the hole. 'Yes!' yelled Flames.

Perez sat up and rubbed her left shoulder.

'Hey, that's not fair!' shouted Nightingale.

'It's okay,' said Perez getting to her feet. She took out her wallet and gave him ten dollars. Flames held the note up and did a victory jig. He was so busy showing the note to his friends that he didn't see her pick up the ball. He turned as she began to bounce it but he was too late and she jumped and popped it through the hoop.

'Question three,' she said, picking up the ball and tossing it to him. 'Had Leon met anyone recently? A new friend? Someone you hadn't seen him with before?'

Flames ran a hand through his hair. He nodded. 'Yeah, there was a girl he'd started hanging around with.'

'What was her name?'

Flames grinned. 'That's another question.' He faked left but broke right. She moved with him and he turned his shoulder to charge into her but she stepped to the side and stuck out her leg and he tripped, sprawling to the ground and letting go of the ball. Perez ran to retrieve it while Flames stood up and brushed his knees. 'Man you are one mean bitch,' he muttered.

She bounced the ball, behind her and then between her legs, grinning at him all the time. 'Anytime you want to give up, just say the word,' she said.

Flames crouched, holding his arms to his side. Her grin widened and then Perez ducked left, turned around and ran to the right, totally wrong-footing Flames. He stumbled and cursed as Perez ran over to the hoop and dropped the ball through the centre. 'How d'you do that?' asked Flames.

'I'm nimble,' said Perez, retrieving the ball and tossing it to him. 'So tell me about the girl Leon was hanging with.'

'Name's Dee-anne. Saw them hanging, talking and walking.'

'Boyfriend-girlfriend?'

'Don't think so.'

'What does she look like?'

'That's another question?'

'No it's not. I asked you tell me about her. Start telling.'

'Longish hair. Pretty. Younger than him. Eighteen maybe.'

'Black?'

Flames shrugged. 'Black like Obama's black.'

'So mixed race?'

Flames nodded. 'Darker than you but a lot lighter than Leon. Saw them in Mickey D's once, playing some stupid game with pencils.'

'Game?'

'They had two pencils, crossed on a piece of paper.'

'Charlie Charlie?'

'What?'

'It's a kid's game,' said Nightingale. 'You use pencils to answer questions.'

'Yeah, well I've got a calculator on my phone does that. But they were staring at these pencils, dunno why.'

'You think they went to college together?' asked Perez.

Flames nodded. 'Yeah, they was often carrying books. Maybe.' He started bouncing the ball, headed to the right, spun around on the spot and then broke left. Perez almost got to the ball but he was too fast, he ran around her and jumped high in the air before dunking it in the hoop. Perez shook her head and gave him another ten dollars before retrieving the ball.

She stood in front of him, bouncing the ball from hand to hand, then bounced it through his legs and ran around him to catch it, jump into the air and throw the ball a good fifteen feet into the hoop.

'Bitch you are good!' shouted Flames.

Perez pointed a finger at his face. 'Less of the bitch,' she said. 'Show some respect to the female that is whupping your arse.'

Flames raised his hands in surrender, then gave her a mock bow. She threw the ball to him and motioned for him to start.

He bent forward, bounced the ball several times, then instead of running he rocked back on his heels and threw the ball at the hoop. It slammed into the backboard and spun off to the side. He cursed and his friends laughed.

'Close but no cigar,' said Perez. She fetched the ball, walked to the edge of the court and began her run. Flames almost got to the ball, but almost was nowhere near good enough and Perez ran by him, jumped and slotted the ball into the hoop.

Flames stood looking at her, shaking his head. 'Who the fuck are you?' he asked.

'Cheryl Perez,' she said.

'You from where, Mexico?'

She laughed. 'Flames, you want me answer a question you've got to sink a hoop first. That's the deal.'

'Can I ask a question?' asked Nightingale.

'Go ahead,' said Perez. 'He owes us one.'

Flames turned to look at Nightingale. 'Tell us what happened to Leon's sister.'

Flames bent down to pick up the ball and began to bounce it slowly between his hands. 'She OD'd. Heroin. She was in a shooting gallery, next block along. Something wrong with the shit, cut with rat poison or some such. She died, three others were in the ICU.'

'When, exactly?'

'Two weeks ago. No, three.'

'Cops involved?'

'If no one gets shot they don't give a fuck, and even then...'

'What about Leon's brother? You said his brother was using, too.'

Flames looked over at Perez. She took out her wallet and handed him a fifty-dollar bill. 'Save you any more embarrassment, why don't we just use cash.'

Flames pocketed the bill. 'The brother wasn't there, but sure, he was a user.'

'But not Leon?'

'Leon was the only one clean,' said Flames. 'His mum used, his dad got shot in a drug deal gone wrong five, six years back. Never been the same since. Leon wanted to make a better life for himself. Death of his sister hit him hard.'

'They were close?'

Flames nodded. 'He made me swear never to sell to her. I respected him so yeah, she couldn't buy from my crew.' He gestured at the block to his left. 'But that's not my territory. They sold to her. Leon tried to stop them but he didn't get anywhere.'

'Where did Leon die?'

Flames pointed off to the right. 'Warehouse two blocks down. Used for long-term storage. He'd been dead two days before anyone found him.'

'Cut to pieces, they said,' said one of the guys standing next to Flames.

'Not literally, though, right?' said Nightingale.

The boy frowned, not understanding.

'I mean he was cut, but not chopped up.'

'I heard he was chopped into little bits,' said the boy.

'Nah, said Flames, he's right. He was cut. Lots of cuts. But the body was in one piece.'

'Any thoughts on who might do that?' asked Perez.

Flames threw the ball from hand to hand. 'I dunno, you hear about the Colombians doing shit like that, but around here drug dealers use guns. Everyone uses guns. Who the fuck uses a knife? You bring a knife to a gun fight and you're fucked.'

'The place where Leon died, he was familiar with it?' asked Nightingale.

'Sure, I guess so.'

'So he could have gone there willingly?' Flames frowned, not following what Nightingale was getting at. 'I mean someone wouldn't have had to point a gun at him to get him there.'

'He'd have had to have broken in, but he wouldn't have had a problem with that.'

'How come?' asked Nightingale.

'Back in the day Leon was a housebreaker. He was a small kid so he could crawl in through open windows, shit like that. When he got older he moved up to locks and stuff but he got caught when he was what, thirteen or fourteen and they put him on a scared straight program where they take kids into prisons and show them what life is like inside. It worked, he's been on the straight and narrow ever since.'

A police cruiser prowled by, a white car with a blue and a yellow stripe across the doors. The occupants, both male and wearing dark glasses, looked over at them and Flames and his friends scattered.

CHAPTER 22

'Do you want to tell me what just happened?' asked Nightingale as they walked back to her car. 'How did you do that?'

'Do what?'

'Whup his arse at netball.'

'Three older brothers and a hoop in the driveway,' she said. 'The deal with my brothers was that they'd only do their share of their chores if I beat them at hoops. And we don't call it netball. It's basketball.'

'It was…impressive.'

She grinned over at him. 'My detective skills you ignore, I shoot a few hoops and you get a hard on. You're such a guy.'

'I'll take that as a compliment.'

'It wasn't meant to be.'

They got into the car and Perez started the engine. 'You think these cases are connected, don't you?' she asked,

'They're similar.'

'How are they similar?' asked Perez. 'Leon Budd was a black male from the Philadelphia streets, Kate Walker was a white girl from Forest Hills.'

'Similar because of the way they died. Cut to pieces.'

'But if you're looking for a connection, usually the connection comes via the victim. I don't see that the same killer would kill a black male in

Philadelphia and a white female in Queens. Geographically it doesn't make sense, victim profile-wise it doesn't make sense either.' She sighed and threw up her hands. 'None of this makes any sense.' She turned to look at him. 'Unless there's something you're not telling me.'

'You know as much as I do.'

She flashed him a sarcastic smile. 'I doubt that.'

Nightingale shrugged but didn't say anything.

'What aren't you telling me, Jack? If I knew, maybe I could help.'

'I'm just sure the two cases are connected.'

'I know. You said. That's why we're here. But I don't see any connection. Other than the fact that the bodies were both stabbed and mutilated. You tell me there's a connection but I don't see it. Which means either there isn't a connection or you're not telling me something. That's your right, of course. You call him Joshua and to me he's Mr Wainwright so I'm guessing he tells you more than he tells me. Which is fine.'

'I need a drink,' said Nightingale.

'I'm driving.'

'I didn't say you needed a drink. I said I did.'

'Okay, but not here, the valet parking is extortionate.' She put the car in gear and drove to a more upmarket area with quaint shops and bustling restaurants. She found a free parking space and they walked to a bar in a side street that offered craft beers and a Happy Hour for cocktails. They went inside, slid onto stools and ordered drinks from a matronly waitress,

'So what aren't you telling me, Jack?' said Perez.

'I don't know much more than you, cross my heart.'

'You keep telling me that the two cases are connected, but I don't see it. Two different cities, completely different victims who can't possibly have known each other.'

'It's the way they were killed that ties them together,' said Nightingale.

'I had figured that out for myself,' said Perez. 'It's the only thing the two deaths have in common. But there are close to two thousand knife murders a year in the US and they're not all connected.'

'The mutilations,' said Nightingale. 'They are quite specific, some of them. Not random.'

The waitress returned with a bottled beer for Nightingale and a glass of red wine for Perez. They stayed silent as she placed the drinks down in front of them and then gave them a bowl of peanuts.

'Excessive,' said Perez as the waitress walked away to deal with another customer. 'Brutal. Over the top. Yes, I get that.'

Nightingale took a long pull on his beer. 'It's more than that, Cheryl. The cuts were done to conceal something else. A sigil.'

Perez frowned. 'A what?'

'A mark. A devil's mark. A calling card.'

Perez screwed up her face. 'Jack, I've seen both sets of crime scenes. There were marks on the bodies but they were different. There was no similarity other than that there were a lot of cuts and stabs. And in Kate's case Donaldson left the knife, in Leon's case the killer took the knife with him.'

'Or her,' said Nightingale.

'What?' said Perez. 'What do you mean?'

'I mean we don't know if Leon's killer was a man or a woman.'

'So you don't think Matthew Donaldson killed Leon?'

Nightingale shook his head.

'Then you are confusing the hell out of me because if there's no connection between the victims and two different killers in different cities – how are they connected?' She drained her glass and put it down in front of her.

'I told you. The sigils. The marks.'

'The marks are different.'

'Yes, they are different. But they're both sigils. Different sigils, but sigils nonetheless.' He took another pull on his beer. 'Say you found a body with the letter A carved into it. And a few weeks later found another body with the letter C. Wouldn't you start looking for a victim with a B?'

Perez cursed and waved at the waitress. She came over and Perez ordered another glass of red wine.

'You're driving, remember,' said Nightingale.

'Yeah, and if you don't open up to me I'll be driving back to Manhattan on my own,' she said. 'You're telling me that both Kate and Leon had these sign things carved into the bodies, and that the rest of the cuts were to cover them up.'

'Maybe.'

'And who would do that?'

Nightingale shrugged. 'That's the $64,000 question, isn't it? I think Leon must have known his killer. He took off his clothes, same as Kate did. And he was a tough kid, grew up on some mean streets and wasn't afraid of standing up to drug dealers, so I'm guessing if he had the chance to fight back he would have. I think like Kate he went willingly. He knew whoever it was who killed him and right up until the last minute he had no idea what was happening.'

'So we've got two similar murders – similar in the way the victims were killed – happening a hundred miles apart and with different killers?'

'I know it sounds unlikely, but yes.'

'And these marks you say are there, they're what? Signals?'

'Sigils.'

The waitress brought over Perez's fresh glass of wine and asked Nightingale if he was ready for another beer. He shook his head and she smiled and left them in peace.

Perez took a gulp of wine. 'Devil marks, you said.'

Nightingale nodded. 'Satanists believe that every devil has a mark. A special mark that can be used to summon them.'

'Satanists? You mean devil-worshipers?'

Nightingale nodded.

'But that's nonsense, right? The only cases of Satanism I've come across are when perps use it as an excuse. "The devil made me do it" and all that crap.'

'It doesn't really matter whether it's true or not,' said Nightingale. 'What matters is whether or not the killers believe it.'

'Okay, but if two killers a hundred miles apart are killing in the same way, there has to be a connection right?'

Nightingale nodded. 'Sure.'

'So if the victims didn't know each other, maybe the killers did?'

'That's a possibility.'

'You don't sound convinced.'

Nightingale shrugged and drank his beer.

'And what's the Charlie Charlie connection?'

'I don't know.'

'You didn't seem surprised when Flames mentioned it.'

'It's a thing among schoolkids.'

'Is it part of this devil worship thing?'

'Charlie Charlie is a game. You can't summon devils with it.'

'How do you know so much about it?'

'I don't,' said Nightingale. 'I know bits and pieces. And one thing I know is that Charlie Charlie is a game, nothing more.'

She took another gulp of wine. 'I thought you might be going to tell me that Charlie Charlie is the link. That it's Charlie doing the killings. How crazy is that?'

'There is no Charlie Charlie. It's a game.'

'So it's just a coincidence that Katy and Leon were involved in it?'

Nightingale screwed up his face. 'That's where it gets complicated,' he said.

'So it is a connection?'

'I don't think for one minute that a being called Charlie Charlie is behind the killings. That would be ridiculous, obviously. But it suggests there's something going on, doesn't it? Both victims have sigils carved on the bodies. Both were involved in the Charlie Charlie game. Both found inside, in places where they probably went voluntarily.'

'And both victims lost someone close to them recently.' She sipped her wine thoughtfully. 'So they were both grieving. Could they have gone to the same grief councillor? Been consoled by the same priest?'

'I don't get the feeling that either of them were religious,' said Nightingale. 'And again, they were a hundred miles apart.'

'So what next?' asked Perez.

'Hand on heart, I don't know,' said Nightingale. 'Let me sleep on it.'

CHAPTER 23

Nightingale waited until he had showered in the executive bathroom before phoning Joshua Wainwright. He had no idea where in the world Wainwright was, but the Texan answered on the fifth ring and sounded bright and breezy. Nightingale quickly brought him up to speed about the two murders.

'So it's definitely about the sigils?' said Wainwright.

'Yes. Kate Walker was using a Ouija board and I'm pretty sure that was how she got involved. And Leon Budd was using Charlie Charlie. Kate Walker was killed by a teenager called Matthew Donaldson and he was taken to a priest because his parents thought he was possessed.'

'Have you identified the sigils yet?'

'No. Not yet.'

'You know what you have to do, Jack. You need to talk to Proserpine. She's the only one who can tell us what we're dealing with.'

'I'm on it, Joshua.'

'The sooner the better, Jack.'

'I hear you. There's something else I have to tell you. Perez knows about the sigils.'

'You told her?'

'I didn't have any choice. She's not stupid, she knew I was keeping something from her and it was going to screw up our relationship. If she doesn't trust me she's not going to help me.'

'She's a hired hand. She'll do what she's paid to do.'

'I know that. But I couldn't keep lying to her.'

Wainwright chuckled. 'It's not a problem, Jack. I assumed you'd have to tell her at some point. She's a smart cookie. I just figured that if she got the news organically she'd deal with it better, rather than springing it on her from Day One. How are you two getting on?'

'She's a good operator.'

'She is that. Just don't tell her too much, though. She was always going to have to know about the sigils, but other than that you need to keep your cards – and mine - close to your chest.'

'Understood.'

'And how close are they to catching this Donaldson kid?'

'They reckon it won't be long.'

'Keep me posted, Jack. And watch your back.' The line went dead and Nightingale stared at the cellphone. 'I intend to, Joshua,' he muttered.

CHAPTER 24

Nightingale was sitting in a diner a short walk from the office block waiting for his scrambled eggs and ham when his phone rang. It was Perez. 'I found Dee-anne,' she said. 'Actually I found four Dee-annes but only one who's the right age.'

'Well done you,' said Nightingale. 'How many people did you have to beat at netball to get the information?'

'Netball? Will you stop calling it that?'

'That's what we call it in England,' said Nightingale. 'Netball. It's a girls game. Same as girls play rounders.'

'Rounders?'

'You call it baseball.'

'I don't think you should be trying to insult the colleague who has spent most of the morning doing your legwork.'

The waitress returned with his order and placed it on the table in front of him. He smiled his thanks.

'So do you want to go out to Philly again? I've got an address.'

'Sounds like a plan,' said Nightingale, picking up his fork. 'Have you had breakfast?'

'Breakfast? It's half past nine, I've been in the office since eight.'

Nightingale looked at his watch. 'I didn't have a great night, the sofa bed isn't that comfortable.'

'You're breaking my heart. When and where shall I pick you up?'

'I'll be outside the office in fifteen minutes.'

'Perfect. Get me a coffee and we're even.'

Nightingale was late. Perez was already sitting in her car with her flashers on when Nightingale hurried up with two coffee containers. 'Sorry.'

'You Brits really can't stop apologising, can you?'

'Sorry.' He laughed and put the coffees in the holders as she pulled away from the curb.

The traffic was heavier than the first time they had driven to Philadelphia and this time the trip took just under three hours. Dee-anne Alexander lived in a public housing block about half a mile from Leon Budd's home. It was a featureless brick building some twelve stories high, one of four in a row. Perez parked in a supermarket car park some distance away and Nightingale didn't need to ask why. She handed him a computer print out. 'Mum's Jamaican originally, dad was white, ran off when mum was pregnant. Mum's since had three more kids with three different fathers. The last one has hung around. Todd Sanders. Dee-anne's enrolled at the Community College of Philadelphia. That's the same place Leon went to. She's studying part time.'

'You think she's home now?'

'Thought we'd try here first then head over to the college.'

Nightingale smoked a cigarette as they walked to the block.

'How many do you smoke in a day?' asked Perez.

'It depends. A pack, maybe. Sometimes less, sometimes more. It depends on what I'm doing. The number of places you can smoke is being cut back every year so it's more a case of lighting up when I can.' He smiled as he recognised the hunger in her eyes. 'You used to smoke?'

'Gave up five years ago,' she said.

'Because?'

'Because I didn't want to die of lung cancer like my grandpa.'

'To be fair, one in six people who die of lung cancer have never smoked.'

'Grandpa was a pack a day man. He rolled his own.'

'But a lot of smokers do just fine. Swings and roundabouts.'

'Swings and roundabouts?' she sneered. 'Where are the positives?'

Nightingale grinned and held up his cigarette. 'Smokers look so darn cool.'

'Says who?'

'Says teenage girls all over the world. Plus they taste good. Plus they give me a lift. Coffee and cigarettes, the breakfast of champions.'

'You're crazy, you know that?'

Nightingale shrugged and took a long pull on his cigarette.

There was a keypad by the side of the door to get inside the building but they only had to wait a couple of minutes before a young woman with a baby in a stroller opened the door from the inside. Nightingale held the door open for her and she smiled her thanks. They went inside where there were three elevators, all spray-painted with graffiti. 'I really don't want to go up in the lift,' said Nightingale. 'Elevator. Whatever. I'll take the stairs.'

'What is it with you and elevators?'

'I just don't like them, It's no big deal.'

'The apartment is on the tenth floor, Jack.'

'I'll meet you up there.' He pushed open the fire door and headed up the concrete stairs. Perez shook her head in amazement and pressed the button to call the elevator.

Nightingale got to the fifth floor before he started breathing heavily and by the time he reached the tenth Perez was already there, grinning at his discomfort. They walked along to the apartment and Perez rang the bell. There was a buzzing from inside and a few seconds later the door opened on a security chain. A middle-aged black woman blinked at Perez.

'Mrs Alexander?'

'Who are you?'

'Mrs Alexander, my name is Cheryl Perez, is your daughter at home?'

'You police?'

'No, we're private investigators, we just...'

The door slammed shut. Perez grimaced. 'That could have gone better.'

Nightingale gestured for her to move out of the way. 'Let me have a go.'

'Use your negotiating skills, you mean?'

Nightingale flashed her a tight smile. 'It can't hurt.' She moved out of his way and he knocked. Nothing happened so he knocked, harder again. The door opened again, still on the chain. This time it was a teenage boy wearing a baseball cap. 'Mom says you're to fuck off,' he said and began closing the door.

Nightingale put his foot in the gap and took out his wallet. He pulled out a hundred dollar bill and handed it through the gap. 'That's for you. Show it to your mum and tell her I've got more for her, we just want a quick chat.'

The boy looked at the money, back at Nightingale, then stamped on Nightingale's foot. Nightingale yelped and pulled back his Hush Puppy. The door slammed shut. Perez looked at him in amazement. 'That was your plan? Offer him a bribe?'

Nightingale shrugged. 'I didn't think I could beat him at netball.'

'Basketball.'

'Potato, tomato,' he said, putting away his wallet.

The door opened again. This time it was the woman. 'How much money you got for me?'

'A couple of hundred dollars,' said Nightingale, taking out his wallet again.

'Five,' said the woman.

'Three hundred,' said Nightingale.

'Four,' said the woman.

'Okay. Four hundred it is.'

'Show me the money.'

Nightingale took three hundred dollars from his wallet and looked at Perez. 'Can you lend me a hundred? I'm good for it.' She gave him five twenty-dollar notes and he waved the money at Mrs Alexander. She reached for it but Nightingale moved it away. 'We just want a few minutes of your time.'

She glared at him suspiciously, then closed the door. Nightingale looked across at Perez. 'It was worth a try,' he said, but then he smiled as he heard the security chain being taken off.

Mrs Alexander opened the door and held out her hand. Nightingale gave her the money and she turned her back on him and walked down a hallway.

Perez and Nightingale followed her. There were two doors leading off to the left. The second one was open and the boy in the baseball cap was sitting at a computer, his face just inches from the screen. At the end of the hallway was a large sitting room. There was a big screen TV showing a soap opera facing a sofa large enough to seat five. Nightingale wrinkled his nose at the musky smell of cannabis. There was a large man sitting at one end of the sofa. He was virtually obese, with rolls of fat hanging over the top of his sweat pants and jowls that gave him the look of an overfed bloodhound. His right eye was almost closed amid a swelling that had gone blue. Three of the fingers of his left hand were bandaged and there was a brace on his right leg. There was a pack of cigarette papers on a coffee table in front of the sofa and an ashtray with a half-smoked joint smouldering away. Mrs Alexander lowered herself down onto the sofa, linked her hands over her stomach and looked up at Nightingale. 'So what do you want?'

The man reached out his hand and clicked the fingers of his good hand. The woman handed him the money, though Nightingale noticed that one of the hundred dollar bills seemed to have gone missing.

'Is Dee-anne here?' asked Nightingale.

'The bitch has gone and if she comes back she'll wish she hadn't,' snarled the man. There was a large purple bong on a side table and he reached for it. He took a deep pull on it, held the smoke in his lungs for several seconds, then exhaled. He passed the bong to Mrs Alexander.

'Are you Todd Sanders?' asked Nightingale.

The man screwed up his eyes as he stared up at Nightingale. 'Who wants to know?'

'My name's Jack. I heard you were the head of the household.'

'In his dreams,' chuckled Mrs Alexander. She took a pull on the bong and ignored the withering look Sanders gave her.

'Have you been in an accident, Mr Sanders?' asked Nightingale.

'You could say that,' said Sanders. He wrenched the bong away from Mrs Alexander.

'It looks painful.'

Sanders didn't answer. He looked at the TV as he drew smoke into his lungs.

'Do you know where Dee-anne is?' Perez asked Mrs Alexander.

The woman shook her head. 'She left.'

'But she lives here?'

'She left,' repeated the woman.

'When will she be back?' asked Perez.

Sanders blew a cloud of smoke in her direction. 'I told you, if she shows her face here again she'll....'

'Did she hit you, Mr Sanders?'

'She caught me unawares,' he said. 'I wasn't looking. Sucker punched me.'

There was a framed family photograph on the wall by the door. A younger Mrs Alexander with four children, two were teenagers and two were toddlers. The oldest boy was the one who had opened the door the second time. He was good-looking and smiling proudly at the camera, his arm around his mother's shoulders. Standing on the other side of the woman was a slight girl who couldn't have been much more than five-three. In front of Mrs Alexander, grinning as if their lives depended on it, were two small boys, toddlers separated by a year at most. They were all smiling at the camera. A happy family. Perez pointed at the girl in the photograph. 'That's Dee-anne?'

Mrs Alexander nodded.

'Lovely girl,' said Perez. 'Nice smile.'

'She's a no-good disrespectful bitch,' snarled Sanders.

'When was that taken?' Perez asked Mrs Alexander.

'Two years ago.'

Perez nodded and looked over at Nightingale. She was obviously thinking the same thing. It must have been one heck of a sucker punch for a small girl like Dee-anne to cause that much damage to a man possibly four times her size.

'What were you arguing about, Mr Sanders?' asked Perez.

'She's a bad kid. A pain in the butt. Answering back. Staying out late. Talking shit to her mother.'

Perez looked over at Mrs Alexander who was trying to pry the bong out of her partner's good hand. He reluctantly released his grip on it and Mrs Alexander took a long pull on it. 'You were arguing with Dee-anne, Mrs Alexander?' asked Perez.

The woman nodded and blew smoke. 'She came in late and wouldn't say where she'd been.'

'How old is she?' asked Nightingale.

'The bitch is seventeen but so long as she lives under my roof she follows my rules,' snapped Sanders.

'Does she have a boyfriend?' asked Perez.

Mrs Alexander shook her head. 'She was too busy at school.'

Sanders scowled up at Nightingale. 'What's she done, anyway?'

'Nothing that we know about,' said Perez. 'We want to talk to her about a friend of hers. Leon Budd. Did she ever mention him?'

Mrs Alexander shook her head. 'She didn't bring her friends home.'

Nightingale nodded. He could understand why. He felt a sudden tug of sympathy for Dee-anne, forced to share her life with Mrs Alexander and Mr Sanders.

'So we're done, right?' said Sanders. 'She's not here, we don't know where she is and we're not expecting her back.' He pointed at the door with his bandaged hand. 'You can let yourselves out.'

Perez looked over at Nightingale and he shrugged. It didn't look as if there was anything to be gained by hanging around. As they walked down the hallway to the front door, the teenager came out. He hurried ahead of them and opened the door for them, then followed them into the corridor. 'What did he say?' he asked.

'Your dad?' said Perez. 'He said Dee-anne had gone.'

'He's not my fucking dad. He's not blood, He's nothing to do with me. Did he tell you why Dee-anne went?'

'They had a row,' said Nightingale.

'Fuck they did. He was touching her. He's been touching her ever since he moved in. I seen how he looks at her and how he's always putting his hands on her. Mom sees too but she's too scared to do anything.'

'You sure?' asked Nightingale.

The teenager's eyes blazed. 'Fuck you, man, you think I'm making this up.'

'He says they argued because she came home late.'

'Fuck that. He went into her room. Then bang crash and he was all smashed up. Then Dee-anne left.'

'Did she say anything to you before she went?'

'Didn't even look at me. Pushed me out the way like I wasn't there.'

'Has she been all right recently?' asked Nightingale.

'Whatchya mean?'

'Did she seem different?'

'If she did, it's not surprising, is it? Not with that fat fuck touching her up.'

'But you said he's been like that for years. Did she ever lash out before?'

The boy shook his head. 'She just kept out of his way and kept her door locked at night.'

'But that night she hadn't locked her door, right?'

The boy shrugged. 'She must have forgot.'

'Was she forgetting much else?' asked Nightingale.

The boy's eyes narrowed. 'What you mean?'

'Did she seem different? Recently? Had she changed?'

The boy nodded. 'Yeah. She was, you know, distracted. Like she had something on her mind.'

'Do you know Leon Budd?'

The boy pulled a face. 'Nah.'

'Did she ever mention him? Budd. Leon Budd. They went to the same school.'

'Nah.'

'Do you have any idea where she might have gone? Does she have any friends she might have gone to stay with?'

The boy shrugged but didn't answer.

'Who is her best friend?' asked Perez.

The boy shrugged again.

Perez sighed and took out her wallet. She gave him a couple of twenty dollar bills.

'Makayla Jackson. She lives in the next block. Ninth floor.'

'School friend?' asked Perez. The boy nodded and hurried inside as if he feared she would take her money back.

Perez headed for the elevator while Nightingale pushed open the door to the stairwell.

CHAPTER 25

Nightingale walked up to the ninth floor to find Perez already talking to Makayla Jackson's mother. The door closed as Nightingale walked up. 'She's at school,' said Perez. 'Community College.' She laughed at how out of breath he was. 'Jack, if you're going to insist on climbing all these stairs you might want to rethink the smoking.' She patted him on the chest. 'I'll see you back at the car.'

Nightingale went back down the stairs. Perez was standing by her car with two coffees by the time he got there and he took his and thanked her.

The Community College of Philadelphia was a ten-minute drive away. Perez parked at a meter in the street and they went inside. They found an office where a very efficient receptionist pointed them in the direction of the lecture theatre where Makayla was supposed to be learning the finer points of Java programming. The receptionist also let them have a look at her photograph on the screen so that they would be able to pick her out.

They got to the lecture theatre ten minutes before the session was due to end. When the doors eventually opened, Nightingale and Perez stood either side, scanning faces. Nightingale saw her first. She was a pretty black girl with short dreadlocks, with a tiger-patterned messenger bag across her chest and a heavy textbook in her left hand. 'There she is,' he said to Perez. 'Best you do the talking or we'll get into the whole "are you English" thing.' She was deep in conversation with a lanky Hispanic teenager and Perez had to interrupt. 'Hi, are you Makayla?' she asked. 'Makayla Jackson.'

She frowned. 'Yes?'

'We just need a few words with you, Miss Jackson,' said Perez.

'Are you police?'

Perez shook her head. 'We're private investigators, we're trying to find Dee-anne Alexander.'

'You don't have to talk to them,' said the teenager next to her. 'They can't detain you.'

Perez smiled at the teenager. 'Law student?' she asked.

'No, but I know my rights.'

'It's okay, Santiago,' said Makayla. 'I'll talk to them. You go ahead, I'll catch you later.'

The teenager looked as if he wanted to argue, but then he nodded, flashed Perez a peace sign, and walked away.

'Has something happened to Dee-anne?' asked Makayla.

'We just want to talk to her,' said Perez. 'Do you know where she is?'

'I haven't seen her for a while. Has she done something wrong?'

Perez shook her head. 'No, we want to talk to her about a friend of hers. We've been to her home but she isn't there. Do you have any idea where she might have gone?'

Makayla looked at her watch. 'I need a cigarette. Can we do this outside?'

'Sure,' said Perez.

They followed her outside. Makayla took a pack of cigarettes from her bag. Camels. She lit one and offered the pack to Nightingale. He wasn't the least bit surprised that she had recognised him as a fellow smoker. Smokers had an inbuilt radar that picked up anyone who shared their habit. Nightingale wasn't a big fan of the Camel brand – he had tried them but much preferred his Marlboros – but he took one and let her light it for him. He nodded his thanks and blew smoke at the sky. Perez waited for them to finish bonding before asking her question again. 'So, do you know where Dee-anne is?'

Makayla grimaced. 'I haven't seen her for a while. Sorry.'

'You're friends, aren't you?'

'Sure. At least we were. BFFs for a long time.'

'But not for ever?'

Makayla blew smoke. 'She changed.' She shrugged. 'People change.'

'And when was the last time you saw her?'

'A week or so ago.'

'In class?'

'No, she's stopped coming to college. I saw her in the street. Called out her name but she didn't hear me. Maybe she had earphones in or was on her phone. She was on the other side of the road and there was traffic. I was going to go after her but I couldn't cross and when it was clear it was too late, she'd gone.'

'And before that?'

'Less than two weeks ago. She was in Wal-Mart. I thought then something was wrong because she didn't seem to be remember me.. Then it clicked and she hugged me and said she missed me but...' She shrugged. 'There was something not right. Like she was in another world. If I didn't know better I'd have thought she'd taken something, but she was always anti-drugs. She'd seen what they'd done to her mother.'

'So she'd dropped out of school?'

'I asked her that and she said she had better things to do with her time. I asked her what and she just grinned and said she wanted to have some fun.'

'Fun?' repeated Nightingale.

Makayla nodded. 'That's what she said. Fun. Then she laughed. Except the laugh didn't sound like her. It sounded like...' She shrugged, unable to finish the sentence.

'Did she have many friends?' asked Nightingale.

'Are you Australian?' asked Makayla.

'Yes,' said Nightingale. 'Could she be staying with a friend?'

'I suppose so,' she said. 'But if she is, I don't know them. No one has mentioned it.'

'What's she like, what sort of person is she?' asked Perez.

'She's lovely. Really caring. I always used to tell her that she cares too much. She was involved in the college's StressLine project.'

'StressLine?' repeated Perez.

'A confidential phoneline that students can call if things are getting on top of them. Like the Samaritans but students doing it for students.' She forced a smile. 'Philly's a tough town at the best of times, and a lot of kids at the college have problems. Family break-ups, drugs, gangs. Plus there's the stress of exams and stuff. StressLine is a free number for you to call so that you can talk to a peer. They run a drop-in centre where you can talk over coffee. Dee-anne was there two or three times a week.'

'Do you know if she met a guy called Leon Budd there?'

'She'd never tell me their names,' said Makayla. 'It's totally confidential.'

'But you heard what happened to Leon, surely?'

Makayla frowned. 'Leon?' Hey eyes widened. 'The boy who was murdered? You think Dee-anne knew him?'

'Well he went to this school.'

Makayla laughed. 'There are something like twenty thousand students here.'

'So you didn't know him?'

'Definitely not.'

'And you don't know if Dee-anne did.'

'She never mentioned it. And like I said, she would never tell me the name of anyone she dealt with at StressLine.' She blew smoke down at the ground, her brow furrowed. 'What do you think happened? Why do you think she's connected to what happened to Leon?'

'We don't know, we're not even sure she knew him. We're just trying to find her at the moment.'

'Well, I just assumed she was at home.'

'She isn't,' said Nightingale. 'The family say she's moved out.'

She nodded. 'That's probably for the best. Her stepfather is a nasty shit. I told her, she should go to the cops but she said he never did anything other than leer and grope and that she could handle it.'

'Where do you think she would go?'

Makayla shrugged. 'I don't know. She could have stayed with me if I'd known.' She flicked ash on the floor. 'Have you tried calling her?'

'No,' said Nightingale. 'To be honest with you, we don't have her number.'

'Her phone has been off for a few days now,' said Makayla. She pulled an iPhone from the back of her jeans and tapped out a number. She held it to her ear and shook her head. 'Straight through to voicemail,' she said.

'Can you let us have her number and we'll keep trying?' asked Perez.

'Sure.' Makayla held out her phone and Perez tapped the number into her own mobile. 'She did tell me about one guy she'd met,' said

Makayla. 'Didn't tell me his name but she said she'd seen him a few times. His sister had died and the guy was distraught. Kept talking about killing himself. I said she should have passed him on to the Samaritans because the StressLine people aren't trained for suicides but she said she was sure he didn't mean it.'

Nightingale looked over at Perez and realised that the same thought had struck them both. Leon Budd's sister had died recently.

'Can you remember anything else she said about this guy?' asked Nightingale.

'Not really. Just that he was really sad and she wanted to help him. She was always doing that, helping waifs and strays.'

'When was this? When did she mention this guy?'

Makayla rubbed her neck as she thought about it. 'Three weeks ago. Maybe four.' She nodded. 'Last month.'

CHAPTER 26

Andy Horowitz parked behind an ambulance and climbed out. Across the road were two black SWAT vans next to which were lined up a dozen beefy men all dressed in black and carrying an assortment of weaponry with a preponderance of AR-15 assault rifles and Mossberg 590 shotguns.

A sergeant jogged over, cradling his AR-15. 'You Horowitz?'

Horowitz nodded. 'Thanks for waiting. Can you give me a sitrep?' He walked around to the rear of his car, opened his boot and took off his coat.

'Perp's in a hotel around the corner. Fifth floor at the back. Booked in this afternoon, hasn't been out of the room.'

'It's definitely Donaldson?'

'We've had a plainclothes guy in there to show the desk guy a photograph and he's sure. He used a credit card belonging to his father to check in.'

'Careless,' said Horowitz. He tossed his coat into the boot and took out a bulletproof vest with POLICE across the front. He put it on and pulled the Velcro straps tight, then took his gun from its holster, checked the actions and put it back.

'He's a kid,' said the sergeant. 'It was the desk clerk who dropped the dime and he said the boy had nothing with him when he checked in.'

'So far as we know he doesn't have a gun,' said Horowitz, slamming the boot shut. 'There wasn't one in the house and the killings have all been with knives or things he's grabbed opportunistically.'

'Understood, but we're not taking any chances.'

'I hear you, I'm just saying that Tasers might be all the fire power you need.'

'We're the professionals here, just let us do our job,' said the sergeant. 'Happy for you to ride along but you need to hold back and leave the tactics to us.'

Horowitz held up his hands. 'Wasn't trying to teach anyone's grandmother to suck eggs, sergeant. And I certainly wasn't trying to minimise the seriousness of this guy. I've seen both crime scenes so I know the damage he can do with a knife or with anything he can grab.'

The sergeant smiled thinly. 'Good to see we're on the same page.'

'So what's your plan?'

'It's a cheap hotel, nothing fancy. One way in, one staircase up and one elevator. There's a fire escape running down the back of the building, accessed from the rear window. We'll take four men up the staircase and two in the elevator. Four will go around the back just in case he heads out of the window. We don't think we can get up the fire escape without making a noise so our guys will maintain surveillance on the ground. I'll leave two at the entrance. Your call where you want to go.'

'I'll stick with you, sergeant, if that's okay.'

The sergeant nodded briskly. 'Not a problem. Just stay behind us and keep your weapon holstered.' He jogged back to the vans and Horowitz hurried after him. He gave his orders in clipped tones then headed towards the entrance, cradling his assault rifle. Seven of his team followed him while four split off and went down a side alley.

Horowitz fell into step next to the sergeant. 'So this guy murdered his folks?' asked the sergeant.

'Looked like a frenzy killing.'

'Drugs?'

'No evidence of a drug problem, but these days, who knows? No drugs in the house and his bedroom looked like the bedroom of a regular High School kid.'

They reached the entrance to the hotel, a single door with a neon sign above it that said VACANCY. To the left was a bellpush with a plastic sign that said 'RING AFTER 10PM'.

The sergeant led the way into a cramped reception area. The Asian hotel clerk sat in a metal cage and he looked up with bored disinterest as the armed cops filed in. 'He's still in his room,' he said. 'When do I get paid?'

'Soon,' said the sergeant.

The clerk handed the sergeant a key card. The sergeant took it, pointed at a narrow stairway and four of his men headed up. Horowitz followed the sergeant into the elevator. Another armed cop joined them. Horowitz pressed the button for the third floor and the door closed. They rode up in silence.

The elevator opened onto a hallway that was as shabby as the reception downstairs. There was a sign on the wall opposite them showing the room numbers to the left and right. The sergeant pointed to the right. The four men who had come up the stairs joined them. Horowitz held back as the SWAT team moved towards the door.

The sergeant carefully slid the keycard into the lock but a red light flashed. He tried it again. Another red light. He put the card into a pocket on his overalls and stepped to the side.

A black officer with a shotgun rapped on the door with a gloved hand. 'Police!' he shouted. 'Open the door!'

There was no answer from inside.

'Break it down,' said the sergeant.

CHAPTER 27

Nightingale was cleaning his teeth when his cellphone rang. It was Perez. 'Where are you?' she asked.

'Office,' he said. 'Getting ready for bed.'

'I'll pick you up outside in five minutes,' said Perez.

'What's it about?'

'Matt Donaldson.' She ended the call.

Nightingale pulled his clothes back on, grabbed his coat and hurried down the stairs. He was halfway through a cigarette when Perez pulled up in front of the block. He dropped what was left of his cigarette in the gutter and climbed into the passenger seat. He had barely closed the door before she sped off down the street. 'What's wrong?'

'Andy's in hospital. Something to do with the Donaldson kid.'

'Andy's in hospital or the kid's in hospital?'

'Would I be driving like this if it was the perp?' snapped Perez.

Nightingale decided that his best option was to stay quiet so he said nothing as she zig-zagged through the traffic, pounding her horn impatiently.

She drove to Bellevue Hospital close to the East River and parked in a multi-storey. Nightingale had trouble keeping up with her as she hurried across the road to the main entrance.

'He's on the third floor so don't give me any crap about elevators,' she said as she punched at the 'up' button. Nightingale could see the entrance to the stairs but decided to stick with her, and he concentrated on breathing slowly and evenly as the elevator went up. As soon as the doors opened he headed out but Perez elbowed him to the side and beat him to it. There was a sign showing the directions of the room numbers and she headed left. Ahead of them were half a dozen uniformed cops and they parted to let her through.

One of them put an arm out to stop Nightingale. 'I'm with her,' he said.

'He's with me,' said Perez and the cop nodded and raised his arm.

Perez opened the door and Nightingale followed her in. Andy Horowitz was in a bed with the head raised. His left arm was in a splint and there was a plaster above his right eye. There were bruises and cuts all over his chest and he was hooked up to a machine that was monitoring his vital signs. A doctor in a white coat was bent over Horowitz, checking his dressings. There were two heavy-set men in suits standing by the window and the older of the two nodded at Perez. 'How are ya doing, Perez?'

'All good.'

The man nodded at Nightingale. 'Who's he?'

'A Brit, he's working with me.'

The man nodded at Nightingale. 'Hey.'

'Hey,' replied Nightingale.

'Pete Taylor and Don Ashley,' said Perez, by way of introduction. 'They work with Andy. How's he doing?'

'I'm not dead, Perez,' said Horowitz. 'I can speak for myself.'

The doctor turned and headed for the door. Perez went over to the bed. 'What happened, Andy?' asked Perez. 'Looks like you got hit by a truck.'

'That kid. He was a machine.'

'A machine?' repeated Perez.

'He was unstoppable,' said Horowitz. There were six guys at his door. Six. Armed to the teeth, Kevlar helmets and vests, the works. They knock, Nothing. They announce they're cops. Still nothing. At that point you figure he's either shitting himself or he's out on the fire escape, right?' He winced and closed his eyes.

'Are you okay?' asked Nightingale.

Horowitz opened his eyes. 'Are you fucking serious? No I'm not okay. I've got a broken arm, three of my discs are out and I've lost my spleen. One of my kidneys is on the watch list and I'm pissing blood.'

'I'm sorry,' said Nightingale.

'Why the fuck are you sorry?' asked Horowitz.

'He says sorry a lot,' said Perez. 'It's a British thing.'

Horowitz nodded. 'Anyway, he wasn't heading down the fire escape. They tried a key card but that didn't work so they kicked door down the door and he was just standing there, his head down, his hair hanging over his face. The door's lying on the floor, there are six rifles and shotguns pointing at him and everyone's shouting. Shock and awe. The fucking works. And he's just standing there, like it's nothing. Then he looks up, real slow. And I swear to you, his eyes had gone red.'

'Red?' repeated Perez.

'Red. Not red like he'd been crying. Red like blood. All hell's breaking lose, everyone's shouting, and he's just standing there. I'd told them he wasn't armed and one of the guys lowers his shotgun and pulls out his Taser. He fires it and the two prongs shoot out and hit Donaldson square in the chest. We hear it crackle and Donaldson just laughs. He laughs. Laughs like he's crazy. Laughs like the Taser is nothing. I got Tasered in training. It's not nothing. I went down like I was poleaxed. He just stood there and fucking laughed.'

He winced again and closed his eyes as he took two long, slow breaths. He opened his eyes again. He focussed on the ceiling as he continued to talk. 'He pulls the barbs out from his shirt, just grabs the wires and pulls. The guy holding the Taser is off balance and he stumbles into the room. Then Donaldson starts to move. Man, I've never seen anything like it. I've seen Navy Seals in action and they're fast but this guy... This teenager. He moves like.. I don't know. Like fucking lightning. He grabs the Taser guy, spins him around and breaks his neck. You could hear it snap through all the shouting. They can't shoot now because the SWAT guy is between them and the kid. Then he throws the SWAT guy at us. That guy is two hundred and twenty pounds minimum and he tosses him as if he was a fucking doll. The SWAT guys hits the team as a dead weight and then Donaldson is heading for the door, heading right at us. The sergeant who was second in line is the size of a small tank. The sergeant pulls his trigger but Donaldson is so fast, he steps to the side and grabs the barrel. You fire a gun and the barrel gets hot but he doesn't seem to feel it. He pulls the guy into the room and then he does I don't know what and the SWAT sergeant flies through the air and slams into the wall. The guy who was behind him fires but Donaldson ducks and rolls and then he comes up right in front of the guy his hands are a blur and the cop's face just turns to mush. Then Donaldson turns and with one hand he throws the guy into the room and with the other hand he grabs the next cop by the throat. I've never seen anything like it. He didn't even look, he just reached out and the next moment he's squeezing his throat. Then he turns and breaks the guy's neck. Snap. Just like that. One handed.

'That leaves two SWAT guys between me and Donaldson. They've got assault rifles and what's he got? Nothing. Just these red eyes that don't seem to be blinking. The first one fires, bang-bang-bang, and all three shots hit the wall because he's moved. He didn't jump or flinch, he just moved from where he was to the side of the guy that was shooting and then he slams him up against the wall. And I mean up. The guy's feet were swinging off the ground and he must have weighed as much as me. Donaldson is doing it one-handed. Then the other guy fires but Donaldson throws the body at him and they both end up on the floor. Donaldson stamps on the second guy's hand and I hear the bones crack. Then I'm the only one left.'

Horowitz winced again. 'Cheryl, you're going to have to ask them to increase my painkillers because my ribs are hurting like fuck.'

'I will,' she said. 'Just tell us what happened.'

Horowitz nodded, clearly in a lot of pain. 'The cops had told me not to draw my weapon but it was clear that it was turning to shit so I pulled my Glock. He came towards me and I had my gun aimed right at him and I pulled the trigger three or four times. He moved out of the way every time. How could he do that? How can a kid move that fast? He was as close to me as you are and I missed every time. I pulled the trigger and he moved and I missed. Then he came at me and started hitting me and I just went out like a light. The guy was a machine. A fucking machine.'

'He didn't do martial arts, anything like that?' asked Nightingale.

Horowitz turned to look at him. 'He played softball. Tennis. That was it. He was just a regular kid. How does a regular kid move that fast?'

'Angel Dust, maybe' said Taylor. 'That's a game changer. We've had a few kids go crazy after smoking joints laced with PCP. They call them water joints and if the dose is too high they go crazy.'

'Maybe,' said Perez. 'But nothing we've seen suggests he was on drugs. Right, Andy?'

'Yeah, but nothing in this case makes any sense,' said Horowitz. 'I mean, what was Donaldson doing killing the girl in the first place? He didn't know her, no connection that we can find, and by all accounts he was a good kid. He wasn't a straight A student but he wasn't failing at school, no drugs, no gang affiliations. How does he go from that to butchering a girl and taking out an entire SWAT team?'

'Sometimes in stressful situations, adrenaline kicks in,' said Nightingale. 'Like when mothers lift cars to rescue their kids.'

'It wasn't that,' said Horowitz. 'It wasn't anything like that. He busted my fucking spleen with one punch. And all the time it was happening, he was smiling.'

'I'm sorry,' said Nightingale. Perez looked over at him and gave him a withering look.

'He wasn't scared,' said Horowitz. 'He wasn't the slightest bit fazed. In fact it looked to me as if he was enjoying it.'

CHAPTER 28

Nightingale lit a cigarette as he walked out of the hospital with Perez. There was a half moon overhead but it was mostly obscured by cloud. Nightingale stopped and blew smoke up at the night sky. Perez had parked in the hospital car park but there was a bar in the other direction and she nodded at it. 'You feel like a drink?'

Nightingale nodded. 'And some.'

They walked over to the bar in silence. Nightingale threw away what was left of his cigarette, pushed open the door and stepped inside. A country and western song was playing on a jukebox. Opposite the door was a long bar of polished wood that ran the full length of the room. By the window was a line of wooden booths, most of them occupied, and at the far end of the room were a few round tables with wooden chairs. 'Bar or table?' he asked but she was already walking to the bar. She slipped onto a stool and nodded at the barman, an anorexically thin blonde guy with tattooed arms. 'Tequila,' she said. 'A shot. Hold the salt but I'll take the lemon.'

Nightingale climbed onto the stool to her left. 'Bottled beer,' he asked the barman. 'Whatever's good.' The barman went off to get their drinks. 'Are you okay?' asked Nightingale.

'If I'm not, what'll you do? Say sorry?'

'I can see you're upset.'

Her eyebrows arched. 'Do you think?'

'I am sorry what happened to Andy. But there's no way anyone could have known.'

Her eyes narrowed. 'Are you sure about that?'

Nightingale opened his mouth to reply but the barman returned and put their drinks down in front of them. Perez downed her tequila shot in one, then picked up a slice of lemon from a small dish and bit into it. She put the lemon peel back on the dish and nodded at the barman. 'Another,' she said. 'And keep them coming.' The barman headed back to the tequila bottle. 'Matt Donaldson was a regular teenage High School student,' said Perez. 'Mr average. Mr less than average, maybe. How does a scrawny teenager end up beating the shit out of a SWAT team? And you saw what he did to Andy? Andy went through two tours in Iraq without a scratch. How does a teenager put him in a hospital bed?'

'Like that cop said, drugs maybe.'

The barman came back with a fresh shot. Perez toyed with it but didn't drink it. 'Not an adrenaline rush, like you said back at the hospital?'

Nightingale shrugged. 'Either are possibilities, I suppose.'

'It was a funny thing to say, that's all. Mothers lifting cars.'

Nightingale shrugged again but didn't say anything.

'I can't help thinking that you know more than you're letting on.'

'I don't know much more than you, Cheryl.'

'We both know that's not true. I was looking at you when Andy was telling us what happened at the hotel. You weren't surprised. He told you that a teenage boy took out an entire SWAT team and you just stood there and nodded like it was the most natural thing in the world. So I'm asking you again, Jack, what the fuck is going on?'

Nightingale took a drink from his beer bottle, then stared at the label. A man with a moustache and a starched collar stared back. 'It's complicated,' he said.

Perez drank her shot, slammed the empty glass on the bar and bit into another slice of lemon. The barman was already picking up the tequila bottle.

'Donaldson wasn't himself,' said Nightingale.

'No shit, Sherlock.'

The barman put a fresh shot and lemon slice in front of Perez and took away her old glass and dish.

'Something has taken over his body. Something that allowed him to be stronger and faster.'

'You're saying he's possessed?'

'There's something controlling him, yes.'

She shook her head. 'I'm not buying that.'

'And I'm not selling it. You asked. I'm being honest. If you want we can stick with the angel dust theory. But we both know Donaldson isn't a druggie.'

'And you think he's possessed?'

'Something like that, yes. Something changed him, obviously. Teenagers generally don't smile while they're taking out armed SWAT teams.'

'So we need an exorcism? A priest? Is that what you're saying?'

Nightingale shook his head. 'Possession is when a spirit takes control. Usually they're low level spirits so some holy water and few Latin chants does the trick. But this boy isn't possessed by a spirit.'

'What then?"

'Spirits can enter humans. That's what possession is. Usually the human has to be in a weakened state or have emotional problems. That's why it's often teenage girls who are possessed. To be honest, true cases of possession are rare. But they happen.' He took a long pull on his beer before continuing. 'I think Donaldson has been invaded by something else. A devil. A demon from Hell.'

'What the fuck are you talking about, Nightingale? Devils? Demons?'

'You're a Catholic. You believe in Heaven and Hell?'

'We're not here to argue what I do and don't believe in. You're trying to tell me that a devil has... has what? Taken over his body?'

'Spirits are here, all around us. You and I can't see them, most of the time anyway. Usually they're sad souls that are trapped here and either can't or won't move on. Often they want something. Sometimes the best way of dealing with them is to find out what they want and do it for them.' Perez opened her mouth to speak but Nightingale held up his hand. 'What has happened to Donaldson is way more serious than simple possession. There are demons in Hell who want out. Some demons can move back and forth at will but the vast majority are as trapped as the souls in torment. The problem is that a demon – most of them anyway – have to be summoned. Someone has to call them by name and usually use their sigil. Their sign. Once summoned, a devil can leave Hell and enter our world. The problem for the trapped devils is that there are billions of them. So how can one arrange to be summoned? One voice among so many?'

Perez frowned. She was clearly having trouble following what Nightingale was saying. Then her eyes widened. 'Is that how come Dee-anne Alexander was able to throw her fat pig of a stepfather around? She was possessed?'

'Maybe,' said Nightingale.

'And the mutilations are part of this?'

'Carving the sigils into the bodies is part of it, yes.'

She drained her glass and winced as she bit into the lemon.

'Maybe you should take it slowly,' he said.

'Fuck you.'

'You're driving.'

'No, I'm sitting in a bar drinking. I can Uber it home and pick up my car tomorrow. But thank you for your concern.'

'Sorry.'

'And stop saying sorry.'

He raised his bottle in salute. 'I'll try.'

The barman put a new drink in front of her and she nodded her thanks. 'So you're saying that Matt Donaldson carved a sigil into Kate Walker's flesh?'

Nightingale nodded. 'That sigil would be to summon a particular devil. I think someone primed Donaldson to be a vessel for the demon. I need to find out who the demon is, then I'll have a chance of defeating it.'

'Primed? What do you mean, primed?'

'I'm guessing that he was lured in. Through that kid's game, Charlie Charlie. The game is like a gateway. Same way that cannabis is a gateway drug. You smoke cannabis and then maybe you move on to cocaine or crack or whatever floats your boat. Kids get drawn into Charlie Charlie and some of them move on to Ouija boards and séances and eventually Satanism. Devil worship.'

'You're saying that Kate Walker primed him?'

'I think so, yes. The demon contacted her through Charlie Charlie then the Ouija board.'

'That makes no sense at all,' said Perez. 'You're saying that Kate did the priming but Donaldson killed her?'

'Not Donaldson. The demon. The demon took over Donaldson and murdered Kate. Then went on to murder the parents.'

'And what about Leon Budd? Do you think a demon killed him, too?'

Nightingale nodded. 'I'm afraid so.'

'But not the same demon?'

'No. A different one. Hence the different sigils.'

Perez cursed under her breath. 'This just gets better and better,' she sighed, and downed another shot.

CHAPTER 29

It was close to midnight when Perez finally decided she had swallowed enough tequila. She sounded sober but there was a glassy look in her eyes and she stumbled as she climbed off her stool. She fumbled in her coat and pulled out a phone. 'Uber me,' she said, giving it to him.

'Where are you going?'

'The address is in there,' she said. Nightingale tapped on the smartphone and opened the Uber app. Five minutes later a white Toyota Prius pulled up outside the bar. Nightingale flicked his cigarette away and helped her into the back. 'Good night,' she slurred.

'Forget it, I'll see you home,' said Nightingale, and climbed in after her.

The driver was Middle Eastern with a neatly trimmed beard and a gold tooth in the front of his mouth that glinted when he smiled at Nightingale in the mirror. 'She okay?'

'Bit too much to drink,' said Nightingale.

'Bull fucking shit,' said Perez, leaning her head against the passenger window.

'She'll be fine,' said Nightingale.

The driver already had Perez's address programmed into his GPS and the traffic was light so they made good time but Perez was fast asleep by the time the Prius pulled up in front of her building. He patted her cheek softly. 'Wake up, Cheryl.'

Her eyelids fluttered open. 'Hey,' she said.

Nightingale helped her out of the car and held her up as the Prius drove away. They were in a tree-lined road with four-storey brown stone houses. 'Which is yours?' he asked.

'That one,' she said, stabbing with her finger. 'Basement.'

Nightingale helped her down a metal stairway that led to a black door. 'Keys?' he asked.

Perez fumbled in her pocket and brought out a key ring with four keys on it. The first key he tried didn't fit but the second did and as he pushed open the door a burglar alarm began to beep. There was a console on the wall and he took Perez over to it. She tapped out the four-digit code and the beeping stopped. He left her leaning against the wall while he shut and bolted the door, then helped her along the hallway to a sitting room with a long low grey sofa in front of a big screen TV. He helped her onto the sofa and she murmured something and then lay down. 'Terrific,' said Nightingale.

There was a kitchen at the far end of the hallway and he took a bottle of water from the fridge and took it back to the sitting room. Perez was already snoring.

There was one bedroom. He flicked on the light switch. In the middle of the room was a wooden sleigh bed, the duvet carelessly thrown over it. There was a pile of clothes on the floor next to a wicker laundry basket and three coffee mugs on a bedside table, along with a bottle of Aspirin and an asthma inhaler. Nightingale put the bottle of water next to the mugs, pulled back the duvet and went back to the sitting room, where Perez's snoring was now slower but louder. He lifted her up. As he carried her to the bedroom she put her arms around his neck and snored into his chest. He laid her on the bed, covered her with the duvet and switched off the light.

Back in the kitchen he made himself a coffee and found some Chinese leftovers in the fridge so he sat on the sofa and ate cold Kung Pao Chicken and rice. Half an hour later he was fast asleep on the sofa.

CHAPTER 30

Nightingale opened his eyes to find Cheryl Perez looking down at him. 'Black or white?' she asked.

'Huh? What?'

'Your coffee? Black or white?'

'What time is it?'

'Nine.'

'White. No sugar.'

She disappeared and returned a couple of minutes later with his coffee. He sat up and took it.

'I didn't dream that stuff about devils and demons, did I?' she said, sitting down on a chair opposite him. She sipped her coffee.

Nightingale shook his head. 'I'm afraid not.'

'We can't tell anyone, can we?'

'Well we can try, but no one will believe us. The greatest trick the devil ever pulled was to convince people he never existed.'

'That's from that movie, The Usual Suspects.'

'They got it from a French philosopher, guy by the name of Charles Baudelaire. "The finest trick of the devil is to persuade you that he does not exist", is what he actually said. He produced a lot of quotable quotes. "I have always been astonished that women are allowed to enter churches, what talk can they have with God?" is another of his.'

'Sounds like a sweetheart.' She forced a smile. 'Thanks for putting me to bed last night. I don't remember a thing.'

'I decided against putting you in your pyjamas.'

'Thanks for that, too. I was pretty far gone.'

'That many neat tequilas in a row will do that to a girl,' he said.

'Yeah, well it was one hell of a night.' She reached for the remote control, switched on the TV and flicked through to a local news channel. 'They'll catch Donaldson eventually. He made a stupid mistake last time with the credit card, he'll show up again.'

'Seeing how easily he shrugged off an armed SWAT team, I'm not sure they'll be able to bring him in,' said Nightingale. 'Not alive, anyway.'

'So what do we do?'

'We wait, I guess.'

'That's it? That's your plan?'

'I'll see if I can track down who these devils are.'

'And how do you plan to do that, exactly?'

'There's someone I can ask.'

'A CI?'

Nightingale smiled at the thought of describing a demon from Hell as a confidential informant. 'Sort of,' he said.

'I'll come with you.'

Nightingale shook his head. 'She's fussy about who she talks to.'

CHAPTER 31

Nightingale popped into a library on 67th Street and waited for ten minutes until a computer with internet access became free. A homeless man with a straggly beard and a length of string around his waist as a belt for his stained coat stood up, grabbed a canvas rucksack and walked away muttering to himself. Nightingale took the man's place. His nostrils were immediately assailed by the departed man's body odour and there were wet stains on some of the keyboard keys. He used the hem of his raincoat to wipe down the keys before he started typing. It didn't take him long to find what he was looking for. Googling 'Wicca supplies New York' gave him a dozen or so possibilities and he chose the nearest, just a twenty minute walk away.

He stood up and an old woman with two full carrier bags who had apparently lost all her teeth took his place. Nightingale used the restroom to wash his hands before walking to Alchemy Arts Supplies, smoking two cigarettes on the way. The store was on the second floor of a former industrial building. There was an elevator but Nightingale took the stairs. It looked more like a discount warehouse than a shop with all the stock piled haphazardly on wooden and metal shelving units that ran the length of the building. There were metal baskets and trollies. Nightingale took a trolley and pushed it slowly down the central aisle. Some of his requirements were easy. White candles, for example. They had more than a dozen shapes and sizes in stock. There were literally hundreds of crucibles and bowls to choose from in everything from lead to crystal, many of them hand-made. He put a large lead crucible into the trolley. Chalk was easy, consecrated salt was harder to find but they had several varieties, along with a whole selection of items that had been blessed by named priests, including crucifixes and holy water. The blessed items were in a locked glass-fronted cabinet and he had to get a salesperson to help him. A young man with a badge that said his name was Zak and that he was happy to help unlocked the cabinet and waited while Nightingale took what he wanted.

A lanky young blonde girl with a badge that said her name was Wind was standing by the cash register. She smiled brightly as he pushed the trolley towards her and he saw that she was wearing brightly-coloured braces on her teeth. 'Any chance of you having a birch branch?' he asked.

'Several,' said Wind. 'All freshly cut.' She took him down the aisle and showed him a shelf with more than a dozen branches from a number of different trees. 'They have dates on the tags showing when they were cut,' said Wind.

Nightingale selected a small birch branch that had been cut the previous day.

'You're doing a protective circle,' she said, casting her eye over the contents of his trolley.

'I am indeed.'

'Not many people go to the bother of consecrated chalk and a birch branch. Belt and braces.'

'Better safe than sorry, I always say.'

'And the crucible. Interesting. Looks like a summoning.'

Nightingale pushed his trolley down the aisle but she kept pace with him. 'You're from England?' she asked.

Nightingale nodded but didn't reply.

'What's the scene like there?'

Nightingale wrinkled his nose. 'I tend to avoid scenes,' he said. 'More of a lone wolf.'

'I can respect that,' she said. 'If there's anything else you need, I'll be at the register.' She walked away, her long blonde hair flicking from side to side.

He found a whole section devoted to herbs in jars and bottles of various sizes and he took what he needed. On the way back to the register he passed a section devoted to cleaning products. Usually he used whatever was at hand but as it was available he took packs of soap, shampoo and brushes and put them in the trolley.

Wind had picked up on the fact that Nightingale wasn't in a chatty mood so she totalled up his purchases in silence. The total amount flashed up on the register's screen and Nightingale handed over one of Joshua Wainwright's credit cards. New cards arrived every month and when they did he would destroy the old ones. They came in a variety of names and backed by different banks but he had never had one refused and never bothered to ask if he had a credit limit. She handed the card back and he scribbled an illegible signature on the electronic pad by the register. Payment done she helped bag his purchases and then finally spoke. 'Come again,' she said.

CHAPTER 32

Nightingale was carrying his supplies into the office when his cellphone rang. It was Wainwright. 'There's been another one, Jack. In New Jersey. Happened two days ago. The victim was a girl. Another teenager. Sara Moseby. The body was cut and slashed but you can make out the sigil on her back if you look carefully.'

Nightingale cursed under his breath.

'If you get over there this afternoon you can see the body for yourself. I have a contact in the Hunterdon County Medical Examiner's Office. I'll text you the name and the address.'

'I'll call Perez.'

The line went dead. Nightingale had Perez's number on speed dial and she answered on the third ring. 'Joshua wants us to take a look at a body out in New Jersey,' he said.

'Any body in particular?'

'There's been another murder, similar to the first two. He's arranged for us to take a look at the corpse.'

'Where are you?'

'The office.'

'I'll be outside in thirty minutes.'

When Perez rolled up in her car, Nightingale was standing outside the office holding two Starbucks coffees. He climbed in and gave her one of the coffees then took out his phone. 'I've got the address,' he said. 'Do you have a GPS?'

'Never use it,' said Perez. 'I'm New York born and bred, I don't need a computer to tell me where to go.'

'Have you been to Hunterdon County before?'

'I've been all over New Jersey. You can't work homicide or serious crimes in Manhattan and not be going back and forth over the Hudson. 'You've seen The Sopranos, right? Half the Mafia lives in New Jersey. Hunterdon County Medical Examiner's Office is in Flemington, right?'

'Wescott Drive,' said Nightingale.

It was mid-afternoon when they arrived at the Medical Examiner's office. It formed part of the Hunterdon Medical Centre, a sprawling community hospital complex to the north of Flemington.

Perez parked and she and Nightingale headed inside. A bored receptionist pointed them in the direction of the Medical Examiner's Office and they followed the signs until they reached another reception area where a brunette in a white coat was bent over a computer terminal. She looked up and peered at them over the top of red-framed spectacles. Nightingale nodded and smiled. 'We're looking for a Medical Examiner by the name of Sam Jenner. Any idea where we can find him?'

The brunette smiled. 'You've found him. Or her.' She pushed her glasses further up her nose.

'You'll have to forgive my friend, he's not used to dealing with women in authority,' said Perez. She held out her hand. 'Cheryl Perez. My sexist assistant here is Jack Nightingale.'

'It happens all the time,' said Jenner, shaking hands with them both. 'It was my dad, he's a sexist pig himself at the best of times and figured a neutral name would be a help career-wise.' She wrinkled her nose. 'And you know what, I'd never admit it to him but he was right.' She turned and gestured at a set of double metal doors. 'Mr Wainwright said to expect you, but we don't have long. How are you on smells?'

'Smells?' repeated Nightingale.

'It's not pleasant in there. Not if you're not used to it.' She reached into her lab coat and took out a small tub of Vicks Vapor Rub. 'I carry this for visitors.'

'Definitely,' said Perez. She took the tub, opened it and smeared some across her upper lip.

She offered it to Nightingale but he shook his head. 'I'm good,' he said.

The Medical Examiner put the Vicks back into her pocket. 'Let me know if you change your mind,' she said. She pushed open the double doors and Perez and Nightingale followed her through. There were two stainless steel autopsy tables in the middle of the room, with circular lighting arrays above them. There was a body covered in a rubber sheet on one of the tables but it was tiny, the size of a toddler. Nightingale turned his eyes away. Jenner pulled open the door to a walk-in refrigerator. There were four racks lined up across the fridge and a single body on one. Jenner drew back a pale green rubber sheet to reveal a teenage girl with mousy brown hair and a snub nose. Her mouth was open. Her skin was pasty white making the half a dozen stab wounds all the more apparent. 'Sara Moseby, sweet sixteen,' said Jenner. The Y-shaped cuts made by the medical examiner during the autopsy had been held together with plastic staples.

'Most of the damage was to her back,' said Jenner.

'Can we take a look?' asked Nightingale.

'There's not much to see, just a lot of cuts and stab wounds.'

'It'd be helpful,' said Nightingale.

Jenner rolled the body onto its side. Nightingale and Perez walked around to get a better look. 'Oh my God,' whispered Perez when she saw the damage. There were dozens of cuts where the flesh had been cleanly parted, and as many stab wounds where the flesh had puckered outwards.

Nightingale looked down at the body. 'You ever seen anything like this before?' he asked Jenner.

She shook her head. 'No, and I hope I never do again. Whoever did this is one sick puppy. You can tell from the way the wounds bled that she was alive for most of the time he was cutting her.'

'But it wasn't sexual?' asked Perez.

'Definitely not. He didn't go near the sexual organs. And no sign of rape.'

Defence wounds?' asked Perez.

'A few small cuts on her hands. It looked to me as if he caught her by surprise. Stabbed her in the stomach and chest and she either fell face down or he turned her over and began slicing and stabbing her back.'

Nightingale squinted at the centre of the girl's back. The cuts seemed random but as he stared at the damage he could make out a shape. Three parallel cuts linked by a curve with another curve across the middle line that had a small point on the end. It wasn't obvious and would only be seen by someone who was looking for it. He pulled out his phone and took three pictures, one with the flash and two without.

'Do you see something?' asked Perez.

'I just wanted a record of it,' said Nightingale as he put his phone away, though he could see from the tightening of her jaw that she knew he had avoided her question.

'What about her clothes?' Nightingale asked the medical examiner.

'They were fine. They came separately in an evidence bag.'

'No blood or cuts?'

The Medical Examiner shook her head. 'They must have been removed before the attack.'

'Do they have a suspect?'

Jenner nodded. 'Bethlehem is a small town. The local Sheriff knows everyone and within hours they were looking for a guy who lives nearby. Steve Willoughby.'

'Bethlehem?' said Nightingale. 'Like the place where Christ was born?'

'The very same,' said Jenner. 'Population four thousand give or take. Mainly rural, God-fearing people. It was settled in the seventeenth century by Irish, Dutch and German immigrants.' She smiled at Nightingale. 'A few English, too.'

'How much do you know about the case?'

'Not much, but Deputy Sheriff Driscoll is an easy-going guy, I'm sure he'd tell you what's going on. I spoke to him yesterday afternoon and he was about to go to the papers with an appeal for information.'

'Is he based in Bethlehem?' asked Perez.

She shook her head. 'Hunterdon County Sheriff's Department is in Court Street. Downtown, a couple of miles away. But he said he'd be out in Bethlehem today.'

Nightingale looked over at Perez. 'We should take a run out there.'

'How far is it?' Perez asked the Medical Examiner.

'Twenty miles. I've got the address of the Moseby farm. As I said, Mark's very approachable.'

'Mark?' said Nightingale.

'Mark Driscoll. Deputy Sheriff. Just mention my name.'

Perez nodded at Nightingale. 'Okay, we can head over there now.'

CHAPTER 33

Nightingale expected Perez to mention the fact that he'd photographed Sara Moseby's back but she drove to the farm in silence. He figured she was using the old interrogator's trick of hoping that he would say something to fill the silence but he resisted the urge and listened to the radio instead during the half hour drive.

The Moseby farm seemed to be centred around a large herd of dairy cows that were grazing either side of a dirt road that led to a cluster of brick buildings. There were a number of vehicles parked on a Tarmac square in front of the main house but none of them looked as if they belonged to a Deputy Sheriff. Perez and Nightingale climbed out of the car and looked around. To the right of the house was a children's play area with a slide and a swing set and a tyre hanging on a rope from a spreading oak tree. There was a young boy sitting on one of the swings, pushing himself slowly backwards and forwards.

Perez parked in front of the house. There was a Ford Cherokee Jeep and a Range Rover and a couple of Toyota saloons.

They climbed out of the car. A large chestnut horse looked over at them and neighed, shook its head, and ran off. 'You go and see if you can talk to the parents, I'll have a chat with the boy,' said Nightingale.

'You might want to rethink that,' said Perez.

'Why?'

'Because generally it's not a good idea for middle-aged men in raincoats to be approaching young boys,' said Perez.

'Point taken,' said Nightingale. 'Plan B it is, then.' He headed towards the house.

Perez walked over to the boy on the swing. He didn't look up as she approached, just continued to stare at the dusty ground as he pushed himself backwards and forwards on the swing. 'Hi, my name's Cheryl,' she said. 'What's your name?'

'Luke,' said the boy. He squinted up at her. 'Are you a police lady?'

'I used to be,' she said.

'Do you have a gun?'

'Not with me,' she said.

'I can shoot a gun,' said Luke.

'Wow,' said Perez. 'How old are you?'

'Ten.'

'I didn't shoot a gun until I was twenty,' said Perez.

Luke nodded. 'Daniel taught me.'

'Daniel?'

'My brother. He's dead.'

'I'm sorry about that,' said Perez.

'He got drunk and crashed his truck,' said Luke. 'My dad said he's a damn fool.'

'You must miss him.'

Luke nodded solemnly. 'A lot. My sister died too.'

'I heard about that.' She looked over her shoulder at the house. Nightingale was knocking on the door.

'They say that Steve killed her but I don't think so because Steve was Sara's friend,' said Luke.

'Steve is your neighbour, right?'

Luke nodded again. 'He was Daniel's friend but he was sort of my friend too.'

'You must miss Sara a lot, too.'

Luke nodded again. 'Now my mom and dad only have me.'

'You're very important to them. They're going to need your help because they'll both be very sad, too.'

'I know,' said Luke.

Perez looked over at the house. A woman had opened the door and was talking to Nightingale.

'Luke, did you ever play Charlie Charlie?'

'You know about Charlie Charlie?'

'Sure. Everyone knows about Charlie Charlie. Have you tried it?'

Luke nodded. 'Sara wanted me to. She wanted to talk to Daniel.'

'Did it work?'

He nodded again.

'Wow,' said Perez. 'Really?'

'It was him. For sure.'

'How do you know?'

'Because he knew me and Sara. We talked to him.'

'How? Charlie Charlie only answers yes and no.'

'Sara got a Wee-Jee board.'

'A Ouija board?'

He nodded. 'With letters and stuff on it. You hold the wooden thing. The planet.'

'Planchette?'

'That's right. The planchette.'

'Weren't you scared?'

'A bit, he said. 'Especially when Sara put a blindfold on me.'

'Why did she do that?'

'It was Daniel's idea.'

'Luke!' Perez turned to see the woman walking quickly across the grass towards them. 'Luke, you come here right now!' she shouted.

'I've got to go,' he said, slipping off the swing. 'That's my mom.'

'Nice talking to you,' said Perez.

Luke ran over the grass to his mother. She put a protective arm around him and shepherded him towards the house.

Nightingale joined her under the tree and lit a cigarette. 'Didn't want to talk. Can't blame her, I suppose.'

'What about the father?'

'Dosed up on anti-depressants. Any joy with the boy?'

Mrs Moseby took Luke inside the house and closed the door. 'He played Charlie Charlie with his sister.'

'Did he now?"

'And she used a Ouija board with him. He says they spoke to their brother, Daniel. He died when he crashed his truck.'

'And what did the dear departed Daniel have to say for himself.' He blew a tight plume of smoke at the swing.

'Luke doesn't know, his sister put a blindfold on him.'

'Same as Kate did to her brother. What's the story with that?'

Nightingale pulled a face. 'I've never heard of Ouija boards being used for private messages. Usually it's a group thing.'

A police car turned off the main road and headed down the drive towards them. 'This'll be Sheriff Driscoll now,' said Perez.

They went to wait for him. Nightingale flicked away what was left of the cigarette when the Deputy Sheriff parked his patrol car behind a red truck. Nightingale knew it was a sure sign of getting older when the policemen started to look young, but Sheriff Driscoll barely looked old enough to drive. He was tall and thin with baby-smooth skin and thick black hair that kept falling over his eyes. He was wearing a dark brown uniform and had a Glock in a leather holster on his hip and black boots that had been polished until they shone. He looked over at them and his hand moved almost imperceptibly towards his gun.

Perez did the talking. 'We're private detectives in Manhattan investigating a murder that's similar to your case here,' she said. 'Cheryl Perez and Jack Nightingale. Sam Jenner suggested we come over and say hello.'

'That's very neighbourly of you,' said Driscoll. His hand moved away 'But why?'

'There are similarities in the case we're looking at. The way the body was mutilated. We just thought we could be helpful.'

'What case is that?' asked the Deputy Sheriff.

'It was in Manhattan,' said Perez. 'You might have seen it on the news. Teenager called Matt Donaldson killed a girl called Kate Walker. Similar MO to your murder.'

'She was found in a loft, right? And they have a suspect.'

Perez nodded.

'So what's the connection? You have a suspect in that murder, we're pretty sure we know who killed Sara Moseby.'

'The wounds are similar,' said Nightingale.

'Similar in what way?'

'A lot of them. Overkill.'

The deputy nodded. 'We definitely have that.'

'Can you show us the crime scene?' asked Nightingale.

'Nothing much to see,' said the Sheriff. 'They took the body to the Medical Examiner's.'

'Just be useful for a look-see,' said Nightingale.

The Sheriff nodded and pointed at a red-painted wooden barn with a steeply sloping roof. 'Over there,' he said.

Perez and Nightingale followed him to the barn. There was a double door one side of which one was ajar. The Sheriff pushed it open further and went inside. Nightingale went after him. Perez stood by the door while Nightingale and the Sheriff went into the middle. It had been used as a storage area. There was a tractor and two quad-bikes and barrels of fuel in one corner, cartons of what looked like spare parts in another. The floor was concrete and was surprisingly clean other than from old oil stains. 'Her father found the body, here,' said Driscoll, pointing down at a rust red patch on the concrete. They'd been out all day at a friend's birthday party. Sara had said she wasn't feeling well. When they got back at just after eight she wasn't in her room and her father saw a light on in the barn. He came over, found her dead. He cradled her as he used his cellphone. There was blood all over him by the time we arrived.'

Nightingale went over to the bloodstain and knelt down. He moved his head from side to side, looking for changes in the surface of the concrete. He could just about make out glistening traces of candle wax. Not much, someone had done a pretty good job of cleaning up.

'Can I help you, Mr Nightingale?' asked Driscoll.

'It's a Sherlock Holmes thing he does,' said Perez.

Nightingale stood up and walked around the bloodstain. He spotted a white smear and he crouched down and rubbed it with his fingers. Chalk. Just a trace.

'Like I said, we have a suspect,' said the Deputy Sheriff. 'Steve Willoughby. He was a friend of the family, lives on the neighbouring farm.'

'You've got him in custody?'

Driscoll shook his head. 'He's on the lam. But he's a kid, he won't get far.'

'Sara's brother died recently, is that right?' asked Nightingale.

'Daniel was killed in a car crash a month back. He'd been drinking, ploughed into a telegraph pole late at night. There was no other car involved, he wasn't wearing his seat belt. Just bad choices coming home to roost. Why would you ask about him?'

Nightingale struggled to think of a reply.

'Might be worth seeing if we can find a link between your perp and ours,' said Perez. 'Emails, websites, social media.'

The Deputy Sheriff nodded. 'Sounds like a plan,' he said. 'What was your perp's name?'

'Matt Donaldson.'

'They nearly caught the guy, right?'

'Close but no cigar,' said Perez.

'I suppose Willoughby could be a copycat,' said Driscoll. 'We'll ask him when we bring him in. Any other similarities you can think of between the two cases?'

'Victim was a young girl,' said Perez. 'Clothes removed. Girl killed and cut up.'

Driscoll nodded thoughtfully. 'Could be a coincidence. But it's worth seeing if we can link the perps.' He turned to look at Nightingale. 'Why were you asking about Daniel?'

'Kate Walker was upset about the death of her boyfriend,' said Perez. 'We thought she might have come into contact with her killer during the grieving process.'

The Deputy continued to stare at Nightingale and Nightingale nodded in agreement. 'It was just a thought.'

'But this Donaldson guy wasn't a bereavement councillor or anything like that, he was just a High School student right?'

'I was just looking for connections,' said Nightingale.

'You say that Donaldson had the girl remove her clothing?' asked Driscoll.

'Asked her or forced her, we don't know which,' said Perez.

'Then maybe it is a copycat,' said Driscoll. 'Sara's clothes were in a neat pile on a bench. We were thinking maybe she'd arranged to meet him for sex and something had gone wrong. An argument, maybe, and then

Steve lost it.' He looked around the barn. 'Though if it was sex they had planned, you'd expect them to choose a more comfortable place.'

'What about the weapon?' asked Nightingale. 'Did he bring it with him?'

Driscoll pointed at a row of tools on a rack by the door. There were shovels, picks, screwdrivers and several knives and cutting implements. 'He took a pruning knife from there. We had the DNA and fingerprints analysed and checked against samples from Steve's bedroom. It's him.'

'How old is he, this Steve?'

'Eighteen, going on nineteen.'

'And Sara wasn't in a relationship with him?'

'Both sets of parents say no. He was at college but they went to the same High School. Steve was a good friend of Daniel, Sara's brother. Their paths would cross all the time, but they were never a couple.' He folded his arms. 'You're wondering why she would take her clothes off if she wasn't his girlfriend?'

'I'm wondering a whole lot of things,' said Nightingale. 'I don't see any easy answers.' He looked at his watch, and then over at Perez. 'We should be going,' he said.

'Before you go, maybe you could give me the name and badge number of the detective handling the Manhattan case,' said the Deputy.

'We've been talking to a homicide detective by the name of Andy Horowitz, but it's not his case. Though he's working the parents.' She held out a hand. 'Have you got a card, I'll get them to call you.' Driscoll took out his wallet and gave her a business card. 'You heard about the problems NYPD SWAT had bringing in their perp.'

The Deputy nodded. 'What was he, high on drugs?'

'Maybe,' said Perez. 'Just, you know, be careful. If you corner the guy, don't assume he'll come quietly.'

The Deputy patted his sidearm. 'I'll be careful.'

Perez and Nightingale said their goodbyes and then walked out of the barn and over to Perez's car. 'Thanks for getting me out of the hole I dug for myself,' he said. 'That was a dumb question I asked., about Daniel.' He climbed into the passenger seat.

Perez got into the driver's seat and started the engine. 'There were better ways of approaching it,' she agreed.

'But you see what it means? Kate Walker wanted to talk to her dead boyfriend, Sara Moseby wanted to talk to her recently-deceased brother. And they both ended up dead.'

'Not just dead. Naked and mutilated. Yes, I see the connection. Plus we have Leon Budd, also mutilated and naked after he talked about communicating with his dear departed sister.'

'I notice you didn't mention that to Deputy Driscoll.'

'Jack, I can barely get to grips with what's happened over the past few days. If we'd dumped all that on to a New Jersey Deputy Sheriff all at once … he'd have thought we were crazy.' She looked across at him. 'You're sure about this? All this possession stuff? I keep wishing, hoping, that we're just dealing with serial killers here.'

'I wish we were, too. But no, this is far worse. Far, far, worse.'

CHAPTER 34

The Willoughby farm was easy enough to find, less than a mile from where the Mosebys lived. They didn't see any cows as they drove up but there were horses and orchards and a sign offering home-produced cider. There was a collection of barns and storage silos next to a large white painted wooden house with a green roof and a wide porch on which there were two large swing seats. Perez parked between two mud-splattered SUVs. 'I don't see why we need to talk to the family,' said Perez.

'I just want to know what state this Steve was in, before and after the killing,' said Nightingale.

'I can't see that the Willoughbys are going to be any keener to talk to us than the Moseby family,' said Perez.

'Nothing ventured, nothing gained,' said Nightingale.

They climbed out of the car and walked to the front door. There was a brass doorknocker in the shape of a horseshoe on the door and Perez banged it several times. A woman in her forties opened the door. It was clear from the haunted look in her eyes that it was Steve Willoughby's mother. She was wearing a baggy sweatshirt that Nightingale knew instinctively had belonged to her son, and faded work jeans.

Nightingale let Perez do the talking. 'We're so sorry to bother you, Mrs Willoughby, we were told that Deputy Driscoll would be here.'

The woman dabbed at her eyes with a handkerchief. 'He's on his way,' she said.

'Can we come in?' asked Perez.

The woman nodded and walked back into the house, leaving the door open.

Perez looked at Nightingale. 'I suppose that counts as in invitation,' she whispered.

Nightingale nodded. 'After you,' he said.

Perez followed Mrs Willoughby down a hallway to a large sitting room lined with bookshelves. Nightingale closed the door and followed.

Mrs Willoughby went over to a window overlooking fields where dozens of black and white cows were grazing contentedly. She stared out, her arms folded across her chest. Nightingale looked around the room. There was a large framed photograph above the fireplace. The Willoughby family. Mrs Willoughby, in a pale blue dress, her husband in a dark suit and a tie, and two teenage children. A boy – obviously Steve – and a blonde girl who was much younger.

'We're sorry to bother you, Mrs Willoughby, but can you tell us what happened the day Sara passed away?' asked Perez.

The woman shook her head. 'She didn't pass away. She was murdered. And the police say that Steve did it.' She didn't turn around and from the way her shoulders were shuddering it was clear she was crying. Perez looked over at Nightingale and narrowed her eyes. The message was clear – she didn't think they should be there bothering Mrs Willoughby.

'How had be been during the days before it happened?' asked Nightingale. 'Was he upset, or distressed?'

She shook her head.

'Was he going out with Sara? Boyfriend-girlfriend?'

She shook her head again. 'They were friends. But there was never anything between them. Steve had a thing for a girl at his college. And when he was at High School all he was interested in was sports. He was the perfect son. I know all parents say that but he really was perfect.'

'Steve was a friend of Daniel's?' asked Nightingale.

Mrs Willoughby turned around to face them. There were tears running down her cheeks but she made no effort to wipe them away. 'That's what I don't understand. He and Daniel were like brothers. He helped carry the coffin at the funeral. How could he be so close to Daniel and do something like that to Sara?'

Perez and Nightingale said nothing but Mrs Willoughby continued to stare at them as if expecting an answer.

'I'm so sorry,' said Nightingale. 'Sometimes people act out of character.'

'What's happening mum?' They turned to see the little blonde girl from the photograph standing in the doorway holding a small dog.

'It's all right, Lisa. You go back to the kitchen.'

'Is it the police? Is it about Steve?'

'Please, Lisa, just go back to the kitchen.'

Lisa looked at Perez. 'Have you found him? It's all a mistake, he wouldn't hurt Sara.'

'We haven't found him, no,' said Perez.

'Lisa, please,' said Mrs Willoughby, firmer this time. 'Kitchen. Now.'

The girl pouted flounced around and stamped down the hallway. Mrs Willoughby forced a smile and went to sit down on a battered leather sofa. There was a box of tissues and she grabbed a couple and dabbed at her eyes. 'We can't believe that Steve would do that. He knew Sara. They grew up together. She shook her head. 'I keep thinking there must have been some horrible mistake, but the police says there's no doubt.' She looked tearfully at Perez. 'There is no doubt, is there?' she asked.

'They have DNA evidence,' said Perez. 'They seem sure that it was Steve.'

'It doesn't make any sense,' she said. She picked up a cushion and held it to her chest. 'None of this makes any sense at all. When Daniel died it was awful but it was an accident. It was... understandable. It was a terrible tragedy but we could understand it. Daniel made bad decisions and paid for them with his life. But what happened to Sara makes no sense. Steve wouldn't hurt a fly. He's the kindest soul you could meet.'

'Did something happen to him before Sara died?' asked Nightingale.

'Nothing,' she said. 'Absolutely nothing. The night before she was over here and they went for a walk. They talked for ages.'

'About what, do you know?" asked Nightingale.

'Steve said she was missing Daniel. That's understandable, of course. But she went back home before it got dark and he came back in for dinner.'

'And he was fine then?' asked Nightingale.

'Perfectly fine. Even filled the dishwasher without being asked.'

'And when was the last time you spoke to him?'

She took a deep breath to steady herself, then hugged the pillow tightly. 'The day it happened. It must have been just afterwards because he came back and there was blood on his shirt. He went upstairs and I went up after him because I thought he'd hurt himself. I kept asking him what was wrong but he wouldn't talk to me. It was like he couldn't even hear me. I kept saying to him, tell me what's wrong, but he just packed a bag and went. I grabbed his arm and he pushed me away, hard. I hit the wall and almost passed out.' She rubbed the back of her head. 'It's still bruised.'

'Did he say anything?' asked Nightingale.

She shook her head. 'He just sneered at me, as if I was beneath contempt. Like I didn't exist. He just walked out of the house and got into one of our trucks and drove off.'

'What about his cellphone?' asked Perez. 'Did you call him?'

'He left his phone in his bedroom,' said Mrs Willoughby. 'He just walked away without a second look.'

'He'd changed?' said Nightingale. 'It's as if he wasn't himself?'

Mrs Willoughby nodded in agreement. 'It was as if he didn't know who I was. As if I'd ceased to exist. It was horrible. Like he wasn't my son any more.'

They heard heavy footsteps in the hallway and a man appeared at the doorway. He was big, well over six feet, broad-shouldered with a thick neck. He was wearing blue overalls and workboots and there was a streak of dirt across his cheek. 'Who are you?' he asked.

'They're with the police,' said Mrs Willoughby.

Perez didn't correct her. 'We're just leaving,' she said. 'We're very sorry about what happened.'

'You and me both,' snapped the man. He looked at his watch. 'The vet's late. Why is he always late?'

'I don't know,' said Mrs Willoughby.

'The fees he charges, you'd think he'd at least make the effort to be on time.'

Perez nodded at Nightingale. Mr Willoughby moved to the side to let them out of the room but made no attempt to show them out. As they walked down the hallway they heard Mrs Willoughby burst into tears.

Perez didn't say anything until they were in the car and driving towards the main road. 'That was awkward,' said Perez.

'It had to be done,' said Nightingale. 'It could have been that Steve was a bad kid who just kicked off. Now we know that something happened to him.'

'And that something was Sara Moseby, that's what you think?'

'You can see the pattern, right?'

'It's as obvious as the nose on your face. But just because I can see it doesn't mean I understand it.'

'Sara lost her brother and wanted to contact him. She tried with Charlie Charlie and the Ouija board with her brother and that led her to whatever it is that has taken over Steve Willoughby. It took him over and killed Sara.'

'So you saw a sigil on the girl's back?' asked Perez.

Nightingale nodded. 'Yeah.'

'I didn't see anything that looked like the other two.'

'They're all different. Like snowflakes.'

'Yeah, but a snowflake looks like a snowflake.'

'Then it's a bad example,' said Nightingale. 'But yeah, I saw a shape among the damage.'

'You said you had a CI who could identify the sigils?'

Nightingale nodded. 'I'm working on it.'

'Are you going to call him?'

'It's a she not a he,' said Nightingale. 'And she doesn't use the phone.'

'So arrange a face to face.'

'I think I'll have to,' said Nightingale. He blew smoke up at the sky.

'Do you want me to come with you?'

'Best not,' said Nightingale. 'She's the jealous type.'

CHAPTER 35

The demon that now inhabited Steve Willoughby's body was hungry, so hungry that every fibre of its being ached. He was hungry for food, for alcohol, for pain, for fear. He stopped and held up his hands and stared at them. He could feel his heart beating and the blood coursing through his veins. He was standing in Central Park, less than a mile from where he'd dumped the truck and was carrying the holdall with the few things he'd taken from the boy's bedroom. There were things he had to do to look after the body he now inhabited. It had to be cleaned and made to look presentable. His teeth had to be brushed, his hair combed, body odour had to be regulated. None of those issues applied in Hades, he thought with a smile.

Two mounted police officers came towards him. Their horses were big and black, their coats burnished to a shine. One of the cops was a man in his forties, the other was a woman maybe half his age. Willoughby stopped and stared at them. The horses pricked up their ears as they caught sight of him. The man's mount stopped and began pawing at the ground. The cop cursed and dug his heels into the horse's flanks but the animal took no notice.

Steve grinned. He could smell the animal's fear. He took a step towards them and growled softly. The woman's horse reared up and she almost slipped out of her saddle. The horse being ridden by the male officer backed away. It tried to turn away but the officer kept yanking on the reins. The horses eyes were wide and fearful and its nostrils flared as it snorted. Steve took another step forward and the female cop's mount reared up again and this time she fell backwards and hit the ground hard. The horse ran off across the park. As the male officer twisted around in his saddle to check that his colleague was okay his horse managed to slip the bit from between its teeth and bolted off across the grass.

Steve walked away, humming to himself. There was a hot dog vendor at the edge of the park and Steve stopped and put his head back as he sniffed in the smells. The meat, the onions, the bread roll, the ketchup. The vendor was a middle-aged Asian, dark skinned with his sleeves rolled up to show forearms matted with thick black hair.

Steve took out his wallet and handed over two dollars. He wolfed down the hot dog in four bites and ran his tongue over his lips.

'Hit the spot?' laughed the vendor.

'Fuck, yeah,' said Steve. He handed over another two dollars. 'Put more of that pickle stuff on.'

'Sweet relish? Sure?' The vendor ladled extra relish over the sausage and onions and gave it to him. Steve devoured it in three bites, then burped his appreciation. There were two German tourists behind him waiting to order but Steve made no attempt to move. 'Another,' he said.

The vendor grinned and began to prepare another hotdog for him.

'Excuse me, please, we want to buy the water,' said the German behind him.

Steve turned to look at the couple. Middle-aged, overweight, carrying guidebooks and with long lensed cameras hanging from straps around their necks. Steve's eyes flashed red. 'Nimm Dir das Feinste vor, Du arschfickender Hurensohn, spreiz' und bums' die Muschi der Mutti...Sie wird Dir für die liebe Kundschaft danken und um mehr bitten,' he snarled.

The two tourists stepped back as if they had been struck, then hurried away. Steve turned back to the vendor and took the hotdog from him. He devoured it in two bites. 'Another he said.' He pointed at a line of bottles. 'And Gatorade.'

'What colour?' asked the vendor, grabbing a sausage and shoving it into a bun.

'Don't care,' said Steve.

'My favourite type of customer.' He heaped onions and relish on the hot dog and handed it over. Steve handed him a twenty-dollar bill and walked away, humming contentedly to himself.

CHAPTER 36

Nightingale spent the best part of an hour scrubbing the concrete floor in one of the meeting rooms. He closed all the blinds and pulled up the grey carpet and tossed it into the open plan office, then carried buckets of water from the bathroom. Only when he was sure that the floor was spotless did he go back to the bathroom and shower. He used coal tar soap and a plastic nail brush to clean under his fingernails and toenails. He shampooed his hair twice and rinsed it for ten minutes, then dried himself on a new towel.

He had bought new clothes from Macy's and a pair of Nike trainers and he put them on and went back to the open plan office. Everything he needed was in a large cardboard box that had once contained cans of dog food. He took a piece of white chalk and used it to draw a circle about six feet in diameter in the centre of the room. Then he used a small birch branch to gently brush around the outline of the circle. The consecrated chalk would probably be enough to contain Proserpine but the birch branch was a safety net that Nightingale preferred to have in reserve. Just to be on the safe side.

He put the branch back in the box and used a new piece of consecrated chalk to draw a pentagram inside the circle so that two of the five points faced north. Then he chalked a triangle around the circle with the apex pointing north and wrote the letters MI, CH and AEL at the three points of the triangle. MICHAEL. The Archangel.

He removed a glass stopper from a chunky bottle of consecrated salt water and methodically sprinkled water around the circle. Then he placed five large white church candles at the points of the pentagram and used his lighter to light them, moving clockwise around the circle. Once they were all lit he put the lighter in the box and took out a Ziploc bag containing a mixture of herbs and a lead crucible about the size of an ashtray. He moved clockwise around the circle sprinkling the herbs over the candle flames where they spluttered and fizzled and filled the air with acrid smoke. He poured the rest of the herbs into the crucible and placed it in the middle of the protective circle. He moulded the herbs into a neat cone and set fire to it with his lighter.

The herbs burst into flames and a thick plume of eye-watering smoke rose into the air. Nightingale straightened up, coughing. The first few times he had summoned Proserpine he had written down the Latin incantation and read it out loud but these days he knew the words by heart. He slowly turned though three hundred and sixty degrees, checking that he hadn't forgotten anything, then slowly and precisely spoke the words that summoned Proserpine. He didn't know for sure what all the words meant, but he knew how to pronounce them perfectly and that was all that was necessary. He raised his voice as he spoke and by he time he reached the final words, he was shouting at the top of his voice. 'Bagahi laca bacabe!'

The fumes from the burning herbs started to spin, faster and faster. The floor began to vibrate and the ceiling tiles shook above his head. There was a flash of lightning and a crack of thunder that made him flinch.

Tears were streaming from his eyes and he wiped them with the back of his hand. Breathing was an effort, he felt as if he was inhaling a thick, treacly liquid and he could taste burned meat at the back of his throat.

The floor shook so violently that he staggered to the side. His right foot hovered over the chalk circle and he pulled it back, knowing that to step outside would be fatal.

'Bagahi laca bacabe!' he screamed again. There were two flashes of lightning that were so bright that he put his hands over his eyes to protect them. When he took his hands away the room shimmered, then the room seemed to fold in on itself and Proserpine was there, standing in a space between the tip of the north-facing point of the triangle and the edge of the circle. She was wearing a long black coat, black boots and a black t-shirt with a hand-drawn pentagram in the centre. Her jet-black hair was long and cut with a fringe and there was so much black eye-shadow that her eye sockets were dark pools of nothingness. Next to her stood a black and white collie sheepdog. It had a black leather collar from which hung an upside down ankh symbol, the key of life. The dog sat down and stared at Nightingale as it panted. 'This had better be important, Nightingale,' she said. 'I was in the middle of something.'

'I thought time didn't matter to you,' said Nightingale. 'You can come and go as you want.'

'That doesn't mean that I don't have plans, plans that are more important than your mindless chatter.'

'I'm pleased to see you, too.'

The dog snarled and Proserpine reached down and rubbed it behind the ears. 'We won't be long, baby,' she whispered. 'Seriously, Nightingale, you're playing with fire.'

'Fire and brimstone?'

The floor shook beneath Nightingale's feet and her featureless eyes stared at him with contempt. 'What do you want, Nightingale?'

'One of yours is killing teenagers.'

She shrugged. 'So?'

'So I need to stop it.'

'And this concerns me, how?'

'I think they're demons looking for a way out, a way from your world to ours. And I thought that was against the order of things.'

She tilted her head on one side. 'And what do you know about the order of things?'

'I know that rules are to be followed. Let's face it, if all the devils in Hell could come and play here on earth, they would, wouldn't they? For the fun, if nothing else.'

'Fun? You think that your kind are fun?'

'I think we amuse you, sometimes. And I'm guessing that even Hell could become boring over eternity.'

'You don't know what eternity is,' said Proserpine.

'I know you see time differently to us. But I'm right, aren't I? Most devils are supposed to be confined to Hell. You're a Princess of Hell so you can come and go as you please, but most devils, they have to be summoned.'

Proserpine stared at him for several seconds, her face a blank mask. 'Tell me what you think you know.'

'Three teenagers have been killed. One boy. Two girls. Butchered. And sigils were carved into their flesh. Three different sigils.'

'You have them?'

Nightingale nodded and he took out a sheet of paper on which he had drawn three sigils – the two that Wainwright had given him and the one that he had seen on Sara Moseby's back. Proserpine held out a languid hand and Nightingale instinctively went to give them to her. At the last moment he realised what he was doing and he jerked back. Any contact with her would negate the protective circle. She smiled at his discomfort.

'I'm hurt, Nightingale,' she said. 'Do you think I'd pull a cheap trick like that?'

'I figured it'd be a scorpion thing. Your nature and all.' He pointed at the first sigil. 'This was a young man killed out in New Jersey.'

Proserpine stared at the sigil with featureless unblinking eyes. 'You are sure about this?'

'I haven't seen it myself, but I'm assured it's accurate. You recognise it?'

Proserpine nodded. 'Oh yes.'

'Do you mind sharing the information with me?'

She looked at him, her face black. 'Lilith. She's a princess from Hell.'

'So if she's like you, why does she need to do this?'

'I didn't say she was like me, Nightingale. She's nothing like me. I come and go as I please but then I have special privileges. Lilith doesn't. If what you say is true, she is breaking her covenant.'

Nightingale pointed at the sigil that had been carved into Kate Walker's back. 'This was the second one. It happened here in Manhattan, last week.'

Proserpine studied it and nodded. 'Xaphan. A second-order demon. He stokes the furnaces of Hell.' She frowned. 'If he has left Hades, there is a problem.'

'A problem?'

'With discipline. His place is there. And there is no way that he should have been summoned.' She looked at the third sigil. 'That's not familiar,' she said.

'You don't know them all?' asked Nightingale.

Her jaw tightened. 'I know them all, of course. Whoever did the drawing did it incorrectly.'

Nightingale looked at it, frowning. 'I copied it,' he said. 'I saw the real thing, in an autopsy room.'

'Then you made a mistake when you drew it,' she said. 'Think carefully.'

Nightingale stared at the drawing, then closed his eyes and tried to think back to what he'd seen in the autopsy room. He opened his eyes and pointed at the left side of the sigil. 'You're right, there was a curved bit here.'

'Curving to the left or the right?'

'To the left, with a barbed thing on the top. Like an upside down fishing hook.'

For the first time Proserpine smiled. 'Baalberith,' she said. 'An archivist. He also has no right being out. It looks as if you're right, Nightingale. Something is happening. Something that most definitely should not be happening.'

'Why the killings?'

'As part of the ceremony for these demons to leave Hell and to walk the earth, there has to be a sacrifice. And their sigil has to be carved into the victim.'

'By the demon?'

Proserpine shook her head. 'By whoever acts as the host. The demon has to be called by name. And at the time and date that is appropriate. Then a sacrifice has to be made. Only then can the demon pass over into this world.'

'Is there any way you can check if these demons have left Hell?'

'Of course.'

'And if they have, then someone must be organising things. Could that be a demon? A demon still in Hell?'

'It's possible,' she said. 'The only way they can get out is if they are summoned. There must be a facilitator, someone who is pulling the strings.'

'Is there a pattern? Is there any link between the demons you've named?'

'None that I can see at the moment,' she said. 'But it can't be happening by accident. I don't see three demons deciding independently to do this at the same time. Someone is behind it.'

'What about this Lilith? The princess? Could it be her?'

'It is possible, I suppose. But she isn't the brightest or best. I can't see that she could have come up with something like this.'

'So how do we leave it?' asked Nightingale.

'Let me find out what's going on. I'll get back to you.'

'I don't need to summon you?'

'I'll find you, don't worry. You're still doing Wainwright's bidding?'

'I do the odd job for him, yes.'

'He's using you.'

'It's symbiosis. We help each other.'

'What do you think you get from him?'

'Protection,' said Nightingale.

'You think he can protect you?'

'He's done okay so far.'

She smiled. 'If it's protection you want, you could work for me. I'd take care of you.'

'You'd want my soul, Proserpine. I went to far too much trouble to get my soul back to squander it so easily.'

'You wouldn't have to promise me your soul, Nightingale. Just promise to serve me.'

'Become one of your minions?'

'You say that as if it's a bad thing,' she said. 'You're already working for Wainwright. You do his bidding. And believe me when I tell you that he doesn't have your best interests at heart.'

'And you do?'

'More than you know, Nightingale.' Now say the words to release me.'

'You'll let me know what you find out?'

'Just let me go, Nightingale. Before I lose my patience.'

Nightingale raised his hands in the air to say the words that would allow her to leave. There was an ear-splitting crack, time and space folded in on itself, and she and the dog were gone.

CHAPTER 37

Nightingale took an Amtrak train from Penn Station to Philadelphia's 30th Street station. It took just over an hour and he was outside the block where Dee-anne Jackson's family lived at nine o'clock in the morning, sitting in the back of a cab. The driver was a Ukrainian and after a few minutes haggling had agreed to take Nightingale to and from the block and wait so long as Nightingale handed over fifty dollars every half an hour. The driver was a smoker so they passed the time listening to the radio and smoking.

Dee-anne's brother finally emerged at ten-thirty after Nightingale had paid a hundred and fifty dollars and was starting to wonder whether he should risk going up and knocking on the door. The teenager had headphones over the top of his baseball cap and was carrying a skateboard. Nightingale climbed out of the taxi and hurried across the road. 'Hey, remember me?' asked Nightingale.

The teenager took off his headphones. 'Say what?'

'I said, do you remember me? I was at your apartment talking to your mum.'

The boy squinted at him and then nodded. 'The British private eye? Yeah. What's up?'

'I need your help. Look, I'm sorry but I didn't get your name.'

'Dwayne.'

'Okay, Dwayne, I'm still looking for your sister. But to find her I'm going to need to have something of hers. Something personal, an item of clothing, something she's touched.'

'For DNA? CSI?'

'Yes, exactly,' said Nightingale, figuring that it was less trouble than explaining what he really wanted it for.

'Why are you waiting here? Why didn't you come up?'

'Because I thought your father would just slam the door in my face.'

'He's not my father,' snapped Dwayne.

'Sorry, my bad,' said Nightingale. 'But you know what I mean, right? He's not going to do anything to help me, is he? The way he was talking, he doesn't want her back in the home.'

Dwayne nodded. 'He keeps calling her "the bitch". I'm coming close to hitting him myself. Or worse.'

'I'd advise against that, obviously,' said Nightingale. 'But maybe you should think about moving out?'

'It's on my list,' said Dwayne. His cellphone buzzed and he took it out and checked a message. 'I've got to go.'

'Yeah, I know, but can you do this for me. Just pop back upstairs and get me something of your sister's?'

The teenager looked at his phone again.

'Please,' said Nightingale. 'She might need help.'

Dwayne's eyes narrowed. 'If she needed help she'd call me.'

'Her cellphones off,' said Nightingale. 'We tried calling her but it goes straight through to voicemail.'

'Yeah. I know.' He tapped the phone against his leg and then nodded. 'Okay, wait here.'

Dwayne headed back inside. Nightingale turned and gave his driver a thumbs up, then took out his cigarettes and lit one. He was half way through it when Dwayne returned. He handed Nightingale a white plastic case. Nightingale opened it. It was a retainer, for straightening teeth. 'She'll need that, if you find her,' said Dwayne. 'And when you find her, tell her to call me.' He put his phone to his ear and pointed at Nightingale.

'I will,' promised Nightingale.

Nightingale took the train back to Manhattan and spent the next hour buying the things he needed, including a white cotton robe, a large scale map and two white candles. He took his purchases back to the office where he showered and changed into the robe. He spread the map out on the floor. The map was double sided – one side showed the entire country, the other was a large scale and showed only New York state. He had the state map upwards. From the pocket of his raincoat he took a small brown leather bag. The bag was several hundred years old but the leather was supple and glossy and it glistened under the overhead fluorescent lights. He untied the leather thong that kept the bag closed and slid out a large pink crystal, about the size of a pigeon's egg. It was attached to a fine silver chain. Nightingale lit the candles and placed them either side of the map. He knelt down on the floor and opened the retainer case. He put it at the bottom of the map, then sat back on his heels, closed his eyes and said a short prayer as he held the crystal pressed between his palms. When he had finished he opened his eyes and let the crystal swing free on its chain. He pictured a pale blue aura around himself as he took slow, deep breaths, then he slowly allowed the aura to spread out until it filled the room.

He repeated her name as he held the crystal over the retainer. For a minute or two it remained motionless and then it began to slowly move in a small clockwise circle over the retainer. The movement was slight, much less than he was used to seeing with the crystal. He figured that was because Dee-anne wasn't Dee-anne anymore. She was Lilith, a princess from Hell.

He whispered a sentence in Latin, and imagined the blue aura entering the crystal, then he moved the crystal over the map. Almost immediately the circling slowed. He raised it higher so that it was above his head and the circling began again, but it was still a fraction of what he normally saw when he was trying to track somebody with the crystal. He lowered the crystal towards the east of the city and the circling slowed, then it quickened when he moved it westwards. North made it slow, south made it circle faster. His best guess was that she was somewhere in the south-west of the city. He put the crystal back into its leather bag. At least he knew she was still in Manhattan. But finding her wasn't going to be easy.

CHAPTER 38

Cheryl Perez pulled the cork from the bottle of Chianti and sloshed it into a glass. She drank some and went through to her sitting room. She pulled open the drawer of a side table and took out the framed photograph of herself and Eric. It had been in the drawer for over a month – a new record. The photograph had been taken on New Years Eve three years earlier. They'd flown to Vegas for the weekend and seen in the New Year at a show in the MGM Grand. The casino's logo was in the bottom right hand corner of the photograph. They were both a little drunk and they were holding hands either side of a champagne bucket that Perez was fairly sure contained their second bottle. Maybe their third. They had got so drunk that they had collapsed on the bed in their clothes and woken up the following morning still clothed and wrapped in each other's arms. 'You bastard, Eric,' she whispered. 'How could you leave me?'

She took the photograph over to the dining table and stood it in the middle. She sat down, drank some wine and then picked up one of the two pencils there. She drew a cross on the page, dividing it into quarters. She wrote YES in the top right and bottom left quarters, then wrote NO in the top left and bottom right. She took another drink of wine, then smiled lop-sidedly at the photograph. 'I know, I know, it's stupid and my soul will burn in Hell, but I have to try, don't I?'

She put the pencil on the paper, along the horizontal line. She picked up a second pencil and balanced it at a right angle on top of the first one. Then she sat back and drank more wine as she stared at the pencils. She put down the glass and linked her hands as if she was in prayer. 'Charlie Charlie, can we play?'

Nothing happened.

'Charlie Charlie are you there? Charlie Charlie can we play?'

Something cold blew against her back and she shuddered. She looked over her shoulder but there was nothing there. But the window behind her was open and the evening was getting chilly. Of course there'd be a draught. She drank her wine and stared at the photograph. She closed her eyes and took a deep breath, then opened them again. 'Eric, are you there?' she said. As soon as the words left her mouth she felt ridiculous and even though she was alone her cheeks reddened with embarrassment.

'This is stupid,' she said, and raised her glass at the photograph. 'I can't believe I'm doing this.' She sipped her wine again. Her eyes were brimming with tears but she refused to cry. 'Damn you, Eric. Damn you for leaving me, damn you for killing yourself.'

She took another drink of wine, blinked away the tears and stared at the pencils. 'Last chance, Eric. Are you there?'

Nothing happened and she shook her head sadly, angry at herself for wasting her time. She was just about to stand up when the top pencil swung to the right so that the point was aimed at YES.

CHAPTER 39

Nightingale had the taxi drop him close to Gramercy Park. He lit a cigarette as the taxi drove off. The park was a large square surrounded by townhouses. There was a metal gate across the entrance. He pushed it but it was locked. 'It's private,' said a woman in a long coat who had just lit a cigarette. 'You have to have a key.'

'A key? Are you serious?'

The woman waved her cigarette at the townhouses overlooking the park. 'It's for the people who live around it,' she said. 'They pay almost ten grand a year for the privilege. There are fewer than four hundred keys, all of them numbered.'

'Sounds like a prison,' said Nightingale.

'You're not wrong,' said the woman. 'You're not allowed to drink alcohol, smoke, ride a bike, walk your dog, kick a ball, throw a Frisbee or feed the squirrels.'

'What can you do?'

'Walk. I think you can sit but I'm not sure.'

Nightingale chuckled. 'You live here?'

'I work in that building over there.' She pointed at one of the townhouses. 'I'm a housekeeper. My boss has a key but as I want to smoke there's no point. You're not from around here?'

'England. But just doing some consultancy work for a client. So this is the East Village?'

'Everything from here to the Lower East Side and across to the river. Everything east of Broadway to the river, between Houston Street and 14th Street. It used to be all Lower East Side until the hippies moved in during the Sixties. Then it became the birth place of punk rock, they say.'

'Do they now?'

'Harry Potter lives around here. I've seen him a few times.'

'You know Harry Potter's a fictional character?'

She laughed. 'Daniel Radcliffe. The actor. And James Bond.'

'Sean Connery?'

She shook her head. 'Another Daniel. Daniel Craig.'

'Ah, you see, there's only one true James Bond and that's Connery.'

'And Lady Gaga. Madonna.'

'Neither of whom could ever play Bond,' said Nightingale.

'You're a funny guy,' said the woman. She held out her hand. 'Tracey,' she said.

'Jack,' said Nightingale. They shook hands.

'So where are the happening places around here?' he asked.

'You want to bump into Lady Gaga?'

'Just wondered what people did here for fun.'

'Fun? Well, there's bars. Restaurants. Still a fair number of live music venues. 'Is it safe?'

'Safe?'

'Much crime. Violence.'

'Exactly what sort of consulting are you involved in, Jack?'

Nightingale flashed her what he hoped was his most boyish smile. 'The client's thinking of moving to New York and he's asked me to check out a few areas for him.'

'Businessman?'

'Sure.'

'Rich?'

'Not short of a bob or two.'

'I have no idea what that means.'

'He's got money.'

'Then maybe think of the Upper West Side. As close to the park as you can afford. This area is still coming up but it has a few rough edges still.'

'But it's quiet, generally.' He waved at the park. 'I mean, this looks great.'

'There were cops and sirens last night. East 7th Street. Bar fight, the papers said. A big one.'

'That happens a lot?'

'Not really. But your client would find it quieter on the Upper West Side.' She took a final drag on her cigarette and flicked what was left into the garden. 'Back to the coal face,' she said. 'Nice meeting you, Jack.'

'And you....'

'Tracey,' she finished for him.

He grinned. 'I knew that,' he said, but she was right, he had forgotten her name. She was already walking away.

Nightingale finished the rest of his cigarette as he walked to East 7th Street. The bar was easy enough to spot. Two men in green overalls were replacing a window and the door looked as if it had been hacked with an axe. Nightingale went in. A number of broken chairs and stools had been stacked against a back wall. Several framed posters had been smashed and they had been taken down and placed by the door. There was a middle-aged man with a receding hairline and a ponytail moving bottles away from a cracked mirror.

'That's seven years bad luck for a start,' said Nightingale. 'Are you open?'

'So long as you don't mind the noise,' said the man. 'What can I get you?'

'Beer'll be great. Whatever you recommend.'

The barman filled a glass with draught beer and put it down in front of Nightingale. 'It's a local craft beer. Not as warm as you English like it, I know, but it's got a good flavour.'

Nightingale took a sip and nodded his approval. 'If you like that, you should drop by on Tuesday night,' said the barman. 'For ten bucks you can sample every brew on tap.'

'I might take you up on that,' said Nightingale. He nodded at the broken mirror. 'So what happened?'

'A bar room brawl. Just like the cliché. Chairs and fists flying.'

'Over what?'

The barman shrugged. 'Over nothing. A few kids who didn't like being carded.'

'What happened?'

'One of them was a girl and she looked real young. So I politely asked to see her ID. I said if she's underage she can have a mocktail or whatever but she says she wants tequila. I say she can have a tequila when she shows me her ID. Then the guy who she was with, who wasn't much older, jumps over the bar and grabs a bottle.'

'Jumped over? Literally, you mean?'

'It was like that street jumping thing the kids do these days. Parkor. He just jumped over, grabbed the bottle and three glasses and jumped back. Then he pours them shots, cool as you like.'

'So there were three of them?'

The barman nodded. 'I said I'd call the cops and they said call them. There was no point, calling cops out for underage drinking, they've got other priorities, right. So I yell at them to get the hell out of my bar. A couple of my regulars came over to back me up. Big guys, they're both into mixed martial arts. Cage fighters. They grabbed the guy and he laughs and they flew through the air. I mean flew. One came over the bar and hit the mirror, the other hit the wall by the door. The little guy threw him twenty feet. You tell me, how does a scrawny teenager do that? That's when I picked up the phone to call the cops but the girl grabbed it out of my hand.' He held up his left hand which was bruised and scraped. 'Her hands were tiny but she had a grip like a vice. She twisted my arm and almost broke it. And she crushed my phone.'

'Crushed it. How?'

'With her hand.' He reached under the bar and pulled out a cellphone. The screen was cracked and there were pieces of the casing missing. 'She just squeezed it and then tossed it away.'

He gave it to Nightingale. 'With her hand? She didn't stamp on it.'

'She was about five feet six and looked like butter wouldn't melt in her mouth.'

'So you didn't call the cops?'

The barman laughed harshly. 'I didn't get the chance. She pulled me over the bar. Pulled me, like I weighed nothing and I was twice her size. Then she threw me against the wall there.' He pointed at the wall behind Nightingale and he turned to look. There was a dent in the wooden panelling. 'My head did that.'

'How many were there?'

'Three. Two guys and the girl.'

Nightingale sipped his beer. 'The cops came eventually, right?'

'A couple of the customers called 911. But by the time they got there the kids had trashed the bar. They took five of them to hospital. Big guys, all of them. The kids didn't even break a sweat.'

Nightingale reached into his coat pocket and pulled out a photograph of Matt Donaldson. 'Was this one of them?'

The barman took the picture and his eyes widened. 'Where did you get this?'

'That's one of them, yeah?'

'Who are you?'

'I'm a journalist,' said Nightingale, quickly deciding that the lie was worth the risk. 'This guy attacked some cops a few days ago.'

'Who is he? You need to tell the cops because all we could do was to give them a description.'

'His name's Matt Donaldson.'

The barman held up the picture. 'Can I keep this?'

'No need,' said Nightingale. 'The cops already have his picture. Check on line, Matt Donaldson. He's wanted in connection with the murder of a girl called Kate Walker.'

The barman nodded and handed back the photograph. 'You're a journalist?'

Nightingale nodded. 'I'm researching a story on teens gone bad,' he said. 'The three who were here. Had you seen them before?'

The barman shook his head. 'We don't tend to get kids coming in, it's not their thing.'

Nightingale finished his beer, put a ten dollar bill on the bar and slid off his stool. 'Hopefully they won't be back,' he said.

'Can I tell the cops your name?'

'Rob Taggart,' lied Nightingale. 'But at the moment I know as little as you do.' He headed outside and lit a cigarette.

CHAPTER 40

Nightingale was standing by the entrance to Gramercy Park when Cheryl Perez drove up. She wound down the window. 'What's going on?'

'They were here. All three of them.'

'Shit. When.'

'Last night. They smashed up a bar.'

Perez cursed under her breath. 'Get in,' she said.

Nightingale climbed in. 'They put some cage fighters in hospital.'

'What are they playing at?' asked Perez.

'They're having fun, by the sound of it.'

'Fun? What do you mean?'

'They're demons, from Hell. This is a playground for them. They're stronger than us, they're faster. They can do pretty much what they want.' He sighed. 'This is getting out of control.'

'So what do we do? Tell the cops?'

'Tell the cops what? That three demons from Hell are now in human form and they're wreaking havoc? One, the cops will think we're mad. Two, what can they do about it? You saw what Donaldson did to a SWAT team.'

'So they can't be killed, is that what you're saying?'

'Not by the likes of us, no.'

'What about silver bullets?'

'That's werewolves.'

'A stake through the heart?'

'That's vampires. You're not getting this, are you? They're not physical monsters, they're devils. The evil equivalent of angels. You can't kill them.'

'So we're back to exorcisms, right?'

'No, because these aren't possessions. They were invited in. That's why they used the sigils. An exorcism won't get rid of an invited devil.'

'So what then? What can we do?'

'You won't like it,' said Nightingale. 'But right now, we need to go somewhere.'

'Where?'

'A shop.' He waved ahead. 'Two blocks down then take a right.'

It took less than half an hour to get to Alchemy Arts Supplies. They parked outside the building and Nightingale took Perez up the stairs to the second floor. 'What on earth is this place?' she asked as she surveyed the rows of shelving.

'It's like Office Depot or Staples, but instead of office supplies they sell stuff for people interested in Wicca and witchcraft and the darker stuff.'

'The darker stuff?'

'People talk about white magic and black magic but really it's all just magic. It's what you use it for that defines it. Like guns. A cop carrying a gun means one thing. A drug dealer or an armed robber with a gun is something else.'

'And why are we here? You want to buy a magic wand? That's your plan?'

Wind was standing behind the register and she smiled in recognition. He nodded at her. 'Need any help?' she asked.

'Just browsing.'

'You know where I am,' she said.

Nightingale took Perez along to the shelves that contained the branches and twigs. He ran his hands through them and selected a couple of holly branches, one of cedar.

'You said a stake through the heart wouldn't work,' said Perez. 'And neither will silver bullets.'

'I said they weren't vampires or werewolves,' said Nightingale. 'What they are is regular people like you and me who've been taken over by devils.' He held up the branches he had selected. 'Holly has been used for centuries to guard against evil, but it's a strong wood, too. Unlikely to break. Cedar also protects against evil.'

'You believe that?' asked Perez.

Nightingale searched through the branches and pulled out a yew branch, as thick as his wrist.' It doesn't matter whether I believe in it or not, what matters is whether or not it works. But yes, I believe.' He held up the yew branch. 'Yew has long been known as the wood of death. There are yew trees in many British churchyards and in many cases they were their before the churches.'

'So you can stab these devils with wooden stakes?'

Nightingale didn't answer. He walked away and she followed him down the aisle and along to the display case that contained the consecrated items. She looked at the bottles of salt, water and various herbs, and squinted at the small cards that said when the items had been blessed, and by whom.

'So all this gear has been blessed by priests?'

'Sure. You're a Catholic, you were baptised, right?'

'Of course.'

'That's you being blessed with holy water. All these things have been blessed in the same way. The strength of the blessing depends on when it was done and who by and under what circumstances. Paying for it isn't the best way, obviously, but sometimes beggars can't be choosers.' He pointed at the register. 'Do me a favour and ask Wind to come and unlock the cabinet.'

'Wind?"

'That's her name.'

Perez went over to the cash register and returned with Wind. She opened the cabinet with a brass key and Nightingale showed her what he wanted.

Perez waited until Wind had relocked the cabinet and gone back to her post before speaking. 'You're serious about this? Holy water and consecrated salt.'

'You believe in baptism? Well this is the same principle. Devils can't deal with Holy Water. Or anything consecrated.'

'So you attack them with Holy Water and the devils go back to where they came from?'

Nightingale looked uncomfortable. 'It's more complicated than that, unfortunately.'

'So tell me.'

'Like I said in the car, you won't like it.'

'What I don't like is the way you keep things from me,' she said, putting her hands on her hips and glaring at him.

He put up his hands as if warding off an attack. 'Holy Water – or anything consecrated – means you can get in close. If it's on a bullet they'll have trouble avoiding it. Soak a stake in it and you can stab them with the stake. But that in itself won't make the devil leave. You have to kill the host.'

'The host?'

'The body they're in. You shoot them with bullets that have been blessed. That means the bullets will hit the target. You have to kill the body before the devil will leave.'

'So Dee-anne. Matt. Steve. They have to die, that's what you're telling me?'

Nightingale shook his head. 'They're dead already. Their souls have moved on and they can't ever come back. The devils have taken over their bodies. If the devils leave, the bodies are dead.'

'Jack, you can't kill them.'

'You're not listening to me, Cheryl. They're dead already.'

'Except they're clearly not. They're walking around, they're talking, they're breathing. If you kill them, then they're dead. And you'll be held responsible.'

'I'm not planning to go public, obviously.'

'You're planning on murdering three people? And by telling me you're making me an accessory before the fact.'

'It's nothing to do with you. I'll handle it.'

She looked at the sticks he was holding. 'And you're planning to use those?'

'I'm not sure. Maybe. At the moment I'm just weighing up my options.'

'You're going to make them into stakes and stab them in the heart? I can't believe we're having this conversation.'

'We're not having a conversation,' said Nightingale. 'You're interrogating me and I'm trying not to tell you too much. It's not your problem.'

'You're going to do it on your own? Take on all three of them yourself?'

'I don't see I've any choice.'

'You can't do it yourself, and you know it.'

'It wouldn't be fair to involve you. I'm used to this sort of thing. You're not.'

'Oh I see. You bring me here to stock up on murder weapons but you're not involving me.'

'To be fair, they're just branches at the moment.'

'We need to discuss this.'

'More than happy to. But not here, obviously.'

Perez looked at her watch. 'You hungry?'

'Sure.'

'I'll cook for you. Nothing special, pasta.'

Nightingale grinned. 'It's a date.'

'No, it's not a date. It's pasta. And wine if you're lucky.'

CHAPTER 41

Perez's apartment was in the basement of a brownstone building in a tree-lined avenue on the Upper East Side. She had found a parking space a short walk away. Nightingale carried the bags containing his purchases from Alchemy Arts Supplies. Wind had wrapped the branches up in brown paper and tied the packages with string and he had them tucked under his arm. Perez unlocked the door and took Nightingale through to a low-ceiling kitchen with a small circular table at one end. 'Drop your stuff on the table,' she said, taking off her coat. Nightingale put his packages on one of the chairs around the table. Perez unclipped her hair and shook it free, then took his coat and hung it up with hers before opening her fridge. 'Wine or beer?' she asked.

'Whatever you're having is fine,' he said.

She took a bottle of Chianti from the fridge. 'I prefer my wine cold,' she said, giving him the bottle. 'There's a corkscrew in the top drawer by the sink.'

She busied herself preparing spaghetti as he opened the wine and poured it into two glasses. He gave her a glass and sat down at the table. He watched as she made a carbonara sauce.

'So how was your day?' he asked. 'Before I called up to ruin it.'

'I'm looking for similar killings,' she said. 'A girl I went to the academy with works at Quantico and she's helping me access the Violent

Criminal Apprehension Program. They've got countrywide information on all sexual assault cases, solved and unsolved homicides, missing persons.'

'Any luck so far?'

'Depends what you mean by luck. Cases like the one's we're looking at are few and far between,' said Perez. 'People get cut and stabbed all the time, but not butchered the way our victims were. There are two serial killers active at the moment who use knives but they are both very precise in what they do. One is on the west coast and he cuts the body up into pieces with the skill of a butcher. The other cuts his victims to death but with lots of very small cuts, probably with a razor. There's been nothing like this for the last twenty years.'

'I guess it was always a long shot.'

Perez sipped her wine as she stirred her sauce. 'But if you go back twenty-three years, there were four similar killings over a two-month period.'

Nightingale's eyebrows shot up. 'Now that is interesting.'

'Isn't it? Two in Miami, one in Richmond, Virginia and one in Washington DC.'

'Connected?'

'Two men, two women. Not kids back then. Middle-aged. No one was ever caught, the only thing in common was the severity of the wounds.'

'What about crime scene photographs or post mortem photographs.'

'We call them autopsies, Jack. Same as you call our sidewalks pavements. And yes, my contact is emailing them to me. I should get them first thing tomorrow. But obviously there's no connection. There can't be. Matthew Donaldson wasn't even born then.'

'No, but demons are eternal. The demons behind the killings then could be at it again.'

Perez went over to him and held out the spoon. 'What do you think?'

He licked it tentatively and nodded. 'Yummy.'

She grinned. 'Yummy?'

'Yeah, yummy.'

She laughed, went back to the stove and finished the sauce before pouring it over spaghetti. Nightingale refilled their glasses as she sat down at the table.

'This is great, thank you,' he said. 'I was getting fed up with takeaway food.'

She shrugged. 'It's nothing special. I have just one house rule.'

'And what's that?'

'No shop talk while we're eating.'

'That's fine with me.'

She held out her hands and he took them and lowered his head. 'Bless us, O Lord, and these, Thy gifts, which we are about to receive from Thy bounty. Through Christ, our Lord. Amen.' She crossed herself.

'Amen,' said Nightingale, and did the same. Nightingale realised pretty quickly that once they took the case and police work out of the equation they didn't have much to talk about. They settled on sharing movies and books they'd enjoyed but even then it was a struggle to avoid discussing crime. Eventually they had cleared their plates and drunk most of the wine. Perez picked up his plate and took it with her over to the sink. Nightingale poured the last of the wine into their glasses. When she came back to the table, she stood in front of him and he could sense that she was nervous. He looked up at her expectantly.

'I need your help with something,' she said.

'Sure, whatever I can,' he replied, but he had a tight feeling in the pit of his stomach.

'Sitting room,' she said.

'Okay.' He stood up and followed her out of the kitchen. She went over to a Chinese-style cupboard, painted with large ornate brass hinges. She opened it and took out a box. Nightingale knew immediately what it was and he had to fight the urge to swear out loud. Perez closed the cupboard door and carried the box over to the coffee table. It was an Ouija board, the Parker Brothers version marketed in the United States in the early Seventies. There was a picture of two hands holding the planchette and above it the words OUIJA and MYSTIFYING ORACLE. Below that, in smaller type, was printed William Fuld Talking Board Set.

'Cheryl, seriously...'

She sat down and opened the box. Inside there was a plastic planchette and board. She unfolded the board and placed it on the coffee table.

'Where did you get it from?' he asked.

'Found it at a flea market.'

'That's a dumb thing to do right there,' he said. 'You've no idea who has used it before. Or what they did with it.'

'So you do believe in it?'

'It doesn't matter whether I believe or not. It's not about belief.'

She was gently stroking the white plastic planchette that came with the board. It was almost as large as her hand with a large circle cut into it. The idea was the planchette would move across the board and stop with the hole over the intended letter.

'Despite what it says on the box, it's not a game,' said Nightingale.

'I want you to show me what to do with it,' she said.

'Why?'

'I want to talk to Eric.'

Nightingale sighed and shook his head. 'It doesn't work like that,' he said. 'It's not Skype. If you open it up, you have no idea who will come through.'

'But Eric might.'

'Eric's dead. You know that.'

'And I also know that people use this to talk to those that have passed over. If there's any chance, any chance at all, that I can reach Eric, then I'll take it.'

'First, it's a very bad idea. But second, you've been drinking and drink and Ouija board's don't mix. Third, to do it properly, and by that I mean safely, there are precautions you have to take.'

'Such as?'

'A safe board for a start. Then you need flowers in the room. Jasmine, lilies, gardenias and mimosa are the best. And you should burn lavender, mastic, orris root and frankincense in a brass bowl.'

'Are you serious?'

'You asked. You need to forget about this, Cheryl. It's not a good idea.'

'I'm going to do it with or without you. I mean it. I've made up my mind.'

Nightingale sighed and leant back on the sofa, rubbing his hands down his face. 'Fine,' he said eventually.

'So you'll help?'

'If that's the only way I can stop you getting into trouble, yes.'

She smiled and held out the planchette. 'Show me what to do,' she said.

'Not today. I told you, alcohol and Ouija boards don't mix. And I'll have to get us a safe board. One that I'm sure hasn't been defiled.'

Perez pointed at the line of type under MYSTIFYING ORACLE. 'Who was this William Fuld?'

'He's credited as the father of the Ouija board but he didn't actually invent it. Talking boards have been around for centuries. But he was a clever marketer and applied for dozens of patents and trademarks that pretty much made his name synonymous with Ouija boards throughout the late Eighteen Nineties and Nineteen Hundreds. Parker Brothers took over his company in 1966 and they kept his name on the sets.'

'And why don't you think this set is safe?'

'Like I said, you don't know who used it before. Suppose it was used to contact a mischievous spirit. Or an evil one. Open it up again and that spirit would be first in line to come through.'

'So what should I do with this one,' she said, nodding at the box.

'Burn it,' said Nightingale. 'And to be on the safe side, scatter the ashes in a church.'

'You're serious?'

'I am.'

'Then I'll do it. But I want you back here tomorrow morning, okay? First thing?'

Nightingale sighed. 'If you insist,' he said reluctantly.

She smiled brightly. 'I do.'

CHAPTER 42

'I'm still hungry,' said Steve. He waved over at a waitress. 'Can I see the menu again?' He was sitting in one side of a booth. Matt and Dee-anne were sitting opposite him.

The waitress came over. She was in her fifties with tightly-permed hair and a name tag that said her name was Hillary. She handed Steve a menu. 'You still hungry, son? You've already had Brooklyn Spaghetti and Meatballs, Country-Fried Steak and the Prime Rib Philly Melt.' She waved at the empty plates in front of him.

'I'm a growing boy,' said Steve. He licked his lips as he studied the pictures. 'What's in the Grand Slamwich?' he asked.

'Two scrambled eggs, crumbled sausage, bacon, shaved ham and American cheese on potato bread grilled with a maple spice spread. It comes with hash browns.'

'I'll have one,' said Steve. 'And a Philly Cheesesteak Omelette. And I'll take a Strawberry Banana Bliss Smoothie.'

'Son, you have one awesome appetite there. And I don't know where you put it all because you're as thin as a rake. What about you guys? Can I get you anything else?'

'An iced tea for me,' said Dee-anne.

Matt shook his head. 'I'm good.'

'Let me get those empty plates to make room for Mr Hungry,' said the waitress. She gathered up the used plates and chuckled as she walked away. They were sitting in a booth at Denny's, away from the window because TV newscasts were still running photographs of Matt. Matt was wearing dark glasses and had a baseball cap pulled down low.

Steve sat back and beat a quick tattoo on the table top with his hands. 'I can't get over how things taste. And smell.' He grinned at Dee-anne. 'Cheeseburgers are amazing, aren't they?'

'You'll get used to it,' she said. 'I went a bit crazy the first few days as well.'

'But you know what I mean, don't you? Everything feels more real with these bodies. The sensations are...' He threw up his hands. 'I can't explain it.'

'Their lives feel more real because they can end at any time,' said Matt. 'They start to die the moment they're born, there is this constant ticking clock in the background which means that every second is precious.'

Steve held up his hands and clenched and unclenched his fists. 'And the feeling you get when you cause pain. It's so much more real here. The way the bones crunch and the blood flows.' He shuddered. 'I fucking love it.' He sat back in his seat and grinned across at Dee-anne. 'We should have done this ages ago.'

'It won't last for ever,' said Dee-anne. 'You know that.'

'That's what makes it so enjoyable,' said Steve. 'The transience of it all. Living in the moment.' He looked around the diner. 'We could kill everyone in here, right now. We could tear them apart, just because we wanted to.'

'We have to take it slowly,' said Dee-anne. 'We have to stay below the radar. We can play but we have to keep a low profile. Fighting armed cops isn't the way to go, and nor is throwing stools in bars. That attracts too much attention. We need to keep it private.'

'Those cops attacked me,' said Matt. 'I was minding my own business and they came at me with guns.'

'I know, but the way you hurt them. They know something's not right.'

'They started it,' said Matt, sitting back and sneering at her.

'You should have just run.'

'They think I'm on drugs. They don't know what's really going on.'

'And we need it to stay that way,' said Dee-anne.

'Why don't we just move?' asked Matt. 'Let's head to the West Coast. They won't be looking for us there.'

'Us?' said Steve. 'They're not looking for us, they're looking for you.'

'There were witnesses at the bar,' said Dee-anne. 'They'll be looking for us all.' She nodded at Matt. 'You're right. We should go. But we have to wait for the Master. He's on the way.'

'How long do we wait?'

'It takes time, you know that. But until he crosses over, we wait here.' She smiled. 'I'm not saying we can't have fun, we just need to be careful, that's all.' She looked at her phone screen and flicked a number of unsuitables on Tinder. Too young, Too hairy. Too weird-looking.'

'Then what?' asked Matt.

Dee-anne shrugged. 'He'll tell us when he gets here.' She kept her eyes on the screen. Reject. Reject. Reject.

'What do you think human flesh tastes like?' asked Steve.

Matt laughed. 'Probably chicken.'

The two boys laughed. The table began to vibrate, then the walls began to shudder. Customers looked around nervously.

'Guys, please,' said Dee-anne, looking up from her screen.

The two boys stopped laughing and the room went still. Dee-anne turned the phone towards them. 'What about him?'

The two boys leaned forward to get a closer look at the man on the screen. His profile said he was forty-five. He was plump with a fleshy neck. His name was George.

'Is he close?' asked Matt.

'Half a mile. Lives alone. Divorced.'

'Looks perfect,' said Steve. He grinned and beat another tattoo on the table. 'I'd better leave some room for dessert.'

George had already approved Dee-anne as a match and within five minutes of her accepting him her phone buzzed with a message. 'Hi. What are you doing?' Followed by a smiley face.

She grinned and held up the phone. 'He's on the line,' she laughed. 'All we have to do is pull him in.'

'Let me,' said Matt, holding out his hand.

'You've got to be careful not to say the wrong thing.'

Matt laughed. 'Look at him and look at you. He's not going to turn you down no matter what I say.'

Dee-anne gave him the phone. Matt read George's message and tapped out a reply. 'Looking for someone to fuck.'

Steve laughed. 'Subtle,' he said.

'This isn't the time for subtlety,' said Matt.

'I'm available,' George messaged back, this time with two smiley faces.

Matt showed them both the phone.

'Too easy,' said Steve.

Matt typed in 'I like it rough, what about you?'

This time they got three smiley faces. 'I like it any way I can get it.'

Matt asked for an address and George replied with a phone number and 'Call me'. Matt gave the phone to Dee-anne. 'He wants to talk to you.'

'Okay, but no laughing. You'll spook him.' She tapped out the number. He answered on the second ring. 'George?'

'Dee-anne?'

'You were expecting someone else?'

'No, of course not. That's really you, in the pictures.'

'In the flesh,' she said. 'The living, breathing, flesh.'

'And where are you?'

'According to the App, half a mile away.'

'Can you come now?'

'I'm just buying some underwear,' she said. 'I can be with you in an hour.'

'An hour's good.'

'Then send me your address and I'll see you in an hour.'

'And it's really you? It's you in the picture?'

Dee-anne laughed. 'Baby, if I'm not the girl in the picture, just shut the door in my face.'

'Okay, okay.' The line went dead and thirty seconds later a text arrived with his address. Dee-anne held up the phone, grinning. 'Got him!'

The waitress returned with Steve's food and put it down in front of him. 'Can I get you anything else?' she asked.

'I'm good,' he said.

'Son, I've never seen anyone eat like you,' said the waitress.

Steve picked up his fork and stabbed a meatball. He popped it into his mouth. He looked over at Dee-anne and groaned with pleasure.

'You sure love your food,' said the waitress, walking away.

CHAPTER 43

The taxi dropped Dee-anne, Matt and Steve in front of a modern three-storey terraced house in a tree-lined street. It was one of six almost identical houses and Dee-anne checked the number on her phone before heading to the front door. Matt and Steve walked down the road and waited outside a delicatessen.

She rang the bell and a few moments later George opened the door. He was older than he looked in the pictures he'd placed on Tinder, and considerably heavier. He was wearing a pink silk shirt and black trousers that were just a little too tight and he smelled of freshly-applied cologne. 'Dee-anne,' he said. 'Welcome to my home.' His hair was thinning and had been combed over to hide the sparsest area. There was a sadness in his eyes, as if he had been hurt before and expected to be hurt again. It was the most attractive thing about him, thought Dee-anne. She stepped into the hallway. The floor was pine that had been varnished like the deck of a yacht. There were dozens of LED lights embedded in the ceiling and unframed oil paints on the walls that looked as if the artists had thrown paint at canvases rather than bothering to use brushes.

'Let me take your jacket,' he said, holding out his hand.

She took it off and gave it to him and he pressed a mirrored panel. It slid back to reveal a large walk-in closet. He hung up her coat and took her along the hallway to a large kitchen, all white marble and stainless steel appliances that had the look of a hospital morgue.

'Champagne?' he asked.

'Why not?'

George pulled open the right-hand door of a fridge that was a head taller than he was and took out a bottle of Bollinger. He showed her the label. 'Vintage,' he said. 'I've been saving it for a special occasion.'

'Well this is certainly special,' she said.

George popped the cork and poured champagne into two flute glasses. He gave her one and then raised his glass in salute. 'To the start of...' He grinned. '..of something,' he finished.

'Of something wonderful,' she said. They clinked glasses and drank.

George smacked his lips appreciatively. 'That hits the spot,' he said. 'Why don't we go upstairs, it's more comfortable.'

He took her up a flight of polished pine stairs that led to a sitting room that ran the full length of the house with windows either end. There were two white sofas either side of a TV screen that showed an image of a flickering log fire. There were more modern oil paintings on the wall, and again they were nothing but splashes of colour. 'You like paintings?' she asked.

'I have a man who buys them for me,' he said. 'They're all investments, really.' He sat down on the sofa but Dee-anne stayed where she was. 'Do you like?'

'The paintings or the house?'

'Either. Both.'

'The house I love. The paintings, not so much.' She shrugged. 'Me, I like a horse to look like a horse and a bowl of flowers to look like a bowl of flowers.' She sipped her champagne. 'So what happened to the wife? Did you kill her?'

George looked startled, then smiled as he realised she was joking. 'What? No. Of course not. She divorced me.'

'No kids?'

'She wasn't one for sex, much. To be honest, Dee-anne, I think she only married me for the money.'

'And did she get it?'

Gorge laughed. 'She's still trying. But I've got some very good lawyers on my team.' He patted the sofa, encouraging her to sit down next to him, but she stayed where she was. She sipped her champagne and looked at him over the top of her glass. 'How old are you?' asked George.

'Old enough,' she laughed.

'Are you sure? Your profile said you were twenty-one but you look younger.'

'And you said you were forty-five but you look older. What are you, George, fifty? Fifty-five.'

'I'm forty-five,' said George, but she could see the lie in his eyes.

She smiled and undid the top two buttons of her shirt, giving him a glimpse of cleavage. She didn't want him getting cold feet, not now. 'You look good, and that's all that matters,' she said.

He put down his champagne flute and stood up. She walked over to him and tilted her neck back. She could still smell his cologne, but it barely masked his body odour. He swallowed and smiled, then he gasped as she rubbed the front of his pants. She felt him grow hard and she released her grip. 'Where's the bedroom?' she asked.

He swallowed again, then pointed at a doorway. 'Upstairs.'

'Shall we?'

'Do you want to finish your drink first?'

She shook her head. 'No, I want to see the bedroom first.'

She put her glass on the coffee table next to his, then took him by the hand and led him to another set of polished pine stairs to the master bedroom. There was a queen size bed with a brass frame. On a table facing the bed was a large television.

'Do you bring a lot of girls back here, George?'

'I don't get many matches,' he stammered.

She stroked him between the legs again. 'I don't believe that,' she said.

'It's true. And never girls as pretty as you. Older ones, sometimes. Fatter. But never like you.'

'You're so sweet,' said Dee-anne. She unbuttoned his shirt and ran her hands through the thick greying hair that covered his chest. He bent down to kiss her but she turned her head. 'Slowly, George,' she said. 'I like to take it slowly. Take your clothes off.'

'What?'

'Take your clothes off, George. And lie down on the bed. I'm going to give you a massage. The best you've ever had.'

'A massage?'

'You look tense. It'll relax you. Now take off your clothes before I change my mind.'

George took off his shirt and folded it before putting it on a chair. Dee-anne opened one of the closets. There was a rack of ties, a few were multi-coloured but the majority were drab stripes.

'What are you looking for?'

She pulled out four ties at random and turned to look at him. 'What do you think I'm going to do to you, George? Now take off your trousers.'

He did as he was told, though he had to sit down on the bed to get them off because they were so tight. He dropped the pants on the chair and looked at her expectantly.

'Your boxers, George. Take them off and get on the bed.'

'What about you?'

She draped the ties over the brass headboard and undid her shirt slowly, then took it off and dropped it onto the floor. She reached behind and unhooked her bra strap, and her breasts swung free as she let the bra fall on top of the shirt.

George's erection bulged at the front of his boxers and he stepped towards her. She smiled up at him and rubbed him. His mouth was open and he was panting and there was a glazed look to his eyes. 'Boxers, off, George,' she said, giving his erection a sly squeeze and then stepping to the side.

He yanked down his boxers, sat on the bed to pull them the rest of the way off, then tossed them onto the chair and lay back. He still had his socks on, dark blue with pale blue diamonds on.

Dee-anne got on top of him, her legs astride his thighs. His erection was standing up like a flagpole and he was panting like a dog in a heatwave.

'Are you ready, George?' she asked.

'Oh, God, yes.'

She giggled. 'Honey, God has nothing to do with this.'

She leant over him so that he could kiss her breasts. His lips found her left nipple and he sucked like a hungry baby. She took one of the ties and quickly bound his left wrist to the headboard.

He broke off from sucking. 'What are you doing?' he panted.

'Hush,' she said, 'suck my tits, I love it.'

He moaned and switched his attention to her right nipple. She grabbed another tie and used it to bind his right wrist. Then she sat up and ground her hips against his erection. 'Get you naked,' he gasped. 'I want to be inside you.'

She stroked his chest, then gripped his nipples. 'So you want me, George?'

'Yes. Please. Yes.'

She tweaked his nipples savagely and he shrieked. Then she quickly bent down and licked his right nipple until he lay whimpering, caught somewhere between pain and pleasure. She moved her left hand between his legs and gently stroked his erection.

'Yes, yes, yes,' he murmured. 'God, this is amazing.'

She moved down the bed, keeping her hand on his erection, then released her grip and quickly tied his legs to the bed.

'Why are you tying me, honey?'

'I want you in my power, George.' She slid off the bed. 'I want to be able to do whatever I want to you.'

'You can,' he whimpered. 'Oh God, you can.'

She laughed, 'Now George, I already told you that God has nothing to do with this.'

She moved to the top of the bed and stood looking down at him, a sly smile on her face. 'Are you ready, George?'

His face had reddened and was bathed in sweat. 'God yes. Just fuck me, please.'

'Is that what you want?'

He nodded frantically. 'Yes, yes, yes. I want it more than anything. Touch my cock, please. Please, baby, please.'

She bent over him so that her face was just inches from his and he could feel her soft breath on his cheeks. 'I'm going to eat you, George.'

'Yes,' he whispered. 'Yes, I'd like that.'

'Well, when I say "I", of course I mean "we", don't I?'

George frowned. 'What do you mean?'

She licked her lips. 'Come on George, you're far too big to be a single serving.' She picked up her bra and put it on.

His frown deepened. 'What are you talking about, baby?'

She picked up her shirt then turned and walked away without answering. He pulled at his arms but they were tied tight. His erection had gone and his heart was pounding as if it was about to burst.

He heard the click of her heels going down the stairs and across the wooden floor, then the sound of the door opening. She was leaving? She was leaving with him tied to the bed? What the hell was going on?

The door closed and he breathed a sigh of relief as he heard her go downstairs. She'd gone. His cleaning lady would be around the following morning, just before lunch. It would be embarrassing but at least she'd be able to untie him.

His stomach turned over as he heard her heels clicking on the floor. She was still in his house? The footsteps went to the kitchen and he heard drawers being opened and closed. She came up the stairs slowly. He heard a laugh, then another. Then she was at the doorway, smiling down at him. 'What's going on?' he asked. 'Is this some sort of sick fucking game you're playing?'

'This is no game, George. This is real life. Your life. What's left of it, anyway.'

There was someone standing behind her. A teenager. Lanky with greasy hair and acne across his forehead.

'Who the fuck's that? Why's he in my house?'

The boy stepped into the room. He was holding a carving knife in his right hand. One of the knives from his kitchen.

George swallowed but his mouth had gone dry. 'My wallet's in my trousers,' he said, his voice trembling.

'That's good to know,' said the boy.

'Take it. Take anything you want.'

'That's mighty hospitable of you,' said the boy. He moved towards the side of the bed and began to run the tip of the knife along George's leg, up to the thigh. He struggled, bucking up and down, but the bonds held firm.

'Why are you doing this?' asked George, his voice trembling.

'Because we can,' said the girl.

'And because we want to,' said a second teenager by the door. He was also holding a knife.

'Please, just let me go, I won't say anything.' He blinked away tears.

The girl smiled. Her pointed teeth seemed to go all the way to the back of her throat. 'But George, that would spoil the fun. We want you to talk. We want you to beg and plead for your miserable life.'

'It won't do any good, of course,' said the boy running the knife along George's thigh. 'But it makes it so much more enjoyable for us.' He lifted the knife and then placed the tip against George's scrotum. His balls shrank defensively and the teenager laughed. He jabbed the knife into George's left testicle and George screamed.

The girl picked up the TV remote and turned on the set and boosted the volume. There was a cookery show on with an overweight Italian man in a chef's jacket whisking something in a bowl.

The teenager grinned as he savagely twisted the knife. Dee-anne moved to the other side of the bed and put her face close to George's, relishing his pain. 'Come on George, you can scream louder than that, I know you can.'

The teenager twisted the knife again and the colour drained from George's face as he passed out.

'You've killed him!' shouted Dee-anne.

'No, he's just passed out,' said the boy, pulling out the knife. He sneered at the spreading yellow stain between Georg's legs. 'And he's wet himself.'

'Wake him up,' said Dee-anne. 'It's no fun if he doesn't scream.'

'I'll get some water,' said Matt, heading for the bathroom,

'Seriously, you need to be careful,' said Dee-anne. 'They break easily. Their necks snap like twigs and they bleed to death so easily. They're fragile, that's why they cling to life.'

Steve nodded. 'That's what makes killing them so much fun,' he said, and he shuddered. He looked over at the bathroom. 'Come on, we're waiting here!'

CHAPTER 44

Nightingale arrived at Perez's apartment just after nine o'clock in the morning. She opened her door wearing tight jeans and a baggy sweatshirt that said SUNY in large white letters. He grinned at the logo. 'Someone can't spell,' he said. 'There are two Ns in sunny.'

'State University of New York,' she said, closing the door behind him. 'My alma mater.'

Nightingale was holding two carrier bags and he gave one to her. She opened it and her eyes widened as she saw the box. 'You got it,' she said.

'Brand new. Never been used.' He grinned. 'And it glows in the dark.'

She put the box on the coffee table and opened it. The planchette was made of white plastic and had the words OUIJA and MYSTIFYING ORACLE on it.'

'Twenty bucks,' he said. 'At Kmart.' He put the other carrier bag on the coffee table. 'I've got the stuff you need, but I'll tell you again, Cheryl. It's not something you want to mess with.'

'If there's the slightest chance that I can speak to Eric, I want to try,' she said.

'There's no guarantee that you'll speak to him,' he said. 'All you're doing is opening up a line of communication, you can ask to speak to a specific spirit but anyone can come through.'

'I have to try,' she said. 'I need to know why he did what he did.'

Nightingale opened his mouth to argue but could see from the look in her eyes that there was no point. 'Okay,' he said. He pulled out several bunches of flowers from one of the bags and gave them to her. 'These need to be in vases around the room. Crystal is best but glass will do.'

She carried the flowers to the kitchen as he took five white church candles from another bag and placed them on the floor around the coffee table, evenly spaced. He went over to the kitchen where Perez was putting the flowers in vases. 'I need three bowls,' he said. 'Crystal or brass. Lead will do at a pinch.'

'Lead?" she said, arching an eyebrow. 'Who has lead bowls in their kitchen?'

'Crystal will be fine. Or glass.'

She opened a cupboard, took out three small glass bowls and gave them to him. He opened a bag of white crystals and poured them into one of the bowls.

'Please tell me that's not cocaine,' she said.

'It's the consecrated salt we bought.'

He opened a second bag and poured sage into a bowl. Then lavender.

He took the three bowls back to the coffee table, then lit the candles with his battered Zippo. Perez placed the flower-filled vases around the room and then sat down next to Nightingale on the sofa. 'Last chance,' he said.

'For what?'

'To recognise that this is not a good idea, on any level.'

She shook her head. 'I'm going to do it, with or without you.'

Nightingale nodded. 'Okay.' He sighed. 'Let's do it.' He sprinkled sage on the five burning candles, then smudged some of it on the board and the planchette. He sprinkled salt and lavender over the board, then wiped his hands on his trousers as he to face her. He took her hands in this. 'Close your eyes,' he said. She did as she was told. Nightingale closed his eyes and began to speak, clearly and loudly. 'In the name of God, of Jesus Christ, of The Great Brotherhood of Light, of the Archangels Michael, Raphael, Gabriel, Uriel and Ariel, please protect us from the forces of Evil during this session. Let there be nothing but light surrounding this board and its participants and let us only communicate with powers and entities of the light. Protect us, protect this house, the people in this house and let there only be light and nothing but light, Amen.'

He squeezed Perez's hand. 'Amen,' she repeated.

'You can open your eyes now,' said Nightingale. 'Now, listen to me carefully, this bit is important. You have to imagine that the table is bathed in a bright white light. Blindingly bright. You have to picture it coming down through the top of your head and completely surrounding your body. Then push it out as far as you can go?'

'I don't understand,' said Perez.

'You have to fill your body with light. Or at least you have to imagine that's what's happening. The light will protect you.'

She nodded. 'I'll try.'

He put his fingertips on the planchette and she followed his example. 'If anything goes wrong, we move the planchette to GOODBYE and we both say 'goodbye' at the same time. We say it firmly. It's not a question, we're not suggesting, we are telling the spirit that it's time to go. Then I'll recite a closing prayer.'

'I understand,' she said.

'It's important. If we end the session any other way, the spirit might not go.'

'I get it, Jack.'

Nightingale nodded. 'Okay then. Now start to visualise the white light.'

'Okay.' She took a deep breath.

Nightingale looked up at the ceiling. 'We're here to talk to Eric....' he began. He stopped. 'Perez wasn't his name, was it?'

She shook her head. 'O'Brien.'

Nightingale looked up at the ceiling again. 'Eric O'Brien.'

The candle flames flickered.

'Eric O'Brien, are you there?' He felt the planchette vibrate, then go still.

'Was that something?' whispered Perez.

'Don't talk,' he said. 'Eric O'Brien, as we sit with you now, we open our hearts. We surround ourselves with the love and light of God's protection. We have released all negativity and we ask you to dismiss all energies that are not of the highest and greatest source.'

The planchette began to vibrate again.

'Are you there, Eric O'Brien?'

Perez gasped as the planchette began to scrape across the board. Nightingale looked over at her. She was staring at her fingers, wide-eyed, and it felt to him as if she was pushing it. He pressed down on the planchette but it continued to slide along the board, towards YES. He pressed harder but there was nothing he could do to hinder its progress. It reached YES and stopped.

'It's him,' she whispered. 'It's Eric.'

Nightingale was reasonable certain it wasn't her husband. It felt to him as if she was pushing the planchette herself – consciously or unconsciously.

'You don't know that for sure. You have to ask it a question that only Eric would know.'

'Like what?'

'Your wedding anniversary. Your birthday. Something like that.'

'Do you want me to ask him?'

'Sure.'

She looked up at the ceiling. 'Eric, honey, please tell him our wedding anniversary.'

The planchette began to move almost before she had finished speaking and Nightingale was more sure than ever that she was pushing. The planchette scraped across the two rows of letters towards the numbers, but then it stopped, seemed to hesitate for a second or so then headed across the letters, stopping so that B was centred in the planchette's hole.

'No, honey, we want the date. The date of our wedding.'

The planchette moved to the right and stopped over the L. Nightingale realised she wasn't pushing, she was frowning as she stared at the L, not understanding what was happening. The planchette moved three letters to the left I. Perez wasn't pushing, Nightingale was sure of that. But he was equally sure that it wasn't her dead husband who was communicating with them. If it had been him the planchette would have gone straight to the date. It moved again, this time down to the lower row of letters, and across to the far left. It stopped over N.

It was moving faster now, and with more confidence, and quickly picked out eight more letters. F-O-L-D H-I-M.'

Perez swallowed nervously. The planchette began to vibrate over the letter M.

'What does it mean?' she asked.

'You know what it means. It wants you to blindfold me so that it can to send you a message that only you can see.'

'Eric, is that you?' she asked.

'Let me ask the questions,' said Nightingale.

'Eric, is that you?' said Perez again.

The planchette jerked across the board and stopped at YES.

'It's him,' said Perez.

'Not necessarily,' said Nightingale.

'Just let me blindfold you and I'll see what Eric has to say,' she said.

'That's not how it works.'

The planchette moved back and then lunged at the YES again.

'What harm could it do?' asked Perez.

'Cheryl, think about it. Why would Eric want you to blindfold me?'

'Because there's something private he wants to tell me.'

The planchette was twitching from side to side now.

'That's not how to do it. Everyone on the board has to be aware of what's going on.'

'You heard what he said. He wants to talk to me.'

'You're assuming it's Eric. Let's ask him for proof first.'

The planchette lunged to the right and stopped over the word NO.

'See?' said Nightingale. 'He doesn't want you to test him. We have to stop now. Before this goes any further.' He looked up at the ceiling. 'Goodbye,' he said firmly. He looked over at Perez. She was glaring at him with undisguised contempt. 'Cheryl, you have to say goodbye.'

She shook her head. 'No.'

'Listen to me. Just say goodbye and we can talk about it. Something's not right here.'

The planchette jerked away from NO, shot to the bottom of the board and then shot back to NO. Nightingale could feel his fingers burning.

'Why won't you just do as Eric asks?' she shouted, her eyes blazing.

'Because it's not, Eric. Can't you see that? Why would your husband want to put you through this.'

'Liar!' screamed Perez. She took her hands off the planchette and as she did it span from under Nightingale's fingers and flew through the air before crashing against the wall. The board span in the other direction and slammed against the kitchen door before falling to the floor. The candles blew out and the three crystal bowls flew off the coffee table and smashed on the floor. Perez sat back, her eyes and mouth wide open.

Nightingale stood up and switched on the lights. He picked up the planchette and the board and put them back on the coffee table. He sat down and held Perez's hands. 'Cheryl we have to say goodbye to the spirit.

This has to end properly.' She didn't resist as he put her fingertips on the planchette. He did the same. He pushed the planchette towards GOODBYE but Perez's fingers slipped off. She was staring blankly at the board. Nightingale cursed and he stood up. 'You've no idea what you've done,' he said.

She didn't appear to hear him. 'Cheryl?' When she didn't reply he gathered up the board and the planchette, put them back in the box and left with it. Perez stayed where she was, staring at the coffee table.

CHAPTER 45

Nightingale stood in the street and smoked a Marlboro as he considered his options. Eventually he pulled out his mobile phone and called Joshua Wainwright. Wainwright sounded sleepy when he answered so Nightingale guessed he was in a different time zone. 'What's up, Jack?'

'I need a gun,' said Nightingale.

'That's not like you.'

'I know. But I don't see any way around it.'

'What sort of gun?'

'Powerful but concealable. And ideally with a history that'll muddy the waters.'

'Where are you?'

'Manhattan.'

'How urgent?'

'The sooner the better.'

'Okay to use this number?'

'Sure. I'm going to be ditching it soon anyway.'

'I'll get someone to call you back.'

'Cheers.' Nightingale put the cellphone back in his pocket and walked slowly down the street, deep in thought. Wainwright was absolutely right, Nightingale wasn't a big fan of guns but sometimes he had no choice other than to use them. In a former life he'd been an armed cop in the UK and he'd been a bloody good shot, but that had been years ago. Walking around New York with a loaded weapon was just asking for trouble, but under the circumstances Nightingale didn't feel he had many options.

He had just finished his cigarette when his cellphone rang. He took it out but didn't recognise the number. 'Yeah?'

'You Jack?'

'Yeah.'

'I'm to give you something you need. Where are you?'

'Manhattan.'

The man laughed harshly. 'I know that. Where?'

'I'm not sure. All these streets look the same.'

'Where are you from?'

'Not here,' said Nightingale.

The man laughed again. 'Walk to the nearest intersection and tell me what signs you see.'

Nightingale walked to the corner and looks up at the road signs. 'Second Avenue and 80th Street.'

'Upper East Side,' said the man. 'Stay where you are and I'll pick you up in half an hour. Forty-five minutes at most. Blue minivan.'

Nightingale whiled away the time smoking and pacing up and down the sidewalk. The minivan turned up after forty minutes. It had blacked-out windows but Nightingale could make out the driver, a grizzled grey-haired man wearing dark glasses. The side door opened electronically as he walked up to the vehicle. There were just three armchair-sized seats inside and a large screen TV behind the driver. There was one man sitting in the back, young with slicked-back hair and wearing a shiny blue suit and a bolo tie with a turquoise stone in the middle. 'Get in,' he said.

Nightingale climbed in and took one of the seats opposite the man. The door closed automatically. 'I'm Jed,' said the man, offering his hand.

He had a gold ring in the shape of a steer's head and Nightingale realised the man was wearing cowboy boots with rattlesnake heads on the toes.

'Jack,' said Nightingale, shaking his hand.

'Mr Wainwright said I'm to give you anything you want, up to and including an RPG.' The minivan pulled out into the traffic and headed slowly south.

Nightingale smiled. 'A rocket-propelled grenade is more than I'll need,' he said, 'I just want a revolver.'

'Don't want to leave casings around? I hear you.'

'Something small, but powerful.'

'How does a .38 Smith and Wesson Special sound?'

'Like music to my ears.'

'I'm guessing you want something clean, something that can't be traced.'

'Actually I'd be happier with something that's got a very messy history. I'm going to be dropping it when I'm done so anything that muddies the waters will be a bonus.'

The man grinned. 'Then it's your lucky day, my friend. I might have exactly what you want.' He pulled a pair of latex gloves from a box and put them on, then twisted around in his seat and opened a toolbox in which there were a dozen or more cloth-wrapped packages. He pulled out one and unwrapped it to reveal a .38 Smith and Wesson snub-nosed revolver. 'Not great at distance, it has to be said. But it's a reliable weapon and easy enough to conceal.' The handle and the trigger had been wrapped in grey tape. 'Supposed to prevent fingerprints but I figure there'll still be DNA so if I were you I'd be gloved up,' said the man. 'This has been used in a couple of drug-related shootings in New Jersey and one of them ended up with an undercover cop in the ICU so you really don't ever want to be caught with it in your possession. But in terms of muddying the waters you couldn't do any better.'

He handed the box of gloves to Nightingale. Nightingale pulled out a couple of gloves, slipped them on, then examined the weapon. It wasn't new by any means but it was in good enough condition. He flicked out the cylinder and sniffed it, It hadn't been fired recently but there was still the acrid tang of cordite. He snapped the cylinder back in place and sighted along the barrel. 'Perfect,' he said.

'How many rounds do you need?'

Nightingale rubbed his chin. The .38 Special took six rounds in the cylinder but only an idiot carried one with a round under the hammer which meant loading it with just five. Nightingale planned to make every shot count and he intended to be up close and personal which meant he doubted he would get a chance to reload. But it was always better to have too many rounds rather than too few. 'Let's make it an even ten,' he said.

'As you're not worried about wear and tear, how about using P plus ammo? As used by the FBI.'

Nightingale nodded his approval. The P plus ammo was designed for the FBI after their agents came off worse in several shoot-outs. The experts came up with higher pressure loadings for the .38 ammunition and initially it became known as the 'FBI load'. It used a hollow-point bullet designed to rapidly expand and do more damage when it hit the target. Newer versions, using a jacketed soft-point round, had proven to be even more effective. 'Sounds like a plan.'

The man opened a metal briefcase, took out a box of shells and counted out ten which he placed in a small plastic bag and gave them to Nightingale.

'How much do I owe you?' asked Nightingale.

'It's taken care of,' said the man. 'Now where can I drop you?'

'Anywhere near 96th Street,' said Nightingale. 'East.'

CHAPTER 46

Camilla Rodriguez fumbled the key from her bag and inserted it into the lock. It was eight-fifteen in the morning so she was a quarter of an hour late but with any luck her employer would have already left for work. She pushed open the door and dropped her bag by the hall table. She closed the door and hung up her coat, then picked up her bag and headed for the kitchen. She heard voices and she frowned. Mr George didn't usually have guests. His mother came to stay twice a year, at Christmas and at Thanksgiving, but other than that he stayed alone. He was an easy man to take care of as he was very tidy and loaded the dishwasher himself every time he cooked. He was a stickler for cleanliness but so was Camilla so they were a good match.

She walked into the kitchen. There were two boys and a girl sitting at the centre island, which was covered in fast food containers. There were half a dozen pizza boxes, cartons that had contained Chinese food, burger wrappers, foil dishes that still had pasta in them. They seemed to be teenagers though there were opened bottles of wine and beer on the island.

'Who are you?' she asked.

'We're friends of George,' said one of the boys. He had a smear of ketchup across his cheek.

'Good friends,' said the girl.

'Did he have a party last night?'

'Sort of,' said the girl.

Camilla didn't understand who the teenagers were or why they were in Mr George's house. She wasn't aware of Mr George having any young relatives, at least none that he would invite to his home. He was an only child and while he had been married for ten years he hadn't had any children.

'Where is Mr George?' she asked.

'Upstairs,' said the girl. 'In the bedroom.'

Camilla frowned. 'Are you relatives?'

One of the boys shook his head. 'Dinner guests,' he said, then he sniggered at the girl.

'He's a very good host,' said the other boy. He reached into a KFC bucket and waved a drumstick in the air. 'Tastes like chicken,' he said, and they all laughed.

Camilla headed for the stairs. They were all laughing and as she walked down the hall it felt as if the whole house was shaking. She looked over her shoulder and the laughter stopped. She held onto the banister as she went up the stairs. The door to Mr George's bedroom was closed and she knocked on it. 'Mr George? Mr George?'

There was no answer so she turned the handle and gently pushed it open. 'Mr George? It's Camilla? Are you there?'

The curtains were drawn and the room was in darkness. She groped for the light switch and flicked it on. Her eyes widened when she saw what was on the bed and her mouth opened though no sound came out. She clasped her hands to her chest. What was left of her employer was sprawled across the duvet, covered in blood. His arms and legs were spread-eagled and she realised that he had been tied but the rest of his body was a mass of ruptured tissue. Her whole body began to tremble and she took a half step back. 'Mr George...' she mumbled.

There were bits of flesh on the floor around the bed, as if wild animals had been disturbed while feeding. One of his eyes was hanging from its socket. An ear had been ripped away from the side of his head and was hanging by a small strip of flesh. Camilla felt the strength seep from her legs and she reached out to hold the door to steady herself.

She heard the scrape of a shoe against the stairs and she looked over her shoulder. One of the boys was there, a vicious grin on his face. 'Still in bed, is he?' he asked.

Camilla opened her mouth to speak but it felt as if there was a vice around her throat.

The second boy appeared behind the first. He was holding a knife. Camilla pushed the door closed but the first boy moved quickly and slapped his hand against the wood. 'Now that's just rude,' he said. He pushed the door and Camilla took a step back.

The two boys stood staring at her, grinning. Their eyes were blood red, she realised. No pupils, no whites, just red. Blood red. She took another step back.

The girl appeared behind them. Her eyes were red, too.

'Please, I want to go home,' whispered Camilla.

The two boys moved apart so that the girl could walk between them.

Camilla moved back, two or three small steps, then the bed hit the back of her legs and she stopped. She tried not to think about what was behind her.

'That's not going to happen,' said the girl. She smiled and her teeth looked sharp, like a cat's.

'Don't hurt me, please,' said Camilla.

'Honey, I can't lie to you. We're going to hurt you, a lot.'

'What do you think,' asked the boy on her left. 'Leg or breast?'

The other boy laughed. 'Oh, breast. Definitely breast.' The two of them looked at each other and chuckled.

Camilla felt the floorboards vibrate under her feet. She backed away from them. She crossed herself and muttered a prayer.

The girl grinned. 'Oh yeah, that'll work,' she said, moving towards her.

CHAPTER 47

Nightingale was shrouded in a fog so thick that he could barely make out his feet as he walked across the rugged terrain. The fog was warm and wet and sweat was beading on his face. He'd lost track of time but it felt as if he had been wandering in the fog for ever. He stopped and listened but there was no sound. He rotated through three hundred and sixty degrees but everything looked the same. There was nothing to see, nothing to hear, nothing to smell. He concentrated on the person he was trying to find but he felt his thoughts slipping away. He closed his eyes, took a deep breath, and steadied himself. 'Mrs Steadman,' he whispered to himself. 'Mrs Alice Steadman. I need to speak with you.'

He felt an almost imperceptible tug to his left so he walked in that direction. The ground was one sheet of stone but his shoes made no noise when they came into contact with it. He lost track of how long he walked. After a while he stopped looking at his feet and just stared straight ahead into the cloying mist. He blinked his eyes and felt drops of water run down his face. He wiped them away with the sleeve of his raincoat. He stopped for a few seconds, listened, and then started walking again. Was he wasting his time? Was it time to call it a night and go home? He looked at his watch but it was blank, just a metallic circle on a brown leather strap. He groped in his pockets for his cellphone but his pockets were empty. No phone. No cigarettes. No lighter. No wallet.

'Is there anybody there?' he called, but there was no reply.

He carried on walking. Then he saw a dark patch in the fog ahead of him. He wiped his eyes with his sleeve and carried on walking. The dark patch grew bigger in size but it was still just a shapeless blob. Then he realised the fog was thinning. It was still there, all around him, but he could see further than before, six feet, maybe eight. The dark shape became clearer. It was a bench. And there was a figure sitting on it. Three more steps and the fog was even thinner As he got closer he saw Mrs Steadman. Purveyor of all things Wicca and a font of all knowledge when it came to magic. She was sitting on a wooden bench, her legs crossed in a yoga pose. Mrs Alice Steadman. She was in her late sixties, a tiny pixie of a woman. She was wearing a black bobble hat pulled down low over her face, a black fleece jacket and black tights. Her black boots had pointed toes and little silver bells on the end. The eyes that looked over at him were the greenest he'd ever seen. 'Why Mr Nightingale, this is a pleasant surprise.'

'I wasn't sure I'd be able to find you,' he said.

'You could have phoned.'

'It's late, Mrs Steadman. I didn't want to wake you. And I need to practise my astral projection.'

She smiled. 'You seem to be doing just fine.'

'It's taken me a long time to find you.'

'Why Mr Nightingale, you know that time has no meaning here. And where are you exactly? Still in America?'

'New York,' said Nightingale.

'And you have a problem?'

Nightingale nodded. 'I need a sympathetic priest. Someone who can bless some equipment for me.' He sat down next to her. The fog had thickened again. He could see her clearly, and the bench, but nothing else. Even the ground was hidden in the mist now, though he could just about see the tops of his Hush Puppies.

'What have you got yourself into this time, Mr Nightingale?'

'It's complicated, Mrs Steadman.'

'It always is, with you,' she said. She patted him gently on the knee. 'You're working for Joshua Wainwright, aren't you?'

He nodded. 'I'm doing him a favour or two, yes. I have to. He protects me.'

'Does he? Or does he put you in danger?' She patted his knee again. 'I've told you before, I don't think he has your best interests at heart.'

'He's all I have at the moment,' said Nightingale.

She forced a smile. 'So it's a priest you want?'

'A priest who won't ask too many questions.'

Her smile widened. 'If priests asked too many questions, they wouldn't stay priests for long. You say New York, so you mean Manhattan?'

'Yes. The island.'

'I'd say the best person would be Father MacDowell. He's in Brooklyn, but that's easy enough to get to. His church is St Mary Of The Angels.'

'Can you talk to him?'

'Not on the astral plane, I'm afraid. But I can phone him first thing in the morning to let him know you're coming.'

'That would be wonderful, thank you.'

'Give him my best.'

There was a loud knocking, off to their left, somewhere in the fog. He ignored it but it got louder.

Mrs Steadman smiled. 'There's someone at your door,' she said.

'I'm not expecting visitors.'

'They sound insistent,' she said.

'I'd better go, then,' said Nightingale.

'I think that would probably best,' she said. 'Do be careful.'

'I will be.'

'I'm serious, Mr Nightingale. Take care.'

Nightingale woke up. He was lying on his back, his fingers interlinked over his chest. The banging was coming from the main door. He rolled off the sofa and padded in his bare feet through the main office to the reception area. It was Cheryl Perez wearing a long coat. He looked at his watch. It was almost midnight. He looked at her through the glass door. 'What's wrong?'

'We need to talk.'

'I was asleep.'

She grinned. 'I can see that,' she said. She held up a bottle of wine. 'I come bearing gifts.'

He realised he was wearing nothing but his boxer shorts and a t-shirt. He unlocked the door and held it open. 'Give me a minute and I'll get changed,' he said.

'Okay,' she said.

He had just started to turn when something hard smacked into the back of his head and everything went black.

CHAPTER 48

Nightingale came awake slowly, blinking and groaning. He tried to lift his hands but they were bound behind his back. He was sitting on a chair in the centre of the main office area. Perez was squatting down to his right, putting the finishes to a chalk pentagram, a five-pointed star surrounded by two concentric circles. It was different to magic circles he'd drawn in the past, with dozens of small symbols in the space between the two circles.

'Cheryl,' he said, his voice little more than a croak. She ignored him and continued drawing. Nightingale looked to his left. There was a black candle in a silver candlestick, There was another to his right. 'You don't know what you're messing with.'

She twisted her head around to look at him. 'Keep quiet or I'll gag you. Or hit you with the bottle again.' She had taken off her coat and was wearing a loose black shirt over black trousers. The top buttons of her shirt were open revealing a good helping of cleavage. She stood up. She was holding a piece of paper in her left hand. Nightingale caught a glimpse of a pentagram before she disappeared behind him.

'This isn't Eric asking you to do this. You have to know that.'

She appeared on his right side, drawing part of the five-pointed star within the circle.

'How would Eric know how to construct a pentagram? How would he know about the black candles? Did he give you a sigil, Cheryl? His calling card?'

She stood up and glared down at him. 'You need to shut up,' she said. 'He said you'd try to stop me. He said you'd lie to me.'

'Who said?'

'Eric.'

'How did you talk to him?'

'The Ouija board.'

'On you own?'

She nodded. 'He came straight to me. It's him, it's definitely him.'

Nightingale shook his head. 'No it's not. I guarantee it's not.'

'You don't know him. You don't know Eric. He wants to come back to me.'

'Through me? Is that what Eric told you? Because it's bollocks, Cheryl. It's not Eric and if you do this, if you go through with it, then you'll die.'

Her eyes narrowed. 'He said you'd say that it was dangerous. He said that you'd lie.'

'Eric said that?'

She nodded. 'He said I should ignore everything you say.' Her gaze softened. 'I don't know why you're getting so wound up. He just wants to borrow your body for a while so that he can talk to me properly. When he's finished, he'll move on.'

'That's what he said, is it?'

'He doesn't want to hurt you. It would be so much easier if you do it willingly.'

'Tell me what he said. Exactly.'

She took a step closer to him. 'He said the Ouija board wasn't a good way of talking. It takes too much energy, he said. It drains him. The best way of contacting him is through a circle like this. And a body that he can talk through.'

'Me? He asked for me?'

'He said he could talk to me through you. You won't be harmed, Jack. He just wants to spend some time with me. He wants to be able to touch me, to smell me, to feel me. He can't do that through the Ouija board.'

'And he told you to take off your crucifix?'

'He said jewellery gets in the way.'

'It's not the jewellery he doesn't like. It's the cross. He's a devil, Cheryl. The cross would block him.'

'You're wrong, Jack. I was wearing the crucifix when we used the Ouija board.'

'This is different. This is summoning him. He gave you a sigil, didn't he?'

'A sigil?'

'A sign. We talked about sigils, remember? He would have got you to write it in blood. Your blood.' He gestured with his chin at the Band-Aid on her left index finger. 'Am I right?'

'It's necessary so that he can cross over. It's his calling card, that's all.'

'People don't have sigils, demons do. People have names. If you talk to someone on a Ouija board, you call their name. You don't use a sigil. Google it if you don't believe me.'

'It's just a way of contacting him, that's all.'

'Listen to yourself, Cheryl. he told you to take off your crucifix. He's asked you to write his sigil in blood. Now he's making you draw a pentagram and light black candles. Does any of that make sense to you. You're a Catholic, right?'

'Of course.'

'And Eric? Was he Catholic?'

She nodded.

'Think about it. Why would a Catholic want you to remove a crucifix and mess around with black magic?'

'Who said anything about black magic?'

'What do you think this is? A pentagram, black candles, writing in blood? Look, you need to focus. He's influencing you, he's muddying your thoughts. You're not thinking clearly.'

'You need to shut up now,' she said. 'I have to concentrate.'

'Cheryl, if you do this, if you allow whatever demon it is to take possession of me, you're dead. If the demon takes over my body, the first thing he'll do is carve his sigil into your flesh. Then he'll kill you. That's what happened in the cases we've been looking at. A victim is selected. He or she performs this ceremony so that the demon can walk this earth. And the demon then kills the victim. That's what you are. You're the intended victim. You do this and you'll be dead on the floor, just like the other victims.'

'You're wrong,' she said. 'You'll see. This is just so Eric can spend some time with me.'

She finished drawing the pentagram, then compared it to the drawing she was holding. 'That should do it,' she said.

'Don't do this, Cheryl,' said Nightingale, but he knew that he was wasting his time. She wasn't listening to him.

She stood at the top of the pentagram and began to read from the sheet. Partly Latin and partly something else. Nightingale shivered as the temperature suddenly dropped. Perez continued to read from the sheet. 'Osurmy delmausan atalsloym charusihoa,' she said. Then she took a deep breath and continued to read the rest of the words. When she had finished she held the piece over the north-facing candle. As it burned she spoke again, her voice louder and more strident. 'Come, Eric,' she said. 'Everything is ready.'

'Show me the sigil Eric gave you.'

'Be quiet, Jack.'

'Sigils are for devils, Cheryl. They're not for you or me or Eric. The sigil that you think Eric gave you, it belongs to someone else.'

'Why would Eric lie to me? He loves me.'

'Because it's not Eric that you've been talking to.'

She ignored him and went over to one of the candles. She held the piece of paper over the flame. White smoke began to fill the room.

'Don't!' shouted Nightingale. 'I beg you.'

She ignored him. 'I'm ready, Eric!' shouted Perez. 'Come to me now!' She winced as the flames seared her fingers but she held on to the burning paper until it had completely burned.

There was a loud crack and a flash of light that was so bright that for a few seconds Nightingale was blinded. As he blinked away tears he saw there was a large figure standing in the smoke.

'Eric?' said Perez uncertainly.

Whatever had appeared wasn't Eric, Nightingale was sure of that. It wasn't Eric and it wasn't human. It was reptilian with yellow eyes and a green forked tongue that flicked out from between razor sharp teeth. Nightingale cursed under his breath. Perez backed away from whatever it was, her eyes wide with horror.

Grey, leathery wings sprouted from the thing's back as it threw back its head and roared in triumph. The floor and ceiling shook and the walls bowed out. Perez looked over at Nightingale. 'What is it?' she screamed. 'What's happening?'

Nightingale didn't answer, he just stared at the creature which had begun to change. It shimmered and rippled and morphed into a dwarf with a mop of unruly black hair. He was wearing gleaming black leather boots with silver spurs and a scarlet jacket with gold button. In his right hand was a riding crop and he swished it from side to side as he sneered at Nightingale. 'Long time, no see, Nightingale,' said the dwarf.

Nightingale swore out loud.

The dwarf grinned cruelly. 'And I'm pleased to see you, too.'

'Who are you?' said Perez, backing away. 'What are you doing here? Where's Eric?'

The dwarf pointed his whip at Nightingale. 'Do you want to tell her, or should I?'

Perez looked over at Nightingale. 'What's going on? What's happening? Who is this?'

'Lucifuge Rofocale,' said Nightingale. 'As nasty a piece of shit as ever walked out through the gates of Hell.'

'But where's Eric?'

'Eric's dead, Cheryl. You were never talking to Eric. It was always Lucifuge Rofocale. He was using you, to get to me.'

The dwarf threw back his head and laughed. 'And it worked, like a charm,' he said.

Perez screamed and charged towards Lucifuge Rofocale, her hands curled into claws. He waved his free hand in her direction, then pointed his index finger at her chest. There was a flash of light and a loud crack and Perez flew backwards and smashed into the wall.

'Cheryl!' shouted Nightingale, trying to twist around to see where she was.

Lucifuge Rofocale walked to the edge of the pentagram. 'So are you ready, Nightingale? Are you ready to give yourself over to me?'

'Not really, no.'

'But you have no choice in the matter, you know that?'

'I thought I had to agree. The possession had to be done willingly.'

'Then you thought wrong,' said Lucifuge Rofocale. He gestured at Perez with his whip. 'It's her permission I needed, not yours. She is the one who performs the ceremony.'

'She's not going to help you now, not now she knows who you are.'

'We'll see about that.' The dwarf turned to look at Perez. 'Apply enough pressure and people will do just about anything.'

Nightingale knew he had to act quickly. He closed his eyes and began to speak the Latin phrase that he had long ago committed to memory. He said the words loudly and clearly, knowing that any mistake, any deviation, would be fatal.

Lucifuge Rofocale realised what he was doing and he whirled around, raising the whip above his head. 'No!' he yelled.

'Bagahi laca bacabe!' shouted Nightingale at the top of his voice. He wasn't sure if it would work, the pentagram was different and he hadn't been able to use the herbs that were usually required for the summoning but he wasn't in a position to be choosy. 'Bagahi laca bacabe!' he shouted again, even louder this time.

There was a loud cracking sound and the room vibrated then there was another crack and a flash and time and space seemed to fold in on itself and Proserpine was there, standing in the space between the two concentric circles that surrounded the pentagram. Her dog was with her, and it growled as it stared at Lucifuge Rofocale.

'What have you done?' screamed Lucifuge Rofocale.

'I'll treat that as rhetorical,' said Nightingale.

Proserpine's hair was shorter and spikier than the last time he'd seen her. She was wearing a long black leather coat that almost touched the floor over black shorts and a black halter top. She had no navel, he realised, her porcelain white stomach was completely smooth and featureless. Her lips were jet black and her eyes were featureless pools and around her neck was a black collar with a black upside-down pointed star at her throat. She smiled at Nightingale. 'Bitten off more than you can chew?' she asked.

'I didn't know who else to call,' he said.

Proserpine turned to look at Lucifuge Rofocale and she sneered. 'I should have known it was you,' she said.

'Should have, would have, could have,' said Lucifuge Rofocale. 'This is none of your business, Proserpine. You need to leave.'

'What you are doing goes against the order of things,' said Proserpine. 'You need to return from whence you came.'

'There is nothing you can do,' said Lucifuge Rofocale. 'I was invited. You were summoned. You are trapped within the pentagram. But I can do what as I wish.' He grinned and strutted up and down to prove his point.

'You have to stop this, Lucifuge Rofocale. You have to stop this now.'

Lucifuge Rofocale shook his head and pointed at her. 'This is nothing to do with you!' he shouted. 'You are a Princess of Hell. You have no authority here.'

'You need to stop this before it goes any further.'

He shook his head. 'Your sister was happy to come along.'

'She will be dealt with in due course,' hissed Proserpine. 'But you are the more pressing problem. Go back now. Go back or you will pay the price.'

The walls juddered as Lucifuge Rofocale roared with laughter. 'Did you forget, Proserpine? There is nothing you can do so long as you are trapped within the pentagram. You can watch if that's what you want, but you can't interfere.'

Proserpine glared at Lucifuge Rofocale, shook her head, then looked over at Nightingale. 'Looks like the ball's in your court,' she said.

Nightingale nodded. He began to rock the chair from side to side, grunting with the effort.

'You think you can escape?' laughed Lucifuge Rofocale. 'How stupid are you, Nightingale?'

Nightingale continued to rock from side to side. 'I'm not trying to escape!' he shouted.

Lucifuge Rofocale's eyes widened as he realised what Nightingale was doing. 'No!' he screamed, but it was too late. With a final grunt Nightingale tipped the chair over and he crashed on his side. His head was just over the outer edge of the pentagram. The protective circle was broken.

Lucifuge Rofocale screamed with rage. 'What have you done?' he yelled.

'He's set me free, that's what he's done,' said Proserpine. She stepped out of the circle. 'And now it's time for you to pay the piper.'

Lucifuge Rofocale took a step back, then he roared and his body seemed to ripple and it grew larger and then shimmered and became the scaly-creature with yellow eyes and fangs and talons and leathery wings. It opened its mouth and Nightingale retched from the stench of its foul breath. A claw lashed out but Proserpine swayed back and easily avoided the blow. 'Did no one tell you it's wrong to hit a woman?' she said. She kicked him in the chest and he staggered back, his wings flapping frantically as he fought to keep his balance.

Proserpine's dog growled and moved forward, changing form with each step. It rippled and doubled in size, its fur became hard and scaly. It growled and leapt and as its feet left the ground it changed again. It had three heads, all dog-like but with huge yellowed fangs and slimy forked tongues and with a line of barbed bony spines. When it hit Lucifuge Rofocale it was the size of a small car. One of the gaping jaws fastened onto Lucifuge Rofocale's left arm and another seized his throat. Green blood spurted from the wounds and Lucifuge roared in pain.

Lucifuge Rofocale span around, his wings scraping against the walls. One of the dog's three heads was barking furiously while the other two held on fast to its prey.

Nightingale couldn't move, all he could do was stare in horror at the carnage. Green blood splattered across the ceiling and Lucifuge Rofocale staggered, his yellow eyes rolling back into his head. The dog – or whatever the creature was – dragged Lucifuge Rofocale to the floor and continued to savage him. The air was split with a crash of thunder and there was a jagged streak of lightning that appeared to spark from Lucifuge Rofocale's chest and then he was gone. The three-headed creature jumped back as if shocked by the disappearance.

'He's gone, baby,' said Proserpine. 'You did good.'

'Do you think you could see your way to untying me?' asked Nightingale.

Proserpine turned to look at him. She made a cutting gesture with her right hand and the bonds fell away from his wrists. He rolled over and got to his feet, rubbing his hands as the circulation returned.

'Did you know he was behind this?' asked Nightingale.

The three-headed monster turned and looked at Proserpine and she blew it a kiss. The three heads growled and then it began to change shape. The three heads became one, the body shrank and the fur returned. It headed towards her and with each step it took it became more dog-like. By the time it sat at her side it was back to being a black and white collie sheepdog with a pink tongue lolling from the side of its mouth. 'Good boy,' she said, and patted it on the head.

'I asked you a question,' said Nightingale.

Proserpine's eyes narrowed. 'If I were you I'd keep a respectful tone in your voice,' she said. 'Seeing as how you don't have any protection at the moment.'

Nightingale looked over at the pentagram. 'To be fair, I breached the circle so that you could attack Lucifuge Rofocale.'

'And how did that feel, getting a woman to fight your battles?'

'I got the impression you're no fan of his.'

'Fan or not, he shouldn't have been here. He'll be punished for that.'

'Good to know,' said Nightingale. 'Now what happens?'

'You have to do what has to be done,' said Proserpine.

'Specifics would be nice,' said Nightingale.

'You have to kill them,' said Proserpine. 'Kill the hosts and the invaders will return to Hell where they will be dealt with.'

'Why can't you do it?'

'Because there are rules, Nightingale. Rules that apply to me just as much as your rules apply to you. They are in human form now so they are your responsibility.'

'But how do I find them? They could be anywhere.'

'You need to find Lilith. The others will be with her.'

'I tried,' said Nightingale. 'I used the crystal but it's too vague.'

'Because the crystal seeks the girl and not the demon,' said Proserpine. 'Hold out your hand.'

Nightingale did as he was told. Proserpine traced a shape on the palm of his hand with her nail. He felt nothing but when she took her finger away he saw that she had cut Lilith's sigil into his flesh. Blood oozed from the cuts.

'The closer you get to her, the more it will burn,' she said.

'Well thanks for that,' said Nightingale.

'You must move quickly,' she said. 'Once they learn what has happened to Lucifuge Rofocale they will flee.'

'I'm on it,' said Nightingale. 'And thanks.'

'Proserpine frowned. 'For what?'

'For saving me.'

Proserpine frowned. 'I didn't save you, Nightingale. I sent Lucifuge Rofocale back to where he belongs. The fact that you are still alive is incidental.'

'Well thanks anyway.'

'You're welcome,' she said. The dog made a soft woofing sound and then space and time folded in on itself amid an ear-splitting crack and a flash of light and Proserpine and her dog were gone and he was alone with Perez. He hurried over to her and rolled her onto her back. There was blood dripping down her chin but he couldn't tell whether she had bitten her tongue or if she had internal injuries. He took out his phone. He wasn't thrilled about calling 911 but he didn't see that he any choice. He was just about to dial when her eyes opened. 'Don't,' she said.

'You need an ambulance.'

'I'm okay. I really don't want to have to explain what happened. Not to a paramedic and certainly not to the cops.' She put a hand up to her mouth and winced.

'You could be bleeding internally.'

'I'm not,' she said.

'You took a hell of a knock.'

She forced a smile. 'I've been hit before,' she said.

'Not by a demon from Hell.' He helped her to sit up. 'Can you stand?'

'I think so.'

Nightingale helped her up and then supported her as they walked along to the office he'd been using as a bedroom. He helped her sit down on the sofa bed and then fetched her a glass of water. 'Jack, I'll be fine,' she said.

'You need to be in a hospital.'

'Who was she, Jack? The woman in black with the dog thing. What just happened?'

'She's my CI.'

'A devil?'

Nightingale nodded. 'We go back a long way. I summoned her and by breaking the circle I let her deal with Lucifuge Rofocale.'

'And who the fuck is Lucifuge Rofocale?'

'He's another devil. He almost took my soul a while back and I think he bears a grudge. He was using your love for Eric to get to me. I'm sorry.'

She forced a smile. 'You really need to stop saying that.'

CHAPTER 49

Nightingale helped Perez downstairs and took her home in an Uber cab. He stayed with her for an hour to make sure that she was okay, then went back to his office. He slept fitfully and the next day took a taxi to the St Mary Of The Angels church in Brooklyn. He shuddered and lit a cigarette as the cab drove away. He blew smoke and looked up at the church. It was a solid grey stone structure with a tall steeple, stained glass windows protected with chicken wire and grey gargoyles at the corners. He went up to the main door but it was locked. There was a wooden noticeboard to the left of the door containing a list of services, a number of contact phone numbers and a note that the priest could be contacted at the house to the left of the church.

Nightingale finished his cigarette before walking to the house and pressing the brass doorbell. The door was opened by a grey-haired man in his fifties with wire-framed spectacles. He had a green cardigan over a shirt with a dog collar.

'Father MacDowell?'

'Yes?'

'My name's Jack Nightingale. Mrs Steadman sent me.'

The priest smiled and opened the door. 'Come in, I've been expecting you.' The hallway was lined with framed photographs of Father MacDowell standing in front of different churches, often with other priests.

There were several photographs that had clearly been taken in the Vatican including one of the priest standing in front of Pope John Paul 11. 'My wall of shame,' said the priest, with a smile. 'Go on through to the sitting room, I was just having coffee.'

The sitting room was a comfortable bolthole with overstuffed leather armchairs that were stained and worn, rugs that had gone threadbare over the years, and bookshelves full of well-thumbed volumes. There was a coffee pot on a small table, along with a cup and saucer and a milk jug.

'Would you care for a coffee?' asked the priest.

'I'm fine,' said Nightingale.

Father MacDowell picked up his cup and finished his coffee. 'Mrs Steadman said you needed my help,' he said as he put his cup back on its saucer.

Nightingale nodded. 'I need you to bless something for me. I'm afraid it's a little… unorthodox.'

'It usually is if Mrs Steadman is involved,' he said.

Nightingale reached into his pocket and brought out a dozen cartridges.

'Ah,' said the priest, raising an eyebrow.

'Is it a problem?'

'Not if you can assure me that your intentions are good.'

Nightingale nodded. 'They are.'

'Then it's not a problem. Come on through to the church.' The priest led Nightingale down a corridor to a heavy oak door. He pulled it open and waved for Nightingale to go first. He stepped into a room built of large grey stone blocks. Against one wall there was a heavy oak wardrobe next to a full-length mirror on an adjustable stand and on another wall there was a row of wooden coat hooks above a line of lockers made from matching wood.

'Give me a minute,' said the priest. He opened a locker and took out an alb, a long white vestment with tapered sleeves. He pulled it on over the clothes he was wearing, checked himself in the mirror and nodded his approval. He twisted a brass handle on another oak door which opened out to the area behind the church's main altar.

The priest held out his hand and Nightingale gave him the cartridges. He placed them on the altar, then walked down the centre of the church to a marble stoup by the entrance, an ornate font with a carved marble angel above it. Father MacDowell took a small glass flask from his pocket, filled it with water from the stoup and brought it back to the altar. 'You know what to say, Mr Nightingale?"

Nightingale nodded. 'I've done this before.'

The priest smiled. 'I'm sure you have. Very well. Are you ready?'

Nightingale nodded.

The priest took a deep breath and exhaled slowly. He closed his eyes. 'Our help is in the name of the Lord.'

'Who made heaven and earth,' said Nightingale.

The priest opened his eyes. 'The Lord be with you.'

'May He also be with you,' said Nightingale.

'Holy Lord, almighty Father, everlasting God, be pleased to bless these objects, that it may be a saving help to mankind, through Christ our Lord.'

He paused and nodded at Nightingale. 'Amen,' said Nightingale.

'Lord Jesus Christ, bless these items that they may be used in your service.' He sprinkled Holy Water over the bullets. 'May they be hallowed in the name of the Father, and of the Son, and of the Holy Spirit, through Christ our Lord.'

'Amen,' said Nightingale.

The priest smiled. 'It is done.' He put the cartridges back in the plastic bag and gave them to Nightingale. Nightingale put the cartridges into his pocket. Father MacDowell reached under his alb and pulled out a rosary with a small crucifix attached. 'I don't know what it is you are planning to do, Mr Nightingale, but I would feel happier if you carried that with you.'

Nightingale took the rosary and rubbed the smooth amber beads between his thumb and fingers. 'Thank you,' he said.

'You believe in the power of the rosary, I hope.'

'I believe in anything that helps, Father. I don't play favourites.'

CHAPTER 50

Nightingale went back to his office and spent half an hour sharpening the sticks he'd bought and dipping them into Holy Water. Then he cleaned the gun and loaded it with the bullets that Father MacDowell had blessed. He showered and changed into clean clothes, then retrieved the pink crystal from the glass bowl where he'd left it covered in consecrated salt. He put the map of Manhattan and Dee-anne's retainer on the desk, said a short prayer and then held the crystal over the map. There was even less of a reaction than the first time he'd tried, but there was enough to suggest that Dee-anne was somewhere on the Upper East Side. He put on his raincoat and put the stakes in his inside pocket and tucked the Smith and Wesson into a nylon holster clipped to the back of his belt.

He walked downstairs and took out his cellphone to call an Uber cab but just as he was opening the app a car pulled up in front of him and the passenger side window wound down. 'Need a lift?' It was Cheryl Perez.

'Shouldn't you be in hospital?'

'I'm fine,' she said.

'Either way, you need to stay away,' said Nightingale. 'You know what needs to be done and it's best you're not part of it.'

'I'm seeing this through to the end, Jack. I owe you that much.'

'You don't owe me anything.'

She shook her head. 'You nearly died because of me,' she said. 'Now get in the car or I'll get out and drag you in.'

Nightingale laughed and climbed in next to her. 'You don't have to do this,' he said.

'We've established that,' she said. 'Now, where are we going?'

'Upper East Side.'

'Specifically?'

Nightingale shrugged. 'I'm not sure.'

'That's not much of a plan, Jack.'

'It's all I've got.'

Perez put the car in gear and headed east.

CHAPTER 51

'How about Chinese?' said Dee-anne. She held the phone out to Matt. 'Jimmy Kwok, lives on his own in the East Village.'

'Why is it always guys?' said Steve, looking at the menu. They were sitting in an Argentinian steakhouse in a booth overlooking the street. 'Why don't we get a girl. We can do more with a girl.'

'Speak for yourself,' said Dee-anne.

'He's right though,' said Steve. 'Why is it always guys?'

'Because I'm the one on Tinder. And it's easier to meet men.'

'We could put our pictures up,' said Matt.

'You could. But then you'd be attracting young girls and the chances are they'd be living with their parents.'

Matt grinned. 'So we could have fun with the parents, too. Make it a family thing.'

A waiter dressed all in black with a neatly-trimmed goatee came over and asked if they were ready to order.

'What's your biggest steak?' asked Steve.

'That would be our tomahawk special,' said the waiter. 'It's forty-two ounces for two to share, dry-aged for a minimum of forty days, seasoned with rosemary salt and broiled at 1,400 degrees then finished in a cast-iron skillet and basted with the chef's special mixture of rosemary, garlic, beef fat and brown butter.'

'Sounds good,' said Steve. 'I'll have one.'

'It's to share.'

'I'm hungry,' said Steve.

'One tomahawk special it is,' said the waiter.

'And I'll have it rare.'

'Rare?'

'Rare. And without the salt. As bloody as it comes. In fact you can send the cow in and I'll kill it myself.'

The waiter smiled and looked at Dee-anne. 'Fillet,' she said. 'Rare.'

Matt nodded. 'Fillet for me.'

'Rare?' said the waiter. Matt flashed him a thumbs-up. 'So one tomahawk and two fillets, all rare. Vegetables?'

'Bring them all,' said Steve.

'There's a large selection,' said the waiter. 'Mashed potatoes, roasted new potatoes, potato wedges, minted peas, wilted spinach, buttered carrots, white asparagus.'

'Perfect,' said Steve.

The waiter raised his eyebrows and walked away shaking his head.

'I like the family idea,' said Matt.

'We have to be careful,' said Dee-anne. ' The Master wants us to stay low profile until he joins us. Killing a family would attract too much attention.'

'Then let's at least play with a girl,' said Steve.

Dee-anne put her phone away. 'Okay,' she said. 'Do you have anyone in mind?'

'I do,' said Steve.

The other two looked at him expectantly.

'They already know I killed Sara Moseby. So if we kill my parents and sister, no one will be surprised. Especially after what Matt did to his parents.'

'How old's your sister?' asked Matt.

'Ten.'

'Nice.'

'Sounds like a plan,' said Dee-anne.

CHAPTER 52

Nightingale felt his palm tingle. 'We're heading in the right direction,' he said. They were heading into the East Village in slow-moving traffic.

'How do you know?' asked Perez.

He showed her the cuts on his hand. 'Proserpine gave me this,' he said.

'You and her have a history?'

'She owned my soul for a while,' said Nightingale. 'It's a long story. But she's as keen as I am to stop the three devils on the loose so she gave me this.' He held out his hand again. 'The closer I get to them, the more it hurts. And it's hurting now.'

'And when you find them, what then?'

'I'll take care of it,' said Nightingale. He frowned. The ache in his palm had subsided a little. 'I think we're moving away from them. Can you head back a block and then head south?'

'No problem,' said Perez.

She took the next right and a few minutes later Nightingale's palm felt as if it was on fire. He stared at the cuts which had started bleeding again. 'You can drop me here,' he said.

'Are you sure?'

'I can't see the pain getting any worse,' he said.

'I'm coming with you,' she said.

He shook his head. 'I'm flying solo on this.'

'There's three of them and one of you, Jack.'

'I'll be fine,' said Nightingale. 'Drop me here and drive off.' He winced as pain lanced through his hand. He looked around. 'We're close,' he said.

'Over there,' she said, pointing ahead of them. 'That's the Donaldson boy, isn't it?'

Nightingale looked over at an Argentinian steak restaurant. Matt Donaldson was standing on the pavement, looking around. Dee-anne appeared at his shoulder, holding a cellphone.

'Pull over,' said Nightingale, but she had beaten him to it and was already heading for the kerb.

Steve Willoughby came out of the restaurant and joined Matt and Dee-anne. All three were looking up and down the street.

'They're waiting for something,' said Perez.

'A car,' said Nightingale. 'They've called a cab.'

'What do we do?"

Nightingale grinned. 'What they do in all the best detective movies,' he said. 'Follow that car.' He pointed over at a white Toyota Prius that had just pulled up next to the three teenagers.

CHAPTER 53

The taxi drove to Willoughby Farm and stopped in front of the main house. The driver was a Ukrainian called Leonid who had driven them from Manhattan to New Jersey in silence. 'You have a great evening,' he said to Dee-anne, who was sitting in the front passenger seat. They were the first words he had uttered.

'Oh, we will,' she said, patting him on the knee. 'But we'll be needing your car later.'

'Great,' he said. 'I can wait here if you want.'

Her smile widened and she gripped his knee tightly. 'You don't understand, baby. We'll be needing your car, not you.'

Leonid frowned and opened his mouth to speak, but before he could say anything Steve reached from behind him and clamped his hands around the man's throat. Leonid's eyes bulged as he struggled and his legs kicked against the pedals but Steve's grip was relentless. Dee-anne and Matt climbed out of the car and walked towards the front door as the kicking gradually subsided.

There was a light on above the front door, and another light on in one of the upstairs windows. Steve joined them, rubbing his hands together. 'You should knock,' said Dee-anne.

Steve grinned. 'A friendly face, you mean?' He chuckled. Dee-anne and Matt followed him and stood either side of the door as Steve rapped the knocker.

A few seconds later a light went on in the hallway and the door opened. It was Mrs Willoughby. Her jaw dropped and she put a hand up to her chest. 'Steve? My God, where have you been? Are you all right?'

CHAPTER 54

As soon as the Toyota Prius had driven across the bridge to New Jersey, Nightingale had guessed where they were going and told Perez to hang back. Once he saw the signs for Bethlehem he had no doubt about their destination so they were about half a mile behind the taxi when it turned into the Willoughby farm.

'What do you think?' asked Perez as they reached the entrance to the farm.

'It's not good,' said Nightingale.

'We should call it in.'

'You saw what one of them did to an armed SWAT team,' said Nightingale. 'You can imagine what three of them are capable of.'

'So we do it ourselves, is that what you're saying?'

Nightingale shook his head. 'There's no we, Cheryl. I'm going in on my own.'

Perez parked behind the Toyota Prius. Nightingale had climbed out before she had turned off the engine and hurried over to the other vehicle. He could tell immediately from the unnatural angle of the driver's neck that the man was dead.

'What's up?' asked Perez as she joined him.

'They've killed the driver and they're inside.' He pulled his gun from its holster and turned towards the house.

Perez put a hand on his shoulder. 'Jack, you can't just storm in through the front door.'

'We don't have time to talk this through,' he said.

'You go through that door and they'll be ready for you. How about this? You go around the back. I'll knock on the door. You get them from behind.'

'Have you got a gun?'

'Of course not.'

'So I'm not putting you in harm's way.'

She gripped his shoulder tightly. 'So far as they're concerned I'll be a neighbour popping around.'

'A neighbour? We're in the middle of nowhere.'

'A cold caller, then. Selling insurance. We're wasting time, Jack.'

Nightingale looked over at the house and nodded. 'You're right. Give me two minutes.' He jogged around to the rear of the building.

Perez watched him go. 'Be careful,' she whispered.

CHAPTER 55

Steve slapped his mother hard across the face and gasped with pleasure as she sprawled across the sofa.

'Leave her alone!' shouted her husband. He charged at Steve with bunched fists and Steve kicked him hard between the legs. Mr Willoughby roared in pain and put his hands around his groin. Steve laughed and brought up his knee, gasping again as he felt the cartilage splinter. The man keeled over, moaning in pain.

Matt put a hand on Steve's shoulder. 'My turn,' he said. He grinned. His teeth were sharp and yellowed and his tongue had become longer and pointed.

'Go for it,' said Steve. He looked up at the ceiling. 'I'm going to have some fun with my sister.'

'Save some for us,' said Dee-anne.

'Of course,' said Steve.

'I'm serious,' said Dee-anne. 'Don't be greedy.'

Steve gave her an exaggerated bow. 'I hear and obey, Princess Lilith.'

Dee-anne's red eyes hardened. 'I'm serious, Baalberith. Play with her by all means, but you must share the death with us.'

Steve nodded. 'I will.' He headed upstairs.

Matt grabbed Mr Willoughby by the scruff of the neck and lifted him up as if he was a soft toy. He tossed him at Dee-anne and she scratched his face then hurled him against a wall. She laughed as she heard a bone crack. 'They break so easily, don't they.'

Mrs Willoughby howled in despair and Dee-anne laughed. She gestured at the crying woman. 'Why don't you have some fun with her. You wanted a woman, didn't you.'

Matt sneered. 'This one is old,' he said. 'Younger is better.'

Dee-anne started to laugh but stopped when she heard a loud knock on the front door. She hurried over to the crying woman and grabbed her by the throat. 'Are you expecting anyone?' she asked.

The woman was too shocked to speak. Dee-anne shook her and asked again. This time Mrs Willoughby managed to shake her head. 'Watch them,' she said to Matt and headed out of the room.

She opened the front door, smiling. There was a Hispanic woman standing there, smiling pleasantly. She was a couple of inches shorter than Dee-anne with olive brown skin and wavy black hair. Her smile widened. 'Hi, my name is Sofia, I'm here today to see if you're perfectly happy with your cable TV service,' said the woman.

Dee-anne matched her smile. 'I don't watch much TV,' she said. Dee-anne reached out and touched the woman on the shoulder. Immediately she knew everything and her smile vanished. 'You're a private detective, your name is Cheryl Perez and you're here to kill me. What a devious bitch you are, Cheryl.' She frowned. 'And you're not alone.'

'Damn right,' said a voice behind her.

Dee-anne whirled around. There was a man standing at the kitchen door. He was wearing a grubby raincoat and holding a gun in his hands. She roared and leapt towards him but he pulled the trigger twice in quick succession and the bullets hit her in the shoulder and she went down.

'Back in the car, Cheryl!' shouted Nightingale.

He turned towards the sitting room door but Matt was too fast for him and came hurtling out. He grabbed Nightingale's throat with one hand and clamped the other over the gun.

Nightingale struggled to breathe and Matt grinned at his distress. Perez stepped into the hallway, picked up a vase from a side table and brought it smashing down on the back of Matt's head. He released his grip on Nightingale's throat but ripped the gun from his grasp. He hit Perez with the gun, smashing it against the side of her head and she went down without a sound.

Matt turned to look at Nightingale and grinned in triumph. He seemed to have grown taller and wider and his fingernails had become talons. Nightingale thrust his hand into his coat pocket, pulled out a handful of consecrated salt and threw it into Matt's eyes. Matt screamed and dropped the gun. Nightingale crouched, grabbed the weapon and fired two shots into Matt's chest. There was a loud crack and a flash of light and Matt's eyes turned from blood red to their normal brown. He fell to the floor, his eyes and mouth wide open.

Nightingale heard a scream from upstairs. A girl. He ran full pelt. He reached the top of the stairs and there was another scream, off to the right. He rushed into the bedroom and a hand grabbed the gun and pulled it from his grasp. He recognised Steve Willoughby from the family photograph he'd seen. His sister was lying on the bed, her nightdress ripped and bloody.

'Who are you?' asked Steve. 'A cop?' His eyes were featureless red pits. He snarled at Nightingale, revealing two rows of pointed teeth.

'The name's Nightingale.'

'And what are you doing here?'

'I'm here to kill you,' said Nightingale, softly.

'And how's that working out for you?'

Lisa was sobbing now, her back to the wall, hugging her knees against her chest. Nightingale looked over at her. 'Close your eyes, Lisa.'

Steve laughed harshly. 'You don't want her to see you die, huh? How sweet is that?' He looked over at Lisa. 'You keep your eyes open, honey. I want you to see me beat this Nightingale to a pulp.' He tossed the gun onto the floor. 'I won't be needing this. It's so much more fun to use your hands, to feel the blood on them.'

Lisa stared at him in horror.

'Do as I say, Lisa,' said Nightingale. 'Close your eyes.'

Lisa did as she was told.

'Don't you dare!' screamed Steve.

Nightingale reached into his coat and pulled out one of the sharpened holly stakes. Steve was still glaring at Lisa and he didn't turn until it was too late. Nightingale rammed the stake into Steve's throat and blood gushed over his hand. Steve's mouth opened and blood trickled over his lips. Nightingale twisted the stake up, pushing it through the top of Steve's mouth and up into the brain. Steve let go of Nightingale's coat and his hands clawed at the stake but Nightingale was pushing harder and forcing him back through the door. Blood was spurting from the wound and from between his lips then there was a loud crack and a flash of light and the smell of singed meat and the life went out of him. His eyes turned from red to brown and his legs buckled and he fell to the ground. His mouth was open wide and now he had the teeth of a regular American teenager.

Nightingale stood looking down at the body for several seconds, panting like a sick dog, then he went to the bathroom and washed the blood from his hands. He hurried back to the bedroom. Lisa was still sitting with her back to the wall, her hands over her eyes. 'Lisa, it's okay,' he said. 'We're going to go downstairs to your mum, okay?'

Lisa nodded but kept her hands over her eyes. Nightingale lifted her to her feet and then picked her up. He had to step over Steve to get out of the room and carried her down the stairs. 'Mrs Willoughby, I have Lisa here,' called Nightingale.

There was no answer. Nightingale wasn't sure whether to take Lisa outside or look for her mother but the decision was made for him when Dee-anne appeared in the sitting room doorway. Her chest was wet with blood and her eyes burned with hatred as she walked towards him.

Nightingale put Lisa down on the floor. 'Keep your eyes closed, honey,' he whispered.

'My hero,' said Dee-anne, as Nightingale stood up.

Nightingale said nothing.

'I'm going to enjoy ripping you apart,' she said, walking towards him. She opened her mouth wide and the stench of her breath made him gag but Nightingale stood his ground, his hands at his side.

'The strong silent type, are you? Who are you, anyway?'

'The name's Nightingale.'

'What are you? A family friend?'

Nightingale shook his head. 'Just a passer-by,' he said.

'I don't buy that for one minute.' She patted the bleeding wounds on her shoulder. 'I didn't see them coming. What did you do, dip the bullets in Holy Water? Get a priest to bless them?'

Nightingale shrugged. She was two steps from him now but he knew there was no point in running.

Dee-anne's hand flashed out and grabbed Nightingale's throat. Her blood-red eyes flashed but then her hand stiffened. 'Proserpine?' she said. She frowned. 'What's happening here?' She let go of his throat and he staggered back against the wall, fighting to breathe. 'You belong to my sister,' she said. 'How can that be?'

'I don't belong to anybody,' croaked Nightingale.

Dee-anne shook her head. 'You belong to her,' she said. 'She owns you.'

'Nobody owns me,' said Nightingale.

Dee-anne sneered at him. 'You just don't know it. You belong to a Princess of Hell which means I can do nothing. It's your lucky day, Nightingale.'

Nightingale put his hand into his right raincoat pocket. He grabbed a handful of consecrated salt and threw it into Dee-anne's face. She shrieked and staggered backwards, temporarily blinded. Nightingale stepped forward and pushed her hard in the chest. She fell, her hands over her face. Nightingale followed her and dropped down on top of her, pinning her arms with his legs. He groped in his inside raincoat pocket and pulled out one of the sharpened stakes.

She was thrashing her head from side to side. The salt had burned the flesh around her eyes and the sockets were filling with blood. Nightingale grabbed the stake with both hands and brought the sharpened end down with all his might, into her throat. There was a deafening crack and bright flash of light and she went stiff, then relaxed. Her eyes opened. They were no longer red, they had gone to blue but there was no life in them. Blood was oozing around the stake. Nightingale let go of it and stood up. Lilith had left the body, he was sure of that. All that was left was the shell that had once been Dee-anne Alexander.

He hurried over to Perez. There was blood trickling from her nose and it ran down her cheek and dripped onto the floor. He bent over her. 'Cheryl?' Her chest wasn't moving and his hand trembled as he felt for a pulse in her neck.

She opened her eyes and relief washed over him. 'I'm okay,' she said. She coughed and Nightingale helped her to sit up. 'Is it over?' she asked.

Nightingale nodded. 'Yeah. And we have to get out of here. But give me a minute.'

He stood up and hurried into the sitting room. Mr and Mrs Willoughby were both on the floor. Mrs Willoughby was curled up in a ball, sobbing softly. Her husband was lying on his back, his eyes closed and his mouth open. There was blood on his neck and his left arm was at an angle that suggested it had been broken but his chest was moving. He went over to Mrs Willoughby and shook her. 'Mrs Willoughby, it's over. Lisa needs you. And you have to call the cops. Do you understand.'

She said nothing and Nightingale shook her again. This time she rolled over and looked at him blankly.

'What's happening?" she asked. 'Why are they doing this? Who are they?'

'You have to focus, Mrs Willoughby. It's over.'

'What about Steve?'

'Steve's dead. I'm sorry. But Lisa needs you. She's in the hallway.' He helped her to her feet and out into the hall. As soon as she saw Lisa sitting with her back to the wall she rushed forward and wrapped her arms around her. Nightingale went back into the sitting room and picked up a cellphone off the coffee table. He took it to Mrs Willoughby but she wouldn't take it from him. 'You need to call 911,' said Nightingale. He grabbed her right hand and thrust the phone into it. 'Your husband needs an ambulance.'

She nodded. 'Thank you,' she said.

'Don't thank me,' he said. 'Just get help, now.'

He left her and went over to Perez, dragged her to her feet and towards the front door. As they slipped out they could hear Mrs Willoughby on the phone, tearfully telling an emergency operator that she needed help.

Nightingale put Perez in the passenger seat of the car then climbed in next to her and drove off. As he accelerated down the driveway he saw a figure standing off to the left. Two figures. A girl dressed all in black and, standing by her side, a black and white collie. The girl blew Nightingale a kiss as he drove by but when he looked in the rearview mirror there was nobody there.

###

About the Author

Stephen Leather is one of the UK's most successful thriller writers, an eBook and Sunday Times bestseller and author of the critically acclaimed Dan "Spider" Shepherd series and the Jack Nightingale supernatural detective novels. Before becoming a novelist he was a journalist for more than ten years on newspapers such as The Times, the Daily Mirror, the Glasgow Herald, the Daily Mail and the South China Morning Post in Hong Kong. His eBooks have topped the Amazon Kindle charts in the UK and the US and he was voted by The Bookseller magazine as one of the 100 most influential people in the UK publishing world. You can find out more from his website www.stephenleather.com and you can follow him on Twitter at twitter.com/stephenleather.

CPSIA information can be obtained
at www.ICGtesting.com
Printed in the USA
LVOW04s1923231215

467652LV00022B/1072/P